BOUND IN BLACK

JULIETTE CROSS

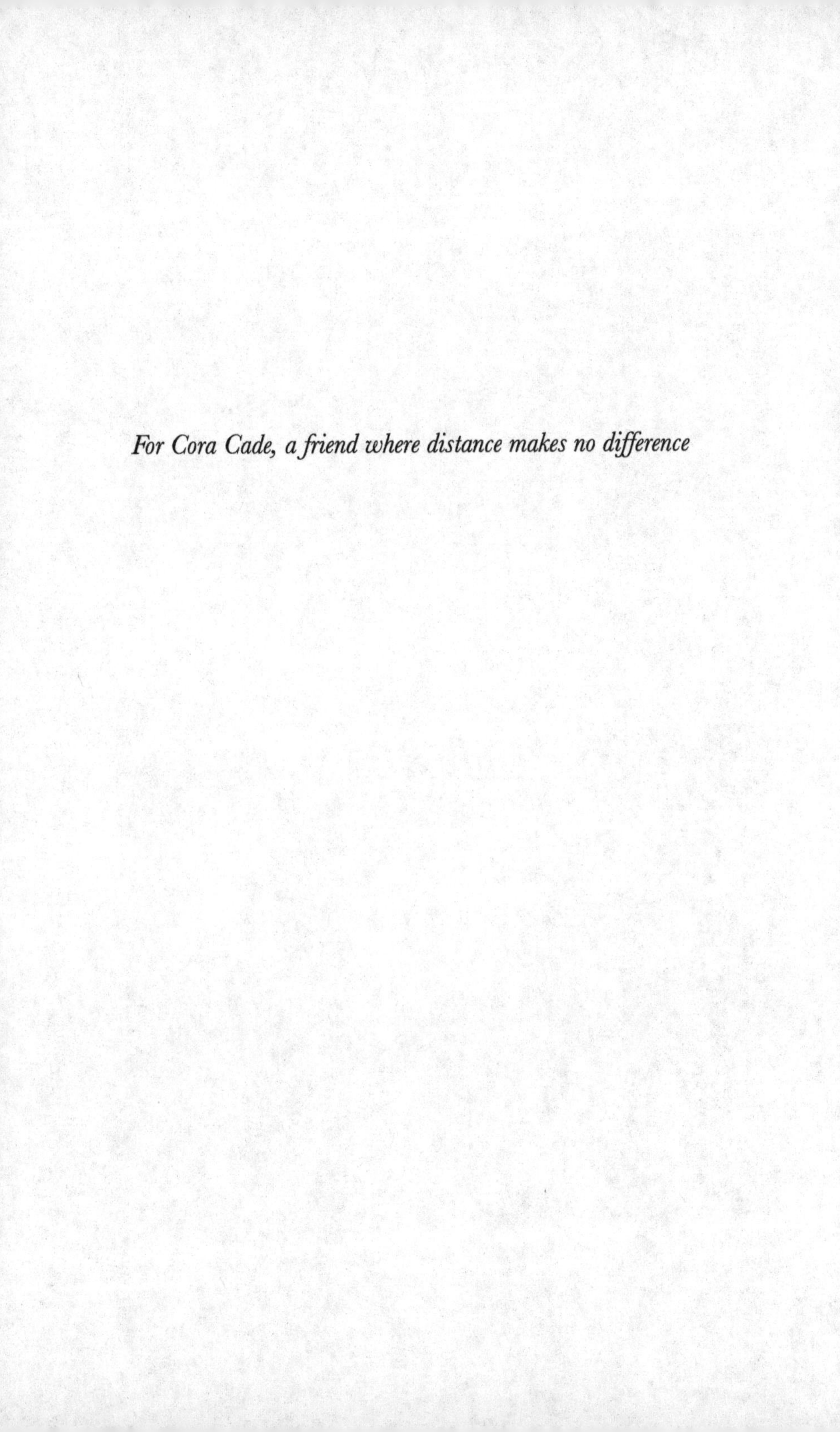

For Cora Cade, a friend where distance makes no difference

THE PROPHECY

The prophecy transcribed by James of Glastonbury in 399 AD as told by the Vessel of Light, known only as Ingrid, the day before she drowned herself in the River Brue.

Beneath the orb that circles round, while hosts of fiends and foes abound,

The Vessel-born shall walk upright, fall from Grace, lose her light.

The sinful reign with demon hand, spread wide the Fallen's mighty band.

But I, the Chalice with full Sight, do see the One to cast off night.

Time will ebb, Time will flow, Light and Dark combat and grow

A ruthless army of good and ill, to war on Land, humanity kill.

When wickedness will rule on land, and all seems lost to mortal man,

One Great War shall begin, upon the hour She stands within

A ring of wordless, mighty breath; amidst the clutch of endless death.

Two great sons of Morning Star; divided, until death will mar.

One will woo the warrior maid, one will cut her to a shade.

Two sisters of the Vessel Light, blood to blood, will evil smite.

Have mercy on the mindless twin, when Wrath is right and Virtue sin.

Sun and Moon, eye to eye; immortals await one battle cry.

For within each heart of Moon and Sun, lies key to rule over all and one.

A door will open beneath the ring, infinite power will it bring.

One look, one word from victor's lips, will smite the
Foe like sinking ships.

But ALL beware, both Light and Dark, for if both
Vessels should not embark

Upon the round of Flamma hosts, to duel to death
among fiends and ghosts,

Then ALL are doomed to eternal night; no devil or
host of heavenly Light

Shall pass to yonder realm or home, an endless walk
under darkened dome.

One last task and heed me well. When Time will
mark the making spell

A sacrificial lamb must die; her blood must pool
under darkened sky,

And rip from hinges the mighty door, then begin the
fated Flamma War.

Prickling of needles under my skin—the unwelcome sensation that meant only one thing. Demons. Once upon a time, it had filled me with tremulous dread. But not anymore.

I waltzed into The Dungeon—the whips-and-chains Goth club owned and managed by Dommiel, high demon of New Orleans—completely indifferent to his red-eyed minions lurking within. Though they were human in appearance, I could feel their sinister aura the second I stepped into the murky den.

As one of the Flamma, a host of either the Light or Dark with supernatural powers, I had the ability to cast illusion, to disguise who I was—a Vessel of Light. With a simple thought, I could've dimmed the effervescent white glow beaming off my skin—my underlight—which always burned brighter in the vicinity of demons.

I could've come here incognito. I could've cast illusion to hide the twenty-seven-inch, razor-sharp katana sheathed at my hip. I could've refrained from alarming my leather-and-leash audience currently giving me death stares. But I didn't.

I wanted every piece of shit here to know I could do damage, if necessary. Every minute wasted was another minute I couldn't reach my destination, another minute lost in finding Jude. My protector, my love…my husband.

No longer hiding my identity, I stalked through the darkened bar like I owned the place. A bulky bartender cut me off before I headed up the stairs, keeping a few steps back.

"Can I help you?" he asked, deep scowl in place.

I inhaled and blew out a calming breath, restraining from showing him the damage a Vessel coming into her power could do.

"Yeah. You can get the fuck out of my way before I sever your head. Or you can escort me to Dommiel. Your choice."

His face slackened from fierce bouncer to shocked idiot. Hesitantly, he sloped off in front of me toward the stairwell. Smart move. I followed, my right hand wrapped around the hilt of my sword in case anyone decided my bad attitude needed an adjustment.

Pulse-pounding, bone-grinding music vibrated the entire second floor. Dancers, if you could call them that, melded together in one mass of moving limbs. A few couples and trios needed to find a private corner before their make-out sessions morphed into an all-out orgy.

The bartender stopped in front of Dommiel's throne. A massive dragon's head—openmouthed and fierce fanged—

hung above the oversized wood-carved chair like a crown. The first time I'd been here, I assumed the head was a magnificent work of art by a local New Orleans sculptor.

Because dragons aren't real, right? Now I knew better.

The beast's head was cut from a high demon's spawn, probably killed in battle against one of the Flamma of Light, someone on my team. Even now, after the head was severed and stuffed, a low vibration of eerie energy swirled in the air. I hadn't detected this before. But back in September, I wasn't the Vessel I was now.

My Vessel Sense, VS, amplified every day, detecting any demon within a one-mile radius. Not only that, my fist and blade packed major force. Still, I knew I hadn't experienced full awakening. Kat, my mentor and friend and the only female hunter I'd met, told me that I'd know when I experienced my awakening. It would be like falling in love.

I definitely knew what that felt like…as well as the tragic heartbreak when that love was ripped from my arms.

I clenched my jaw, willing away those thoughts, and focused on the task at hand.

Dommiel sprawled atop his throne with the latest blonde propped on his lap. With a clean-shaved head and wearing his usual attire—black slacks and white button-down with silver cuff links—he was a contradiction in appearance. If he hadn't pierced every part of his face—lip, lids, nose, tongue, and the entire cartilage of both ears—he'd be hot.

Metal-face didn't turn me on, but some girls were into that. For example, the buxom woman now whispering in his ear, pressing against him with her ample cleavage pouring out of a red patent leather corset.

Dommiel cupped her breast with the one hand he had, brushing his thumb casually along the exposed skin above the too-tight casing. He turned his head when I approached.

His groupies didn't move, though tension rippled in the air. Dommiel's familiar—a black-eyed raven—perched on the dragon's head and watched me.

For a second, I wished I'd brought Mira. The white hawk that I'd created the day Jude was taken away had become my pale shadow wherever I went these days. But I didn't want any of these freaks trying to hurt her in this confined space.

Before her creation, when I was steeped in a well of grief from losing Jude, I hadn't known Vessels could create spawn of Light. If demons could beget creatures of darkness, then it made sense I'd have the power to create one of light. Only, no Vessel had ever done it before. George, the commander of the Dominus Daemonum—the Masters of Demons—said it was because no Vessel before me had ever come so close to her awakening.

When I glanced up at the beady-eyed bird, I wondered what it would do if I'd brought Mira with me and let her poke out one of those evil eyes. I suppose it would've started a shit storm, and that wasn't why I'd come here.

Standing tall, hands at my sides, I looked at Dommiel. "I come in peace."

He considered me for about five seconds. "If this is peace, woman, I'd hate to see war."

"Yes. You would."

In our past dealings, Dommiel had used his sardonic tongue to cut me and keep me in line. I waited for his next smart-ass remark, but something in his gaze told me he recognized this visit was different. I hadn't come to threaten or coerce him into doing my bidding. I had a genuine offer of partnership— one I never thought to present to a high demon.

With a heavy sigh, he squeezed his blonde's breast still cupped in his hand, then gave her a quick deep-throated kiss before pushing her off his lap. He stood, revealing the silver hook on the stump of his other arm, which had been concealed till now.

"This better be good, Vessel." He stepped in front of me, leading me past a guard and down a dark hallway. "I haven't had a taste of her yet and was quite looking forward to it."

"It looked to me like you just got a taste."

He shot me a piercing look over his shoulder. "Okay. Let me rephrase. I haven't yet fucked her until she can't talk or walk. And I was about to take off that edge when you showed up."

"Too much information, Dommiel."

He led me down some narrow stairs, then gestured aside another guard outside his office. I'd been here before to negotiate a sort of truce and mutual business offer on my last visit. This time, I came to offer much more.

Jude wouldn't approve. But I'd do anything and everything to get him back. Selling a small piece of my soul was no hardship if it meant I'd have the chance to save my love from eternal hell.

Dommiel sank into the chair behind his wooden office desk. The furniture seemed out of place. Beyond these walls, mind-blasting music pounded through the club and demons writhed among humans, tempting them to fall farther into their den of sin. But here, in this average-looking office with a comfortable sofa and a low-lit lamp casting a warm hue on the walls, I could've been standing in a normal office building, not a demon's lair.

Resting his hook-hand and arm on the desk, he gestured palm up with the other. "So what do you want? Another favor? More intel? I'm all out of favors, and I know nothing new."

Taking a seat on the edge of the sofa, I shifted the katana so that it didn't poke me in the hip. I paused, staring at my laced fingers hanging between my knees, my wedding band glinting in the light. I searched for the right words that would persuade him.

"I need your help."

A dumbfounded demon is funny to behold. If I didn't have so much anxiety churning my guts into a pool of acid, I would've laughed.

"Wait a minute," he said. "Your asshole boyfriend storms into my place and practically slits my throat for looking at you the wrong way. He then cuts my hand off so I'm stuck with this fucking thing for the rest of my immortal life." He thrust his sharp hook in the air for effect. "And then, you and your bitch of a hunter friend—"

"Kat."

"Whoever...the two of you blackmail me into offering up

information that could've put my head on a platter or gotten me sent to the deepest level of torturous hell. And now…now you want *my* help? Damn, woman. You have some serious balls."

A normal person would've flinched and cowered from the wave of heated rage seething from the high demon across the desk, but all I could feel was elation.

"That's where I want to go."

"Where? What are you talking about?"

"I need you to take me to hell. To find the soul eater Lethe. I need to go to Erebus."

Soul collectors, also known as soul eaters or rivers of the underworld, kept their captives in Erebus—the darkest pit of hell. These five supernatural creatures served neither the Flamma of Light or the Dark, only themselves. Jude had bargained with Acheron once. They were reasoning monsters, but monsters all the same. And there was no way in or out of Erebus but through one of them. I needed Lethe. She was the one to take Jude. She was my best link in finding him.

Dommiel stared at me, speechless, obviously trying to decide whether I was serious or insane. I was probably both.

"Lethe?" he asked. "Why would you need to find her?"

I heaved out a heavy breath, my fingers linked tight and squeezing. "She has Jude. And I'm going after him, and I'm bringing him back."

2

Dommiel tilted his head, expression still and grave. "So…the rumors are true. The almighty hunter is gone."

"What rumors?"

He shrugged one shoulder. "Demons talk."

I frowned, hating that demons were talking about… Wait a minute. "How the hell are demons spreading rumors?" There's no way George or any of the Dominus Daemonum would tell a demon where Jude was. Unless one of them was a traitor. Who was spreading rumors?

Ignoring my question, he turned another on me. "How did the hunter let himself get taken by Lethe? He's too crafty for that. Was he tricked?"

Anger burned hot in my belly. Yes. He'd been tricked, but I hadn't come here to give Dommiel a lifeline of information.

He stood and rounded the desk toward the door. "Well, my sweet Vessel, it seems our meeting is over."

I rose to my feet. "I'm not done."

"There's nothing you can say to persuade me to help the bane of my existence escape from hell, just so he can return and lord over my domain, then abuse me further."

He wiggled his hooked hand in the air and spun toward the door.

"Hear me out, Dommiel…please."

My pleading tone stopped him halfway across the room. His shoulders stiffened, then he turned, his hand on his hip. "Fine. What are you prepared to offer? And it better be good."

I reached inside my leather jacket and pulled from the inner pocket a raven's black plume. The very one Dommiel had given me. I held it up for him to see.

"This wasn't from your pet raven, was it? This was one of yours, whenever you transformed. Wasn't it?"

Dommiel's heavy gaze shifted to mine. He nodded slowly. I'd known it all along. The last time I'd needed his help, I had to coax him into giving me information. Well, coax is too kind. It was more like blackmail.

He gave me information about the whereabouts of certain demon lords. In return, I assured him that Jude would protect his right to rule in New Orleans. But I knew this was different. First of all, Jude was no longer here, so I didn't have that bargaining chip, and I also knew that Dommiel would prefer the hunter who chopped off his hand to be rotting in hell more than anywhere else. But I also had insight that Dommiel didn't have.

He sucked his lower lip into his mouth, his teeth tapping the silver stud, making a ticking sound. Nervous habit, apparently.

He eyed the feather in my hand, a curious expression in place. "What do you plan to do with the gift I gave you? Burn it in a cauldron and put a spell on me? It doesn't work that way."

"I'm not a witch, Dommiel."

"That remains to be seen." He leaned back in his chair. "I don't know what your plans are, but there are reasons all hosts of heaven *and* hell steer clear of Lethe. If she ensnares you, you will forget everything…everyone. You won't even know who you are anymore, much less anything that mattered to you before."

A lump swelled in my throat. "So I've been told."

"So if Lethe took Jude, then you've lost him forever. Even if you found him, he won't know who you are. He won't care that you've come to save him, because there'll be nothing to save him from. She'll have wiped his mind clean of memories long ago."

"Goddamn it, Dommiel! I'm not asking for your opinion on Lethe and her prisoners. I'm asking you to help me find her."

He stepped back, watching my hand, which I'd wrapped around the hilt of my katana. My aggression amplified tenfold every time I thought of Jude being kept captive in that dark, forbidding abyss. When helpless anger overwhelmed me, my hand always went to the sword, wanting to maim and destroy, wanting someone to pay for what had been done to Jude, for what had been taken from me.

"Are you okay?" Dommiel snapped me from my reverie. His thoughtful expression looked almost like sympathy.

I straightened with my chin in the air. "I've been told she lurks around the deepest levels of hell, and I can't trust anyone else to take me there. No one who actually knows how to get there."

He laughed, propping his hand on his hip. "You trust me?"

"I'm willing to." I held up the plume again. "I'm offering a blood vow. To seal our deal."

A blood vow was a truce I'd learned about a month ago when we had to meet with Prince Bamal, high demon of New York, and his men. The only way a Flamma of Light and Dark could parlay without fearing that death and mayhem would break out between the parties was to agree to a truce using a blood vow. The two leaders of the gathering would seal their blood onto an object while casting a particular spell, *Sanguis Promissionem*. There was no way to betray the blood bond, even if one wanted to.

After vehement protests on George's part and guilt-laden coercion on mine, George had instructed me how to cast the spell. He couldn't help me get into hell and find Lethe, and he had no other plan to get me there. Eventually, he had to succumb to my strategy of bonding to Dommiel with the blood vow. There was no other way.

I could sift into hell where I'd been before, the Black Forest, but I'd been told this dark woodland stretched on forever in the underworld. I could search for eternity and still never find Lethe, and so never find Jude. I needed an insider—a demon.

Dommiel shook his head slowly back and forth as he bit his lip again, the metal stud clinking against his teeth. "I can't believe you're serious."

"This isn't a temporary deal, Dommiel. I'm offering you a permanent truce. More than that. I'm offering…friendship."

"You and me? Friends?" He snorted. "The irony is laughable."

"Yeah," I agreed. "But I'm not laughing. I'm dead serious."

"I see that. And why would I want to be friends with the Vessel of Light who proclaims to be the one who will turn the tide of the coming war against my own kind? If you haven't noticed, I'm a demon."

Everyone knew the Great War between heaven and hell was coming, the one to be waged on earth for dominion over this world and all its inhabitants.

"It never escaped my attention. But since you bring up the coming war, let me say this. The war won't be decided in a day, a week, or even a month. We all know that this war will last many years, even with my power on the side of Light. And there will be many casualties. I'm willing to offer you protection. Both from Flamma of Light—hunters, sentinels, and even angels—as well as the high demons on your side who will fight you for dominion over New Orleans."

Dommiel's lips tightened into a line. The silver stud in his bottom lip stood straight out.

"Do you know how attractive this city will become to the high demons looking for new territory when all hell breaks loose?" I asked with a laugh. "Literally?"

"So what? I've got plenty of men here to protect my domain."

"If you believe that, Dommiel, then you're a fool. Bamal will wipe your ass off the map. He'll cut off your other hand just for fun, to teach you a lesson, and make you one of his minions. He's always coveted New Orleans. How do I know? Because Jude told me. You won't stand a chance with him, and you know it."

"And you're offering protection."

"I'm offering more, if you're actually listening to me. I'll count you as one of my friends."

"Why would you do that? I'm a demon lord. You're a Vessel."

"I'll do anything to get Jude back."

He froze at my words, at the stark vulnerability leaking from my voice. I gave him honesty in a way I thought no one ever had. My heart was breaking every second that Jude was in that pit of hell where I couldn't reach him.

"I'd befriend a demon. I'd pledge my devotion to defending you, even against other Flamma of Light, if you would extend me the same consideration."

He shifted his weight from one foot to the other, measuring me. "A friendship?" He said the word as if it were foreign to him. I suppose it was.

"I wouldn't betray you, Dommiel. Can you say the same about your demon brethren?"

He walked closer to me and took the black plume from my hand, twirling it slowly by the tip. "If we're to do this, then I'll need a possession of yours."

"Yes. I know."

I reached around the back of my neck and unclasped the chain of my St. George medal, the one my mother had given me years before she died.

When I'd lost the opal necklace Jude had given me and after I'd discovered my mother had been a Vessel too, I'd put my medal back on and not taken it off since. At first, the discovery about my mother had broken my heart. But then I realized her suicide was a sacrifice for me and Dad.

Like every Vessel before her who'd been targeted by demon lords and had not yet been taken as a slave, she chose the only other way out to protect her family. Death.

I held out the medal cupped in my palm. Dommiel placed the feather on his desk, then lifted the medal by the chain, letting it dangle.

"This is precious to you?" He quirked an eyebrow.

"Yes. Very."

"If I do this, we still must keep this...friendship a secret."

"Believe me. I won't be bragging to all the hunters that my new bestie is the demon lord of New Orleans. They have trust issues just as much as your minions."

His silver-studded brows bunched together in a frown. "They're not minions. They're my soldiers."

"Whatever. Do you want to argue about semantics, or do you want to do this thing?"

He closed his eyes. The sensation of pins pricking under my skin intensified as he seemed to be summoning his demonic power.

All Flamma gave off a specific signature, an aura I sensed by smell or touch. High demons typically had unique signatures, but Dommiel's was a jacked-up version of what all lower demons emitted. Powerful but not as strong as a demon prince like Bamal. Without my help, Dommiel could soon become slave to someone higher up the food chain.

Reacting to the demonic charge revving in the room, my underlight glowed moon bright. He'd closed his eyes for only a few seconds, but the electricity sparking in the air was palpable. When he opened them, his irises were pools of liquid red. He lifted his hand and opened his mouth, revealing a row of razor-sharp teeth, including two canines extending beyond the others.

Clamping down on the fleshy part of his palm, he pierced the skin and held out his hand, now leaking black blood from two punctures. The medal was still cupped there.

"You'll have to assist, I'm afraid." Wagging his hook in the air, he quirked an eyebrow at me.

I took the medal and wiped it along the oozing punctures. After smearing the medal on both sides, I placed it on top of the feather on the desk. Dommiel walked around to the other side.

"Stand across from me."

I moved closer, facing him from the opposite side.

"Place your hand on top."

I did, covering the two objects, except for the tip of the feather sticking out. He leaned forward and covered my hand with his palm. His blood oozed a trail, slipping over my hand to the objects beneath.

"Do you know the words?" he asked.

"Yes," I said with a tight nod, my pulse pumping faster.

"Then let's do it," he replied with the wickedest Cheshire cat grin—his fanged smile both menacing and playful.

We spoke the words together in Latin, the common tongue of heavenly and demonic hosts.

"Bound by blood pure and true, to do no harm through words or deeds…"

As the words poured from our mouths in unison, his crimson gaze burned brighter. My underlight did the same, reacting to the sealing of our blood oath.

"I pledge my life upon this bond."

Upon the final word, a resounding crack snapped in the air above our coupled hands. A swirl of red smoke curled up from under our palms, mine pressed into the objects, Dommiel's pressed into the back of my hand. The tendril wove a figure eight between our wrists, skimming a cold caress along my skin. No, not a figure eight.

"Infinity," I whispered as the mystical vapor trailed the underside of my wrist, sending a shiver through my body.

"Yes," said Dommiel. His fangs had retracted. His eyes had faded to their normal dark hue. "It worked. My first eternal blood oath."

He lifted his hand and opened his desk drawer, then pulled a handkerchief from inside to wipe his palm. I tucked the feather inside my jacket pocket.

The objects were merely token reminders of our blood oath, the vow now sealed in our skin and flesh. The compulsion to keep one another from harm would override all else if either of us was in danger.

"Well, then. When did you want to leave? I have a few things I need to wrap up here… Well, one voluptuous thing, actually," he said with a smirk. He scooped my chain into another drawer of his desk and locked it with a key in his pocket. "But I could meet you for this little tumble down the rabbit hole later tonight."

I straightened the belt holding my katana and shook my head. "Not yet. I need to see a few people before we go."

"I thought you were anxious to get there…to find your man and all that." Sardonic Dommiel resurfaced.

"I'm more anxious than you know, but I'm not going in blind either. I need to speak with someone."

"Ahhh. You have a few tricks up those leather sleeves?"

"I do, as a matter of fact."

"Care to share?"

"Hell, no."

"Then I'll escort you to the door."

"No need. I'll leave from here, if you don't mind. Your wards are weak, Dommiel. You should amplify them if you don't want the unwanted sifting in and out."

He arched the brow pierced with two studs and three gold hoops. "You can sift?"

I saw no need to keep the truth from him. Word would get around if it already hadn't. Apparently, demons were just as bad gossipmongers as humans. "Yeah. I can sift."

"Well, well, well." He leaned back against his desk, crossing his arms, his silver hook jutting out on one side. "Getting friendly with an angel, are you?"

"Not so friendly anymore." I planned to kill him as soon as I found him.

Dommiel chuckled. "Do tell."

"Not on your fucking life."

His grin softened to an expression of pity, as if that brief bit of conversation explained everything.

Thomas. The green-eyed angel who'd professed to be my guardian and who'd betrayed me worst of all by setting Jude up to take my fall—he was the cause of all this. And while he'd been in hiding ever since that day, sooner or later I'd find him. Our meeting wouldn't be pretty.

I'd trusted him. He'd given me the power to sift, a vital ability allowing me to move between time and space. He'd claimed to love me.

Was it my rejection of him that made him betray me and take away the one I loved most in the world?

Of course, Dommiel couldn't know all those things, but he was much more intelligent and perceptive than others believed him to be. This was why I knew he'd accept the blood vow, why he'd agree to take me into the deepest realm of hell even though it could cost him his life. He was smart, and he was a risk-taker. He'd be a valuable asset on my side.

Dommiel crossed one foot over the other at the ankle, shaking his head. "You know, the more you learn about our world, Genevieve, the more you'll come to understand that everyone —Light or Dark—has their own agenda foremost in mind."

He wasn't telling me anything I didn't already know. But his words made me smile.

"Does something amuse you?"

"You used my name."

"I did?" He frowned in surprise. "I did."

"I'll be in touch…friend," I teased.

"Now, let's not go crazy, woman."

I winked before sifting away into the Void. The black abyss pulled me through nothingness, gray blurs whirring by me as I passed Flamma sifting to their destinations. I pinpointed mine, zapping onto solid ground in Jude's courtyard, where two gas lanterns still burned bright from when I'd lit them earlier.

The sounds of the French Quarter at night wrapped around me, even in this enclosure—a squeal of laughter, the upbeat rhythm of trumpets from the jazz band at the outdoor café one street over, the honking of horns along Decatur. Here, the world was right—bustling along at an exhilarating pace.

In my heart, the world had stopped the moment Jude was taken by Lethe.

I walked to the pile of stone rubble against the wall where Jude had swept these remnants of his battle with a demon spawn, a Fury who'd broken through Jude's wards into this courtyard over a month ago. He'd intended to finish cleaning up the mess, but then…

After he was gone, I couldn't make myself do it, needing every reminder of his presence I could possibly latch on to. Like any person who has lost a loved one so dear, I hadn't touched a thing. I wanted it frozen in place.

I bent to the shattered remains of Eros and Psyche. The lovers were no longer clinging to one another in a sensual embrace. I picked up the larger piece of Eros, still mostly whole but cracked down the center of his face. Still beautiful, the fracture sent a terrifying chill up my spine. A premonition of what I might find when I did finally make my way to Jude.

Hold on, my love.

I placed the beautiful broken god back into the pile of rubble and stood, rubbing my hand over my lower abdomen. My body hadn't yet shown any change, at least on the outside. There was no visible sign of the life I carried within me.

But I could feel her essence growing brighter, connected to me along with my VS. I don't know why, but I knew I carried a daughter. Jude's daughter. A twinge of love filled my whole being as I pressed a hand to my belly.

"Don't worry, little one. I'll bring him home. I promise."

3

Evanescence blared through Jude's studio as I performed the kata I'd learned from my father when I was five. Deepening my concentration, I moved with swift, fluid steps as Amy Lee crooned about wounds that wouldn't heal and pain that was just too real—melodious words that resonated through my blood to my bones.

I unsheathed my katana leaning against the wall and worked through a routine of my own creation, including both defensive and offensive moves. For the past three weeks, while I waited for George to locate the archangel Uriel and arrange a meeting, I'd done nothing but train for my upcoming journey. My body was honed to a sharpened weapon.

Funny, I was pregnant, and I was in the best shape of my life. I'd always imagined that when I was expecting, I'd sit on the sofa and eat bonbons all day, watching reruns of *The Office* and getting fat.

Of course, I never imagined I'd be pregnant at twenty and that the father of my child would be suffering in the bowels of hell. Sitting my lazy ass on the sofa was no longer an option. Besides, I was only five or six weeks along. No one could tell I was with child. And I planned to keep it that way until I could bring Jude back home.

I twisted and swiveled on my back foot, slicing the blade through the air with a zing at an imaginary enemy. As I spun toward the door, my heart leaped out of my chest.

"Shit! George, don't *do* that."

George stood in the open doorway, his shoulder leaning against the frame, arms crossed. "Pardon me, but I tried your cell. You were obviously preoccupied."

Though his charming English accent revealed no anxiety, the taut line of his shoulders and pinched brow told me otherwise.

I sheathed my katana and set it on the table, pressing Stop on the iPhone hooked up to the docking station. Sure enough, two missed calls and a few texts waiting. I'd put incoming calls on silent. After clearing the missed calls, I smiled at the profile pic I'd used for George in my contacts—the roaring dragon, Smaug, from *The Hobbit* movie.

When I'd first learned that he was the one and only legendary St. George the dragon slayer, I thought history had gotten this legend all wrong. First of all, I had to come to grips with the reality that dragons did indeed exist. They were titans, the largest of the spawn created by the most powerful high demons.

And second, I had to rearrange my preconception of saints. The debonair man staring at me through aquamarine eyes with well-groomed chestnut hair and who spoke like James Bond was not what I'd imagined a saint would be like. Besides the fact that I'd never planned on meeting one.

"Please tell me you have news, George. You've spoken to Uriel?"

"Yes."

"Can we meet? And soon. I'm losing my fucking mind the longer we wait."

"Go change, Genevieve. He's waiting for us."

"He's here?"

"Not here." George shoved off the door frame and headed up the hallway with me trailing behind. "But close by. And he doesn't like waiting, so hurry."

"*He* doesn't like waiting. I've been waiting for him for weeks!" I stormed past George into the living room and into Jude's bedroom, where I'd moved most of my clothes into his closet.

"He is an archangel."

I wanted to *scream*, to vent my frustration on George. Yes, I understood that we were edging toward an apocalypse, but somehow that didn't matter to me. The only thing that did was getting to Jude and saving him.

Within three minutes, I'd retied my hair into a tight ponytail, slipped on a pair of jeans, and one of Jude's black T-shirts. As always when I wore one of his shirts, which was every day, I pulled the collar up past my nose and take a deep breath. If I wasn't wearing one during the day, I slept in one. I didn't care what I looked like, only that I had something that belonged to him close to me.

Breathing in his scent didn't make me sad. It soothed my nerves. It reminded me that he was waiting for me, and I needed to hurry the fuck up and find him and bring him back.

Then I wouldn't have to smell his shirts to feel close to him. I could hug myself to his chest, bury my face in his neck, and tell him how desperately I loved him. That I'd missed him. That we have a baby on the way.

Wiping the stray tear that slipped free, I rushed to the back and grabbed my katana. Then I strapped the harness on my back, shrugged into my leather jacket, and met George at the door.

"Let's go."

I held out my hand for him to sift me to Uriel's location. He shook his head. "No. He's nearby. Let's go."

He put his hand on my back to urge me forward. The second his hand made contact, a blast of Flamma power pulsed through my body. I fell into a memory of George's past with frightening speed.

I walked down a darkened hallway, adrenaline pumping quickly through my veins. I reminded myself that I was seeing through George's eyes, sensing everything as he did in this moment. The stone corridor was from an old building, a fortress or castle of some kind. Torches lit sconces along the wall, flickering long shadows across the stone.

A sound came from an open doorway up ahead. I stopped, my heart beating faster. I knew that sound. A soft moan grew louder and longer in a steady rhythm. A woman in the midst of pleasure. Profound pleasure.

I stepped forward, tightening my grip on the heavy sword in my hand. A chill of apprehension sucked the air from my lungs. I dreaded what I would find.

The moans of ecstasy grew louder. A masculine voice whispered. A husky feminine one replied, "Yes."

A dim glow of light spilled from the open door as I stepped through the archway, freezing at the sight. Heartbreaking pain nearly knocked me to my knees.

Within a palatial bedroom, including a four-poster bed with a luxurious green coverlet, a fire blazing in the hearth, and a wrought-iron chandelier hanging from the ceiling, were two people, straight ahead against the far wall of the bedroom.

Wrists shackled by two chains on the wall, the object of my heart's desire had her arms spread in a V, her legs wrapped around the waist of a nude man, her ankles locked at his back. The dark-haired man thrust his powerful frame, the muscular line of his back rippling as he pumped inside her.

Though bound in place, the chains jangling, she tilted her head back against the wall, her mouth open, groaning in pleasure, not in pain. Her expression was not that of a prisoner or a woman being violated against her will. The man lifted her thighs higher and whispered something else close to her ear. Her sweat-drenched, white-blonde hair spilled over her shoulder.

She replied with a groan, saying, "Yes!"

He pounded harder and faster.

My blood burned through my veins. I whipped the blade with a resounding whir in the air. She opened her eyes on a gasp, her glittering green gaze capturing me over her lover's shoulder—deep shame and sorrow written there.

I stumbled away from George as I came out of the vision with a violent push, falling backward against the wall.

Kat. The Dominus Daemonum who'd become one of my dearest friends since I'd stepped into this world. She was the one bound against that wall, being pounded into ecstasy. I knew without asking that the man in the vision was Damas, the demon lord who'd captured her. But I'd assumed she'd been kidnapped and held against her will. That didn't appear to be the case.

George's eyes widened with concern. "Are you all right?"

"Yes, I…I saw another memory. It was—"

"No need to tell me," he said, grasping my arms to keep me from sliding down the wall.

The last time I'd been in one of his visions, it had left me a sobbing mess. This time, my stomach flipped in revulsion, wanting to empty its contents.

Regaining my balance, I stared at him, my heart breaking all over again. I knew he loved Kat. I had no idea when he'd found her in captivity that he'd found her like that.

"Whatever it is, Genevieve, keep it to yourself. I don't want to know what horrors you've seen in my head."

Yes. Definitely horrors. He warned me there would be consequences when he shared his power with me so that I could keep Danté from soul-sifting me out of my body at will. I had no idea I'd see some heartbreaking memory from his past every time we bumped into each other. I realized the carefree charm he wore like a coat was more like a mask.

"I'm fine," I said, shoving off the wall. "Let's go. Don't want to keep the archangel waiting."

I followed him down the stairs and locked the door, trying to rub away that vision burned in my brain. I would never judge Kat, of course. Our sins were our own. But there was so much more to the story I didn't understand. How could I possibly ask her about such an obviously shameful part of her past with George? One I knew she must regret.

It was around five o'clock as we exited Jude's home, then stepped through the courtyard and the darkened alcove onto the street. The crisp December air nipped at my cheeks and nose. Heavy clouds pressed down, dimming late afternoon to deep gray.

I zipped up my jacket. Hands in pockets, I strolled alongside George, who picked up the pace heading toward Jackson Square.

Holiday wreaths hung on almost every door. One door decoration was shaped in a fleur de lis wrapped in red, green, and gold ribbon. Silver lights wrapped the wrought-iron railings. A life-size Santa stood in another arched entry. We set off the motion sensor as we passed, sending Santa into a robotic dance to the song "Have a Holly, Jolly Christmas."

Christmas. This had always been a time of pure joy for me. The season of love, kindness, and generosity of spirit. Yet now…I was filled with none of these feelings.

A black mantle enveloped me, smothering all emotions but one—vengeance. Only when every foul creature had paid in blood would I be free of this driving need for revenge.

"How are you holding up?" asked George, breaking into my thoughts.

"Fine."

He gave me a sidelong glance. "You look thin."

"Do I? I haven't felt much like eating lately." I clenched my jaw in frustration. "I'm holding up as best I can. I'll be fine as soon as I get Jude home again."

I recognized the tone of desperation in my shaky voice, but there was no way around it. One thought consumed me. Find Jude. Save Jude. Nothing else mattered.

Well, except his child. And I wouldn't let anything happen to her. Whenever fear crept into my mind about where I was going and the danger I'd encounter, my VS would instantly sing to me along our bond, telling me that all would be well, that I must go.

I just needed to keep the world from knowing about the baby. If word got out that the one and only Vessel of Light was carrying the child of the original Dominus Daemonum, I couldn't imagine the conflicts that would provoke.

"You know there's no guarantee that we'll get him back," he said, his tone soft and sympathetic.

"George—" My voice was a sharpened blade. "Do not for one second start giving me the odds of success. There is no other option. You know that. After what I've seen in your head, you should—"

I bit my lip. His penetrating scowl deepened as we strode at a quick clip. I huffed out a breath of white vapor and focused ahead.

"You should know," I said more quietly. "You should know what it is to need a loved one and to go after him—or her—at all costs."

He clenched his jaw, striding faster as we stepped into Jackson Square. "Whatever memories of mine you've seen, Genevieve, they are for you alone."

"I know… Trust me. I wish I hadn't seen them at all."

George veered to the right, heading up the steps to St. Louis Cathedral.

"We're meeting an angel in church?" I asked.

"An archangel."

"A bit cliché, don't you think?"

"It's the only place he feels comfortable enough meeting with so many demons infesting this city."

Holy ground was one of the places demons were still forbidden. Sometimes I marveled at the rules demons were forced to follow—no stepping on holy ground, no possession of a human on holy days. Odd that demons followed any rules at all.

But it seemed a force greater than their wicked will controlled them with compulsion. Like the blood oath. I rubbed the palm of my hand that I'd used to form the bond with

Dommiel. I wondered if demons would still follow the rules after the war had begun.

"Uriel is afraid of demons?" I asked.

"Not hardly. He just has no time for them. They're such a nuisance."

We stepped into the vestibule, the silence pressing in around us, except for the muffled sound of singing from inside the sanctuary.

"Busy man, is he? I mean archangel."

"Indeed."

I followed George through the double doors into the sanctuary. Beautiful choral music echoed loud and strong. A black-clad priest led a children's choir in "Carol of the Bells" near the altar. In accompaniment with angelic singing, the surroundings were truly heavenly from the intricate scenes of saints painted on the ceiling to the vibrantly colored panels of stained glass windows depicting parables from the Bible.

Latin words had been painted in huge bold letters above the altar: *Ego sum via, veritas et via.* I am the way, the truth and the life.

At least here I needn't worry about a demon sneaking up on me. But after Thomas's betrayal, I was wary even around angels.

We walked by the statue of Joan of Arc in her gilded armor. Her stalwart stance, chin held high, ready to face evil with weapon in hand, shot a pulse of positive energy through me. She had burned at the stake for what she believed in. I hoped it wouldn't come to that for me, but if she could confront the wicked with such strength, so could I.

A few old ladies huddled in pews, saying their afternoon prayers. One wore a lace veil atop her head and prayed intently with closed eyes, her rosary beads clicking. I wondered if I spent a little time calling for help from above whether or not my quest would be successful. But then again, I guess I *had* called for help. George steered toward the one who'd answered my call, sitting in the back corner pew, away from prying eyes.

As happened every time I was in the presence of Uriel, my VS zinged to life. I mumbled the cast of illusion to coat myself in a shield where humans couldn't see my skin glowing like Tinker Bell. There was also the sword strapped to my back.

While New Orleans housed the most eccentric of people, openly carrying a weapon was still frowned upon. My cast of illusion could hide what I didn't want others to see.

George ushered me into the pew first. Uriel's aura of power pulsed outward in a jolting wave. But I sensed something beyond the constant buzz of archangel potency. It was subtle but there all the same—a signature of summer fields and sunny days. A surprising aura, but also apt somehow.

I slid into the pew next to him, trying to see through his cast of illusion to his magnificent gold-tipped wings. My VS was definitely growing stronger. The first time I'd met him, I didn't even know he had wings. Now, I could push through his cast and see the outline. Even illusory, they still took my breath away.

"Hello, Genevieve." His deep voice rolled languidly like water over rocks. The dim lighting shone on his golden locks.

"Hi. You've been busy, I was told."

"I apologize. I know the urgency of your mission. But there were other things too pressing that I couldn't leave undone."

"Like?"

His electric-blue gaze flickered to George, then back to me.

I arched a brow. "Is it some super-secret angel stuff that doesn't involve me?"

"No. It definitely involves you. Those in hell aren't the only ones who sense the stirrings of war."

"Is that so? I imagine that has started quite the shit storm."

The corner of his mouth quirked up into a slanted smile. "Yes. You could say that. There are many Flamma of Light who believe you are the Vessel spoken of in the Prophecy of Glastonbury."

"Ha! Finally." I nudged George with my elbow. He remained silent. "Flamma on our side are listening. It's a freaking miracle."

Uriel raised a hand to still my excitement. "Even so, the war will not end on the night of the Blood Moon. It will begin that night."

After much deciphering between Kat, George and me, as well as through consultations with other hunters, we had deduced the "red sky" mentioned in the prophecy referred to a total lunar eclipse. It just so happened that astronomers had begun announcing that we were due to have a total lunar eclipse, the kind often called the Blood Moon or the Hunter's Moon, on December thirty-first.

New Year's Eve. The marking of a new year and a new world.

"And while you will play a vital role as a weapon of Light, the war will be unfathomable in its devastation to this earth."

I swallowed the lump forming in my throat, thinking of my father, of my best friend Mindy, of her mother. I would protect them any way I could when the time came. But I feared the future all the same.

"I know what you're thinking," said George. "How could agents of good allow death and destruction to come to this world?"

I nodded in agreement and said, "Why should humanity suffer? They aren't part of this war."

"Oh, but they are," said Uriel. "They will choose one side or another and play their part."

"But what of the innocent who are killed? It's not their fault."

"Every war suffers the death of innocents," replied Uriel, his tenor dropping lower as he gazed on the altar. "Civilian casualties are an ugly reality."

I followed his gaze and watched the lovely young faces of the children now singing a soft rendition of "Silent Night." What would happen to them?

By instinct, I placed my palm over my abdomen, until I caught Uriel's keen gaze follow my movement. I pulled my hand away quickly. The archangel's mouth lifted in a knowing smile.

I straightened and cleared my throat. "I'm sure George has apprised you of where I plan to go."

He sobered at once, schooling his features into grave planes. "You seek Jude in Erebus. And you need my assistance."

"Yes."

He tipped his godlike face forward, dipping his chin in acceptance. "I will grant it."

George arched a brow at my surprised reaction.

"Wait. You don't plan to try to talk me out of it?" I asked, baffled.

"Of course not. I trust you know your path. If I can help you, I will."

Speechless because I'd planned on having to persuade him through a lengthy and bitter debate, I shifted in the pew to face him more easily.

"I have a way to find Lethe—"

"How?" interjected George.

Uriel waved him off before I could respond. "That is not our concern."

"Of course it is," George said vehemently, the charm and wit gone. He held on to the pew behind me with a white-knuckled grip. "What if she—"

"George," the archangel said with remarkable patience, "we

know that she will use every precaution to journey there and back safely."

"But—"

"Stop." Uriel raised a firm hand in the air. Though he spoke forcefully, his expression showed only understanding and sympathy. "Sometimes you must trust blindly. Give her the unconditional loyalty she deserves. Which I've given you in the past," he added pointedly. "We've discussed this before, my friend."

Suddenly, this conversation wasn't just about me anymore. George's chiseled jaw softened as he lowered his gaze in resignation. "You're right. Go on, Genevieve."

Hesitantly, I turned back to Uriel. "I'm sure George has already told you Jude was taken by Lethe. I need to know what to expect on the other side. I need to know if there's a way to escape the loss of memory."

I refused to believe Jude could forget me entirely, but I couldn't focus on that right now. I needed to take every precaution of getting in and out of there with my memory intact. After all, what if I actually did make it inside Lethe, only to forget why I'd gone there in the first place? The thought filled me with dread.

"In ancient times, a sentinel of Light began telling the myth of the Rivers of the Underworld."

"But they weren't entirely myth," I corrected.

"Exactly. The soul collectors are like rivers running into the same deep ocean."

"An ocean of souls?" I swallowed, but my mouth was bone-dry.

"Erebus is, in fact, the abyss where all souls meet who have been consumed by one of the five soul eaters."

A streak of cold lightning shot through my veins. If this was true, then Danté would be in that abyss. So would countless other hate-filled souls seeking someone to spend their wrath upon.

"So I don't need to find Lethe?"

"I still think it best to take her as your portal. Erebus is so vast that it's believed souls linger near their portal entrance. We can follow the logic that Jude would be nearby. But there is another matter."

George leaned forward beside me, listening intently.

"The Veil of Lethe." Uriel leaned one arm along the back of the pew in front of us, bracing himself as he spoke. "That's what you must worry about."

"Something tells me I don't want to know about her veil."

"You already do," he said with a sad smile. "The Veil of Lethe is what a soul passes through to get to the other side. It is what erases all memory from anyone crossing over."

"And is there a way around it?"

He shook his head. "If you are seeking Jude, you must take the same path he did. There is no other way into Erebus through the portal of Lethe except to pass through the Veil."

I sighed and sat back in the pew, watching the choirboys disperse from the stage area. A grandmother led her grandson down the aisle. And though he looked around eleven years old, he held her hand openly with pride. A mother spoke with the priest, both of them smiling as the mother gestured toward her son.

I wondered if he was a sentinel like Father Clementine, who'd married Jude and me in Sussex. Was this smiling priest a protector of this place? These people?

"There must be a way," I mumbled, more to myself.

"There is."

My attention snapped back to Uriel. "Tell me."

"There is an elixir. One that is precious and not of this world," he continued, "but I will have to do some desperate bargaining to acquire even a drop."

"Do it. Beg, borrow, steal. Oh, wait… That might not be your style. But I'll offer eternal favors to whoever to get that stuff."

Uriel glanced toward the altar, where the crowd had dissipated and the priest was gathering sheet music from the stands. "Let's stretch our legs into the vestibule, shall we?" he suggested with a wave toward the door.

We strolled out of the sanctuary. The grandmother and grandson lit a candle together for a lost loved one before scooting into the cold evening. I'd refused to light a candle for Jude over the past three weeks of stricken grief. He was not *gone*. Lost, but not gone.

Uriel stood strong and tall. The candles flickered behind him, playing on the edges of his wings, which I could see as if through a gossamer web. His golden underlight shimmered by candlelight.

"I will do everything I can for you, Genevieve," he said with heartfelt conviction, offering his hand for me to shake.

When I took it, his power rippled through me like a flame, not so dissimilar from what I sensed from Jude. But then again, Uriel was his maker. He was the maker of all the Dominus Daemonum. The one who gave the hunters a second chance at redemption.

I sandwiched his hand between both of mine. This man, this archangel, had given Jude a second chance at life when he'd saved him from hell at his making. And now, he offered to save him a third time.

"You have no idea how much this means to me," I whispered. "Please. *Please* do everything you can to get that elixir."

The room lit with golden radiance as he lifted his cast of illusion. I let go and stepped back in complete awe as he spread wide his white, golden-tipped wings.

"I promise, Vessel of Light. I will do everything in my power."

With a whipping crack, he sifted away, leaving George and me alone in the dark and cold corridor. For a full minute, we said nothing in the wake of Uriel's magnificent exit.

"So you have a way in. But what about a way out?" asked George.

When George, Jude, and I had battled a horde of demons at Glastonbury Abbey, I'd been able to summon a human's soul that had been buried deep in his own body for almost two centuries. The demon who'd taken possession of him in the early 1800s was expelled from the body when I beckoned the human's soul forward. It was an innate power I didn't know I could wield. I hoped with all my heart this power could also summon a soul eater from whatever realm she currently wandered.

"I have a plan." It was a risky one, but I had confidence it would work.

"Would you like to share this plan with me?"

"Not really."

With an exasperated sigh, he tucked his hands in his coat pockets. "Fine. I trust you know what you're doing."

I hoped I did.

"Shall I escort you back to Jude's?" he asked.

"No. I have dinner plans with my dad and Mindy."

"Do you want some company?"

I laughed as we stepped outside, the nightlife beginning to buzz through the Square. A tarot card reader had set up her round table with purple muslin scarves draped on top. I wished I could take a seat and have her pull a fortune card that said everything would be all right. But there was no fortune teller to give me any guarantees.

"It was difficult enough to explain Jude to my dad," I said, offering George a friendly tap with my elbow, hands in pockets. "I wouldn't know where to begin with you."

"Very well," he said, the charm returning to his tone. "I know when I'm not wanted. Let it not be said I ever pressed myself against a lady's wishes."

I pulled George into a hug. Hesitantly, his arms came around me.

"Thank you, George. I know this is hard for you. I know you miss him too. Just trust that I know what I'm doing."

"I do, darling girl." He gave me a good squeeze. "I do."

4

"Ohhhh, whooaaaa, sweet child of mi-eeeiiiine." Mindy drew out Axel Rose's chorus in exaggerated glee. Pretty much how she hopped through all aspects of life. I loved the girl. "I love Way-back Wednesday. They play the coolest stuff."

I zipped my coupe through evening traffic down St. Charles Avenue, nearly missing a UPS truck making his holiday route well into the evening. I felt a pang of guilt, not yet having bought one Christmas gift. I loved this time of year. Usually, I'd be the first one to have my shopping done, gifts wrapped and under the tree.

"Earth to Genevieve?" Mindy snapped her fingers in front of my face, then turned down the radio.

"What did you say?"

"Jeez, girl. Talk about distracted. Now I know why you complain when I'm in Dave depravation mode."

Her boyfriend, Dave, did indeed seem to complete her world. When he was gone, she could pout and whine better than anyone. But Mindy could always make the best of things, no matter what. Of course, there was no making the best of things when your man wasn't simply on holiday with his rich parents in Aspen.

"Sorry," I said, trying for a truly repentant smile. "My mind's been wandering a little."

"A little? You obviously don't know the meaning of the word. I knew you were into Jude, but I didn't know you had it this bad."

"Yeah. I've got it pretty bad." I careened around a corner, heading into my dad's subdivision.

"Have y'all talked about, like, marriage and stuff?"

Mindy's wide blue eyes got that glassy look any time the mere mention of white, satin, or wedding cakes came up in conversation. I couldn't help but laugh.

"Yeah. We've…discussed it."

The words stuck in my throat. The memory of Jude standing in front of me in a small church in England, his expression adoring as he vowed to love me for the rest of my life nearly made me choke on a sob. I glanced out the other window and blinked away the tears to get myself together.

This burden of knowing he was gone from this earth—though still alive—was even harder because I couldn't tell my best friend. Mindy could at least console me and assure me everything was going to be all right. Even if I didn't know if it would.

"Y'all have talked marriage already?" she asked excitedly. "Wow, he is really into you, Gen."

"Mmhmm." I fisted my hands tighter on the steering wheel.

"Oh, sorry. I know it's hard, but he'll be back from this business trip soon, huh?"

"Yeah. Soon." I pulled up the driveway and came to a stop behind Dad's Ford truck. We both got out.

"Don't be depressed. It's not forever."

I winced as we walked up the driveway. "I'm not depressed. I'm just—" Exhausted, terrified, angry.

"I know you miss him. I get it. It's just funny to see you so wrapped up in a guy." She tied the wrap of her long cream cardigan tighter around her waist.

I'd left my sword at home tonight, carrying only the concealed daggers in my boots. Jude had cast a protective ward around my dad's house and I'd demanded George strengthen them recently, so I packed light when I came home.

Sometimes I needed to be the girl I was before this all started. Of course, I could never let my guard down completely. But I felt lighter all the same as we walked through the back gate to the entrance off the kitchen.

The second I stepped inside, my VS hummed a steady electric charge. It always did when I was at my dad's. Something to do with the wards Jude had set around the house or something.

Dad stirred a pot over the stove, giving us a beaming smile when we walked in. "There are my girls!"

He tapped the wooden spoon and set it aside, then pulled me into a big bear hug. He smelled of roux and Old Spice and home. Yet again, I swallowed a sob. He brushed a kiss on my cheek, then gave Mindy the same treatment.

"Now aren't I the luckiest man alive to have such pretty dinner dates?"

Mindy giggled, always falling for Dad's silly charm.

The back door opened behind us. "Greetings to the house. I come bearing gifts."

"Erik," I said with a smile.

He waved with the French bread in hand. Erik was a family friend and basically an adopted son for my father. His own parents had died years ago up north. When he came down here to work in wetlands research, Dad had given him a job at the dojo, and Erik had just wheedled his way into Dad's heart. And mine. I had no other siblings. Erik was the brother I never had.

"So." He arched a brow at me after a swift hug. "The prodigal daughter returns?"

I punched him in the shoulder. Though tall and gangly, he was fitter than his physique let on. I'd sparred with him often enough to know.

"I've only been away from the dojo a few weeks."

After Jude was taken, I was unable to focus on helping out at the dojo. I'd been planting the seed of my biggest and most elaborate lie yet, that I'd enrolled in a student-abroad program for next semester.

So I explained I'd been tied up with application essays, paperwork with the arts and sciences department, and packing what I'd need for a full semester abroad. Dad had accepted my lies without the batting of an eyelash.

Erik…not so much. He knew I was up to something, but thankfully, he never pried too much. Just enough to annoy me.

It wasn't entirely untrue. I would be abroad. As a matter of fact, I'd been spending most of the past few weeks at Jude's cottage on the Isle of Arran in Scotland. *Our* cottage, I should say.

Mira would be growing antsy if I didn't return soon. We hadn't been separated this long since her birth.

The agonizing moment when Jude was ripped from my life, I'd sifted directly to the cottage and curled on the floor in a ball of grief. A burning warmth had traveled from inside my abdomen up out of my chest. The glowing orb of brilliant white light transformed into Mira—a snowy white hawk. But not an earthly hawk. My spawn. A fey being made from the Flamma of Light. I'd been with her on the island most of the time since Jude had been gone.

I'd only recently come back to town to see Dommiel. When I went to Jude's house in the French Quarter afterward, I needed to be surrounded by his things, to feel his presence all around me. I'd slept in his bed, remembering the many nights we'd lain there, talking, kissing, cuddling, making love.

Mindy and I were roommates, but we'd both been shacking

up with our boyfriends for months now. She only commented once since he'd been gone, asking where Jude was. Since his business of authenticating rare weapons often took him traveling out of state, I had an easy excuse. As long as Mindy and I checked in with each other daily by cell, there were no worries between us.

"And where's this famous boyfriend of yours?" Erik smirked. "I figured he'd be here for the last supper and all."

"God, Erik," I said with a frown. "Don't make it sound so dire."

"Yeah, she's only going to England," said Mindy. "Omigod!" she squealed. "I can't wait till Mardi Gras break! I'm making Mom buy me my plane ticket to London for Christmas."

My dad clutched his chest. "Mindy, sweetheart. I'm an old man. Please don't make that sound again."

"You're not old, Mr. Drake. You're like fine wine. Men like you get better with age."

My dad actually blushed. "Well now…on that thought, I better finish dinner for my ladies. And, of course…you, um, Erik."

I smiled. My dad flustered was possibly the most adorable thing in the world. For a strapping forty-something man who did indeed seem to grow finer with age, he had no clue how his bashfulness made him even more endearing.

"Smells good, Dad. Gumbo?"

"Seafood gumbo." He opened the fridge and pulled out a pint of raw oysters. "Why don't y'all grab a beer and head into the living room. It'll be ready soon."

I grabbed three Heinekens for us before taking his advice. Dad already had the television tuned to the holiday music station. Michael Buble crooned "Let It Snow," which I always found to be ironic for us down here in the Deep South.

It never snowed. If it did, it was once in a very long while, *maybe* leaving enough sleet-snow to scrape off cars to build a mini-snowman. Still, the song meant the holidays no matter where you lived.

Mindy plopped onto the leather sofa. I did the same. She took a deep swig. I pretended to drink mine, refusing to give Mindy a reason to interrogate me why I wasn't drinking. She might play ditzy sometimes, but she was quite perceptive. She smiled, then wrapped an arm around my shoulder.

"I'm going to miss you."

"I know. I'm going to miss you too." My stomach flip-flopped when I thought of where I was really going.

As much bravado as I showed to George, I was terrified I'd go into the underworld and never return. I blinked back the sudden tears stinging behind my eyes, unable to hide them this time.

"Awwww." Mindy leaned in for a one-armed hug, both of us still holding our beers. "Don't be sad. You're going to have such an awesome time. I just wish you could go after Christmas."

Another lie. I needed to cut ties now. As soon as Uriel got what I needed, I was heading into hell.

"I know. But they like to get you set up in your hall of residence and get the orientation over with before the semester begins."

Erik sat on a loveseat on the other side of the coffee table. He brushed his brown hair, which always seemed to hang in his eyes, off his forehead. He sipped on the Heineken. "So what are you studying?"

"Oh, the usual."

"Like?"

"Honestly, I haven't chosen the courses yet. My advisor gave me a list to choose from that would meet the requirements on my transcript." Lie. Lie. Lie.

"Mm-hmm."

I pretended I didn't know what he was alluding to, admiring the brightly lit Christmas tree we'd decorated together a few weeks back.

"I've got to go potty," said Mindy, setting her beer down and bouncing toward the hallway.

Erik shook his head at her. "She just says whatever she thinks, doesn't she?"

"Yep. Never had a filter. Seems to work for her."

"Must be nice," he said, draining the rest of his beer and setting it on the coffee table.

"How's work in the Wetlands?"

"Work." Always the introvert.

My VS thrummed a steady stream through my body. It wasn't triggering a warning of any kind, but every time that line to my power was revving higher than normal, it put me on alert.

Erik leaned forward, elbows on his knees, hands clasped. "Are you okay, Genevieve? You don't quite seem yourself these days."

Something about his observant gaze sent my adrenaline higher. A familiar awareness shivered through me. He didn't give off the pulse of power of an angel, but there was just something niggling at the back of my mind.

"Erik. Are you…"

I had no idea what I was going to ask him. Are you an otherworldly host of Flamma? The question in my mind sounded ridiculous. I couldn't possibly ask it aloud.

"Am I what, Genevieve?" he asked. Just when I thought he'd answer my question in the affirmative and put my sudden suspicions to rest, he said, "Am I hungry? Yes. I'm starving."

"Well, that's good," said Dad, stepping into the living room and wiping his hands on a towel. "The rice is done. Let's eat."

"Awesome," said Erik, taking his empty beer bottle and disappearing into the kitchen.

My pulse slowed, the shot of adrenaline dissipated, my VS humming steady.

Was I crazy? Paranoid? I was seeing sentinels, angels, and demons wherever I went these days. The next thing I knew, I'd be accusing my dad of being a saint. And while he was an earthly saint to me, I doubted he could hide that kind of secret.

I needed to get back to Arran. That was the one place I could meditate and build my strength, focus my power. I needed to see Mira. My connection with the snow-white hawk grounded me in a way that defied explanation.

I pasted on a smile so I could get through dinner, then get the hell out of New Orleans.

5

I stepped lightly down the dark, stone corridor, drawing closer to the pool of light up ahead and the feminine sounds of pleasure. The eerily familiar moan of the woman drew me faster to the open archway.

Inside the chamber lay a dark-haired woman in bed beneath a fair-skinned, black-haired man. She clawed the man's back as he lay between her legs, thrusting hard. Her ankles wrapped the back of his thighs, encouraging him.

I stepped closer, for they hadn't seen me, hadn't heard me. The man whispered down at the woman pinned beneath him as she writhed in ecstasy.

"Am I your master?" He rolled his back like a snake, slamming inside her with brutal force. She cried out.

"Yes," the woman whimpered.

He fisted her hair and pulled, arching her neck.

"Say it again."

"Yes."

Cool wind and the bite of winter wafted over me, sucking the breath out of my lungs. I recognized the two lovers coupled in sweat and lust and violent submission.

"You don't need him. Only me. I am your master," he repeated in a silky whisper, pumping harder, faster.

"Yes. You are my…"

"No!" I shrieked.

They stopped and peered toward the doorway where I stood. I stared back at the smoldering face of Thomas and my own, then snapped awake.

I sat up, panting. "Never," I choked out on a hoarse sob before looking out the cottage window, where a gray dawn rose. My heart pumped hard at the nightmare.

I rubbed my palms over my face, glad I'd sifted back here to Arran after dinner with Dad and Mindy last night. But I also sensed the immediate loneliness that accompanied living here without Jude.

I'd had dreams of Thomas before. The sultry, seductive kind that heaped a boulder of guilt on my back. This was different, a horrifying nightmare of my submission to darker temptations. This was my subconscious torturing me with my fears as the time to enter the underworld drew closer.

Still…the dream put me on edge.

I threw off the layers of quilts and trudged into the bathroom of the cottage Jude and I had shared for a blissful week-long honeymoon. Hard to believe that was a mere three weeks ago.

After cleaning up, I slipped on a pair of thick wool socks and wrapped the blue, black, and green tartan around my shoulders. I shuffled into the kitchen and lit the stove with the lighter I'd had to buy for the cabin.

We hadn't needed it before. Jude could conjure fire at will. He'd never told me how he'd gotten that handy ability. Actually, I'd never asked. One of those many questions still on my "ask Jude" list.

My stomach rumbled, and a subtle wave of nausea squeezed my gut into a knot. I patted my still-flat abdomen.

"I hear you. I'm coming."

Morning sickness had settled in this past week. But as long as I ate as soon as I awoke, the nausea faded. I filled the kettle under the faucet, staring out at the bleak gray sky. Clouds pressed low and heavy.

A white dot in the distance drew closer. Mira winged out of the clouds, soaring directly for the cottage.

As was her way, she sifted straight through the stone wall facing the sea, flapping her snowy wings and settling on the wooden table. She dropped a mussel from her beak and fluttered her feathers. Setting the kettle on the stove, I walked over and calmed her with soothing caresses.

"It must be cold out there."

She blinked her gold-bright eyes slowly as I smoothed my palm from her head down her back, giving me a greeting chirp.

Over the past weeks, I'd learned to interpret meaning behind her sounds. She chirped again with a soft blink of her eyes, a happy sound she often made—such as when I'd offered her raw oysters for dinner or when I'd given her the warm nest of loose yarn and torn quilts for her to sleep on in the cottage.

Her clicks and chirps meant nothing to the average person, but to me, it was like interpreting a toddler's grunts and coos. The thought made me pause and brush my palm over my abdomen, wondering what our child would look like. I hoped she looked like her father.

"I see you brought your breakfast inside." Mira blinked heavy lids, letting them fall closed. Her cold feathers warmed under my touch. "Let me see if I can get this place a little warmer."

Picking up the fire poker, I stirred the black embers, finding a few reddish coals still glowing in the ash heap. I stepped outside for some kindling in the pile next to the door. A blast of frigid air and a few snowy flakes whooshed in through the open door.

"Brrr!"

I set to piling the kindling and blowing on the embers. Smoke billowed a corkscrew plume up into the chimney. Within a minute, a flame lit. I fanned it higher, then piled on a peat log.

Clack, clack, clack.

Mira tapped her beak on the mussel, digging out her breakfast from the broken shell. I shivered and looked away, not wanting to watch her swallow the slimy creature.

Whereas I could usually eat a dozen raw oysters and relish the slippery delicacy, pregnancy had made me queasy about such things.

When the kettle whistled, I poured myself a steaming cup of water and dunked a bag of Earl Grey inside. After adding a touch of cream, I curled into a ball in the seat closest to the window and lifted Jude's gray wool sweater hanging over the back.

Hugging the sweater to my chest, I nuzzled my nose into the soft threads and inhaled deeply. I closed my eyes and sipped my tea in the morning silence.

Deepening my concentration, I reached out to him in my mind, in my heart. From almost the moment we'd met, he'd been able to tell when I was in trouble, able to sift to me at will.

While I couldn't sense danger now, I knew he was alive. The thread that bound us was unbroken. Stretched thin and frayed in the middle, but still strong. Still *there*. That's all I needed. The barest flicker of hope.

"Good morning, Jude," I whispered, starting my morning ritual. "Mira is eating her disgusting breakfast on your table again. But I don't think you'd mind. You'll love her when you finally get to meet."

I sipped my tea, the warm liquid sliding down my throat, heating me from the inside out.

"There's something else I need to tell you, but it'll have to wait until we're face-to-face."

I opened my eyes and stared out at the gray pall pressing down on the world. My underlight glowed as always when I sought Jude across our frail connection.

"Hold on, my love. I'm coming soon."

I set my tea on the table and brushed his wool sweater over my cheek, needing the touch and scent of him as I needed breath in my lungs.

There was never any reply or any inkling given that Jude might sense me across our supernatural bond. Yet…I felt him all the same, never wanting to leave this state of fusion across dimensions. But I allowed myself only this time in the mornings with him. Otherwise, I'd curl into a fetal position on the floor and never return, like I almost had the moment he'd been taken.

This wasn't an option. Our child needed me to be strong. And so did Jude.

My cell phone dinged, signaling a text. I wiped away the tears from my cheeks and the grief settling hard on my heart. Finding my leather jacket on the sofa, I dug out my cell to find a text from Kat.

Kat: *Where are you? Not at your apartment or Jude's. I checked. At your little hideaway again, wherever that is?*

Jude had kept this cottage on Arran hidden from everyone for centuries. I was the only one he'd brought here. I'd summoned George three days after Jude had disappeared with Lethe, but I'd made him promise to keep this place secret. Apparently, he had.

It had nothing to do with trust. Jude just wanted a place of his own where no one could find him. After being alive for almost two millennia, I could imagine he had a few privacy issues. I figured he'd forgive me for the one transgression whenever I brought him back home.

Me: *Yeah. You want to meet up?*

Kat: *Sure. But not here. Gorham and Razor are being profound assholes these days, and they're up to something. I'll meet you at Jude's.*

Gorham was duke of the underworld who served Bamal in New York. Razor was Gorham's right-hand man. If those two were up to something, it wasn't good. Last time they were misbehaving, Gorham had used his essence, a form of spawn, to enslave young girls in some sort of prostitution ring.

Demons were permitted to use their influence on humans to do their bidding, but never with mind-controlling essence. That was when hunters could step in and punish the wayward offenders.

Me: *Meet me in an hour?*

Kat: *No. I need to rendezvous with Dorian first. How about dinner tomorrow night?*

I hadn't considered the time difference. While it was early morning here, it would be middle of the night in the States. We agreed to meet in New Orleans at six o'clock.

I set my phone back in my pocket and curled back in my window seat. Mira perched on the edge of the table, her talons digging into the wood. She chirped for attention. I petted her with slow, even strokes. But she wouldn't settle, angling her head at me with wide eyes.

"No. I won't leave you here this time."

She made a cooing sort of purr.

"I know. You're tired of being left behind. Well, if there's any place I can get away with having a white hawk for dinner company, it would be in New Orleans."

El Gato Negro was rather empty tonight. Tucked away on the farthest end of Decatur, it attracted more locals than tourists. I was fine with having a small audience, having waltzed in here with a wild bird on my shoulder. Kat waved to me from a table tucked in the corner. She grinned like a fiend when she saw I'd brought company.

"Mira!" she said as soon as we sat. "She actually brought you out of hiding?"

"Hi, Kat. Good to see you, too." I scooted my chair up to the table.

She laughed, her platinum-blonde ponytail sliding forward as she picked up a tortilla chip from the basket and held it out for Mira. She chirped in my ear and snapped at the chip, crumbling most of it on the table as opposed to eating any of it.

"I think she's just being nice." I tried to get a look at her, but it was too hard from this angle. "She doesn't actually eat corn chips."

"Looks to me like she does," said Kat with a smirk cracking her pretty face.

"Drinks, ladies?" asked a petite brunette with fuchsia bangs and neon nail polish.

"We'll have two margaritas on the rocks," replied Kat.

"Um, actually, just a Sprite for me."

"What's wrong?" asked Kat.

I shrugged. "Just a little upset stomach."

Kat nodded. In all honesty, I'd become closer to Kat than Mindy the past few months, since my eyes had been opened to the world of angels and demons living amongst us. But this was one secret I couldn't tell her, for the same reason I loved her so much.

She'd do anything to protect me and my baby. Sending us into hell with nothing but some angel elixir for protection wouldn't satisfy her own sisterly instincts to protect me—us.

Besides, I'd been informed that no demon hunters could go where I was going. When demon hunters expelled one of the damned, a piece of the darkness was left behind, tainting them. Residue, we called it. This was the reason for the inky black swirling the irises of demon hunters. They carried the smudge of sin from demons they expelled, the darkness leaking into their blood, even their eyes.

Every so often, they called the soul eater, Styx, who ate the residue, releasing the hunter from the weight of sin for a while. But it was never enough. The chance of hunters making it out of hell was much lower than it was for me. Expelling demons for me was more like a cleansing, as I wasn't paying a penance as they were.

And anyway, this was a mission of stealth, not guns blazing and swords swinging. I'd have Mira, and that would have to be enough.

"Okay, one margarita and one Sprite." The server looked up from her pad, catching sight of Mira.

"Um, she's part of a performance I have later," I lied, knowing it would sound real enough in a city like this.

The waitress shrugged with a wink. "She's pretty." Then she sauntered off to the bar.

"Of course she is," said Kat in baby talk, scratching under Mira's beak. "So what performance do you have later?" she asked. "The Lady and the Hawk?"

"That has a nice ring to it. I think that was a movie. *Ladyhawke*, actually. Mira, hop down over here please."

She did, perching on the vacant chair to my right, huddling into a ball, her orange-gold gaze narrowed but watchful.

"Really? That was a movie?"

"Yeah. Seriously old one. With the guy who played Ferris Bueller."

"Who's Ferris Bueller?"

"You have to know who Ferris Bueller is, Kat. What is it with you demon hunters? You've been around longer than I have, but you know next to nothing about pop culture."

"Soo-rry. It must've been a tragically important film."

"Yeah. It was. To every teenager who ever lived. John Hughes understood the stolen joys and abject misery of adolescence better than anyone."

"Who's John Hughes?"

I froze with a chip dipped in salsa halfway to my mouth. "I can't believe you just asked me that question."

Our server set down a jumbo margarita glass rimmed with salt, and a Sprite. "Here you are." She handed me a straw.

"Thank you. Excuse me, do you know who John Hughes is?"

She scoffed, which sounded more like a snort. "Of course I do. Director of *Breakfast Club, Pretty in Pink, Some Kind of Wonderful*. I mean, come on. Everyone knows who John Hughes is."

"See!" I glared across the table.

Kat tossed the straw out of her glass and took a big gulp of her margarita. "Oh well. I think I'll survive."

"It's okay," I told our server who seemed baffled. "She's foreign. I'll amend this tragedy as soon as possible."

"Right. So what can I get you ladies for dinner?"

Kat ordered some quesadillas, and I ordered the largest burrito they had with extra everything on top.

"I thought you had a stomachache," said Kat with a suspicious expression.

Oops.

"Oh well, yeah. But I think maybe I'm just overly hungry." After we handed over the menus, I crossed my arms on the table and leaned forward, eager to change the subject. "Tell me what's up with Gorham and Razor. You said they were up to something."

Kat plucked the lime wedge from her drink and sucked on it before folding it in a napkin. "For one, Gorham hasn't been to his club in over a week."

"I'm assuming that's unusual for him?"

"Very. One thing about Gorham is he loves his little kingdom on the seedy side of the city. But he's been disappearing for days and up to a week at a time with Razor."

"No idea where they're going?"

"Nope, but they report to Bamal's tower on a regular basis. They're scheming. And no sign of Bamal's Vessel at all. Not since the incident in Paris."

A few weeks ago, the civilized world was turned upside down when a terrorist bombed the Eiffel Tower in Paris, killing hundreds of tourists. What authorities didn't know was that the woman shrouded in a black burka, concealing her identity, was in fact a Vessel of a demon prince intent on wreaking havoc upon the human world.

"They're keeping her hidden and safe for the night of the Blood Moon, aren't they?"

"Definitely." Kat swirled her straw in her drink. "But while all is quiet on that end, there's demon activity everywhere. Clubs, parties, weddings, even at damn fundraising events. You know, I had to expel four demons from a charity ball for children with cancer last week. They were stirring animosity among the two top patrons who happened to hate each other. It was an all-out brawl by the time I got there."

"*Damn.* That's bad. I'm surprised Dorian let you go for even a night," I said.

As her partner hunter in New York, he was an excellent warrior, but they needed more than one watching Bamal's territory.

She tossed her straw aside and took a gulp of her margarita, which made my mouth water. "Well, he's worried about you too, believe it or not, and wants me to be sure you're okay without…" She put her drink down with an uncomfortable clink.

"Without Jude," I finished for her.

Kat leaned forward into the light and pulled something from a loose strand of my hair. She inspected the piece of kindling. I supposed I hadn't cared to take care of myself much these days.

"Sticks, Genevieve? Are you ever going to tell me where you've been going? And why you smell like sheep and the sea?"

I shook my head. "Not until we get Jude back. It's his secret."

"I bet you told George."

Her otherworldly eyes swirled more green than black, twinkling brighter at the mere mention of George.

Gazing at her now, I could only think of her pinned to the wall while Prince Damas ravaged her…all to her delight. She caught me. I stirred the ice in my glass with the straw, cubes tinkling as they circled.

"What?" Kat sat back in her chair, expression wiped of all humor. "What's that face mean? Tell me."

I squirmed but sat up straighter, trying to find the courage. I wanted answers only she could give me. I could never breathe a word to George of the vision I'd seen. To know what I'd witnessed in his mind would devastate him even more than Kat.

"Tell me, Gen."

I tucked my hands between my crossed legs to keep from fidgeting. "You know that I sometimes see visions or memories of George's."

"Yes." I could practically feel her heartbeat speeding erratically.

"I saw one...of you...when he went to find you with Damas."

She dropped her head forward. "What did you see?"

"You were in a bedroom in a castle, I think."

The place had felt so familiar, like Danté's fortress, where he'd abducted me.

"You were chained to a wall, but—" I couldn't complete the thought aloud.

She sat up slowly with a sad laugh. Shaking her head, she grabbed the margarita and drained it in three gulps.

"Of all the visions of me to see, you picked that one."

"I didn't pick it. I have no control over what I see. My VS just lights up, and I can't stop it."

"It's okay."

She spread her fingers, palm down, on the table, then rolled up her long sleeve. It had never registered that Kat always wore long-sleeve tops—usually black. I just figured it was some kind of personal demon-hunter uniform she instilled for herself.

But when she rolled the other sleeve up her forearm and flattened both palms on the table, I realized why. I'd seen her in a dress before, when we went to dinner with George and Jude the first time, and at the Crescent City Masquerade Ball. Both times, she'd worn bangle bracelets or cuffs on both wrists. I'd only thought it her fashion sense, not pretty camou-flage for what she hid beneath.

My heart plummeted.

Ringed around her pale wrists were circular silver scars. Kat rolled her wrists on the table, palms up, showing me how they wrapped in a complete circle.

"I'm reminded every day of what happened there. These dungeon bracelets"—she rolled her fists in the air, the lamp-light shining on the silvery rings—"they remind me of my own weakness."

"Weakness?" I asked too loudly. The couple two tables over glanced in our direction. Mira's eyes popped open. Kat shushed me with a finger to her lips. She pushed her sleeves back into place, then petted Mira's snowy head till she closed her eyes again.

"How can you possibly say this shows weakness?" I asked.

"Because Damas had won," she said casually, continuing her attentions to Mira, who dozed again. "Prince Bamal plays the big man in New York. But mark my words, when his brother finally resurfaces for this war, *that* is who we'll truly have to battle for our very souls. He plays dirty, and he always wins." Her voice cracked.

"You don't have to talk about it."

"Here we are." Our server set down our plates. "One pulled-pork burrito with everything, and the gulf shrimp quesadillas."

Kat dropped her gaze to her lap. I gave Fuschia Bangs a half-hearted smile. She got the message and disappeared.

Kat lifted her chin, swallowing hard. "I want to tell you. I've held it in too long. George doesn't understand." She fiddled with the napkin in her lap but took a deep breath and held my gaze. "Damas doesn't torture. He doesn't maim or hurt to get what he wants."

"But he handcuffed you."

"To keep me from running away. I tried…at first."

Fuschia Bangs popped up to the table and set a second margarita in front of Kat. "Looked like you needed another. It's on me." She winked and jerked her chin at the good-looking guy behind the bar with a tattoo snaking up the side of his neck. "The bartender and I are friends…with benefits."

"Thanks," I said.

Kat knocked back two gulps. Regaining her composure, she resettled in her chair, her face hard and cold.

"Damas is the king of them all when it comes to deception. He makes promises. He seduces. He's extremely intelligent. And above all, he's patient. I had no idea who or what I was up against until it was too late."

She bit her lip at another memory that seemed to flash through her mind.

"I didn't know I was the prize he'd wanted all along—a reward in this game he'd been playing against George. When I"—she flipped her sleek ponytail to fall down her back —"when I was handcuffed in his lair, he fed me, even bathed me right there in his bedchamber. He took care of my every need. He talked to me and told me stories."

She paused. A crooked smile lifted one side of her mouth.

"Stories that made me pity him, then later feel more for him. I was kept in captivity a very long time. After a while, I thought I'd never leave."

The last she whispered.

"He never forced himself on me. Ever. He wasn't like his dickhead brother, Danté. Besides, I think he enjoyed the conquest. Making me want to submit."

Danté had kidnapped me and had certainly planned to take me by force. That was, until Jude showed up and chopped off his head, then fed him piece by piece to Cocytus, the banshee-like soul eater. I shivered at the memory of her gulping down his body. He got what he deserved, but it was a gruesome vision all the same.

"What was he like?" I prompted Kat gently, as she'd slipped away to her haunted past for a moment.

"He just slowly crept into my mind, then my heart. I'd get angry and scream at him that George would come for me. He'd give me this sad sigh and tell me George would never come. That George never loved me. That he'd already forgotten me as time wore on."

This was the first time I'd ever heard her mention there was once love between them. Perhaps still was. I knew they'd shared a past, but love?

"After a while, I started to believe him and all his beautiful lies that followed. I was so alone, so desperate to feel anything but the aching emptiness. I longed for affection, for comfort. One day, he unchained me. I didn't try to run. I never even left his bedroom. Then one night, he had a particular look in his eyes —an expression I'd seen often enough on men. Though up until that night, I'd only had two lovers, my then-deceased husband…and George."

She glanced up for my reaction. I kept my cool and let her spill her heart.

"Damas told me I needed to be cuffed for my own good. He didn't trust me. I cried and begged and told him I was completely devoted to him. He smiled when I said things like that. God, the thought makes me sick now."

She inhaled a deep breath then spit out the last of it quickly.

"Once I was chained, he put his hands on me without asking for the first time. He whispered in my ear. I'll never forget his words. 'I need to bind you, Katherine. Now, you will submit to me, because you have no choice. Now, you will let me fuck you the way you want me to, because you have no choice. Now, you will beg me to be your king, your lover and your master.'" Her voice wobbled when she added in a whisper, "And he was right."

Two tears slipped down her pale cheeks. I reached over and grabbed one hand. She let me take it.

"I was weak, Gen. And I'll never forgive myself."

She pulled her hand from mine and let out a soft sob into her napkin. I was thankful we were sitting in the secluded corner so she could have some privacy. She needed a minute or two to let it all out.

"How long were you kept there in captivity?" I asked.

She shrugged a shoulder. "Decades."

"Decades?" For a second, I'd forgotten that she, like all Flamma, were ageless. But…decades? With a silver-tongued demon prince.

"When I went in, it was the early 1800s. When I left…when George came and took me away, the United States was on the verge of the Civil War."

"And New York needed a demon hunter, didn't it?"

"Yes. And I needed to be far away from my homeland and all memory of what I was before."

I wouldn't give Kat cheap or false words. She knew the truth of what had happened, and there was nothing I could say to erase or change it. But I sure knew of one way to make her feel better. Something I'd been itching to do myself.

"What do you say we scarf down this delicious Mexican food that you're crying all over, then go kick some demon ass?"

She dropped her balled-up napkin and grinned at me through watery eyes.

"Hell yeah."

6

Mira refused to sift back to Arran when I told her she couldn't go where we were going. Instead, she perched herself on top of the building as we crossed the street toward the basement-level club I knew too well. Stubborn bird. But I loved her.

The beefy bouncer at the door was the same guy I'd seen other times I'd visited Tartarus. One of those nights happened to be my twentieth birthday—the first time I'd laid eyes on the dark and beautiful Jude Delacroix and the first time I'd nearly been killed by a demon. Best and worst birthday ever.

"Long time, no see," said the bouncer, eyeing my ID.

"You missed me, Sunshine?"

I have no idea why I found it fun to tease straight-faced behemoths like this guy, but I did. His chiseled features cracked into what was sort of a smile before he nodded me through the door. Kat followed.

We beelined for the bar. I ordered a Killian's Red, though I had no intention of drinking it. I needed a prop to fit in.

Music pumped a heavy beat even though the crowd was thin. No attention whores danced in the cages up on platforms on either side of the dance floor tonight. Just a few black-clad regulars milling about and a group of frat boys at the bar knocking back shots to the cheers of a gaggle of plastic blondes.

We sat on the end of the bar with the best view of the club, scanning the place for demons. I reached out with my VS, sensing nothing.

"You don't have your sword, do you?" asked Kat.

Most Flamma, strong ones like Kat and me, could see through casts of illusion when we concentrated. Right now, she was staring at my back like it was about to catch fire.

"There's nothing to see. No. I didn't bring it, but no worries. I'm armed." I patted the boot I propped on the middle rung of her barstool.

"Do you even need it?"

"I don't know. But the steel helps me channel the power. I—"

Both our heads snapped to the dance floor. The sudden presence of demons seemed to signal us at the same time.

"What the fuck is he doing here?" I murmured.

Among a throng of dancers grinding to some death-metal tune was Bleed and one of the guys from his band, Gallow's End.

Bleed. What an asinine name. Perfectly fit the owner. Last

time Kat and I had seen him in that demon club on Bayou Sauvage, his long, sleek hair was dyed midnight blue. He'd changed it to deep purple.

Two stumbling-drunk girls were clinging to him and the tall, lanky guy I recognized as his drummer. Their eyes shimmered red in the smoky dark of the club.

That was one thing lower demons didn't have to worry about in New Orleans. With so many freaks in the city joining artificial vampire covens, there was no need to disguise red eyes or sharpened fangs. Both of which were the distinct outward features of a lower demon inhabiting a human.

The young brunette who looked barely eighteen hung on to Bleed's arm. He made a signal to Drummer Boy, who escorted another girl wearing a short miniskirt.

They veered toward a back entrance, taking their fully intoxicated dates with them. Knowing Bleed was into kink and violence and certainly not above forcing his will on the weak and vulnerable, I nudged Kat.

Without a word, we were off the stools and following the four through the storage room, which indeed had a back entrance for deliveries. The door to the alley creaked closed.

Bleed said something, obviously witty and wonderful because the girls giggled in unison. I reached into my boot and pulled out my sharpened stiletto. Kat pulled out a similar but thicker blade, sheathed on a vest harness covered by her jacket.

Kat cracked the door, peering outside. We heard the distant shuffling as the four moved farther off.

"Hurry," I whispered.

We slipped through the exit and stalked after them. They rounded the corner of a darkened building. Although we were walking in the open, this part of the business district was deserted after hours.

In the French Quarter, you could find crowds on every street well into the wee hours of the morning. But this area near the business district was only busy during the daytime. Perfect place to commit some heinous crime on unsuspecting, underage and intoxicated girls.

By the time we reached the next block, Bleed and Drummer Boy had lured the girls down a dark alley. Talk about cliché.

"Where issit?" slurred the brunette. The other girl's giggle echoed off the alley walls.

"Right over here," said Bleed. "I'm going to show you."

I could hear the sneer in his voice. I grabbed Kat's arm, and she looked back at me as we edged closer to the corner of the alley. *Sift*, I mouthed. She nodded.

Holding up my left hand, I put up one finger, then two, then three.

We sifted into the alley a yard away from them. There was no telling what Bleed had in mind, because we interrupted whatever it was he had planned. Somehow, he didn't look surprised to see us, which put me on edge. My VS zinged to life, igniting my underlight to full throttle.

The brunette pointed at me, her hair a mess, her lipstick smeared. "Hey. You look like a fairy."

She and her friend burst into laughter, one of them bending her knees with the weight of drunken hilarity. They'd definitely put more than alcohol in their systems. Or they'd had four too many of whatever they were drinking.

"Go," I told the girls. "Get out of here."

"Whu…why?" hiccupped Miniskirt.

Whispering the words to break through a cast of illusion, I slashed my dagger in the air toward Bleed, who'd not said a word. For the briefest of seconds, the outer shell of the beautiful human he hid inside vanished, revealing the fanged, bony, pasty-gray demon he truly was. Three seconds later, the veil that cloaked the demon in dark beauty hid the beast within once more.

The girls—slack-jawed and wide-eyed—simply stared in horror until Bleed hissed at them. They squealed and stumbled away toward the street, the brunette breaking a heel but not stopping.

"There now, Domina," said Bleed, speaking to Kat, whom he favored over me. My feelings weren't hurt, trust me. "Now that you have us all to yourself, what shall we do?"

"I think it's time to send you back to your playpen, once and for all," she answered with stoic grace.

The gangly one was already backing away, but not Bleed. "I would like nothing more than to bask in the tortures you have planned for me," he said in a sultry tone, inching closer to her.

"Not this shit again," I said, remembering how last time he'd begged her for a little S&M treatment.

He ignored me. "Word has spread, Domina, that you have certain tastes. Delicacies that align with my own desires."

"I'm riveted," said Kat. "Please. Do tell what demons are saying about me."

The salacious grin that spread across Bleed's face as his hand slipped down and cupped his crotch sent a grotesque chill over my body.

"That you prefer…chains in the bedroom. I too enjoy bondage, Domina." The asshole hadn't noticed that Kat had gone rigid with rage, just as she always did two seconds before she was going to strike. "Perhaps we could enjoy each other—"

She sliced out with a leap, but he moved like lightning, prepared for her attack. He ended up behind her with one arm wrapped around her waist. The other hand whipped out and grabbed her wrist holding the dagger. He whispered something I couldn't hear. Before I could even react to help her, she doubled over and flipped him on the pavement.

Drummer Boy took off running. "Kat!" I screamed, taking two steps after him.

She hovered over Bleed, who lay there, grinning like a fiend, on the ground. "Go." She waved me off. "Get him!"

I took off. The dude didn't look like much, but he sure as hell could run with those long-ass legs. I sprinted after him down the alley, coming out onto another well-lit but abandoned street in the business district.

The frosty air filled my lungs, stinging as I sucked in each breath. His cackling laughter echoed to the right. I caught his lanky figure rounding a corner. Another alley.

As soon as I ran into the lane, a familiar signature wafted over me. Winter wind and new-fallen snow, ice castles and midnight blue—a potent seduction of ice and heat. The sight, sound, smell, color of winter emanated not from the atmosphere but from the man—the angel—standing five feet from me.

Drummer Boy was gone. In his place stood Thomas, the one I'd longed to find, to exact vengeance upon him for his betrayal, for what he'd done to Jude. For what he'd done to me. But for several seconds, all I could do was stand there and stare at him, convincing myself he was real and not another mirage.

Black hair curling at his nape like Michelangelo's *David*. Sea-green eyes deeper than any ocean. Fair, flawless skin that rivaled that of Raphael's most perfect painting. And a physique that had indeed been born of heaven. He was the embodiment of breathtaking beauty, and yet all I could do was imagine how quickly I could plunge my dagger into his heart.

I wanted to show him the depth of my rage, of my grief, of my loss. But I kept still.

When he moved closer, a mere foot from me, all I could do was stand there, literally shaking in my boots, trembling from the myriad emotions shooting through my frame. Before I killed him, I wanted answers.

"Genevieve." Even his voice was beautiful. I cringed, wanting my name off his tongue. "You are so lovely. I've missed you. I—"

"Shut *the fuck* up. I can't believe you'd just walk up and pretend like nothing happened." I shook uncontrollably.

"You have a right to be angry—"

"You got that fucking right."

"Please…Genevieve. Calm down for a minute."

He raised his palms in supplication, as if gentling a wild animal. That was when I noticed the air around me was moving. A torrent of wind swept in a circle, lifting my hair.

I gripped my dagger so hard, my bones cracked and my skin pinched against the hilt. A sharp sound crackled in the air. Electricity snapped in a halo around…me. He was using something to try to calm my ire, but it wasn't working.

"What did you do with Drummer Boy?" I asked.

"Who?"

"The guy I was chasing. The lower demon."

"I banished him back to hell. I took care of him for you."

"Don't do me any fucking favors. I remember the last one you did."

A tear streaked down my face as I remembered. Jude had cupped my face in his hands, mouthed the words *I love you*, then leapt into that foul creature, Lethe.

"Don't do *anything* for me anymore. I swore I'd kill your ass the first second I saw you again."

He lowered his palms to his sides as the wind died. "I understand your anger."

"You understand nothing. Were you trying to trap *me*? Or Jude?"

His eyes cast downward in a moment of remorse, though I knew better. "I knew Jude would be there. I knew he would take your place."

"It's as I thought, then." I lunged, slamming his body into the brick wall. Before I could shove my dagger into his chest, his wrist wrapped mine, my blade an inch from the fine linen of his shirt.

"Don't, Genevieve. Please listen." His plea, filled with anguish, made me pause.

One fist in his pretty shirt, I kept my weight angled against him, waiting for his grasp to relent. Panting fiercely, my breath white in the night air, I said all that my heart screamed.

"You took my husband from me. You sent him to some torturous circle of hell where I can't...I can't see him, can't hear him, feel him. I *hate* you, Thomas. I wish I could make you feel the pain I feel now. Even if I killed you, it wouldn't change anything that you've done. He'd still be gone." I choked on a bitter sob.

His grip held hard on my wrist. But his other hand came up, gently brushing the loose strands of hair from my face, his fingertips trailing my cheek. I pulled away from his hand.

His eyes pooled with unshed tears, electrifying them to an unnatural glossy green. I was transfixed by the moment...by him.

"He doesn't deserve you."

"And you do?"

His mouth tilted on one side, cracking his cool facade. "I

suppose not. I only wanted… I love you, you see. A desperate man will do what he must to win his lady."

I jerked back out of his grasp, needing his hands off me. His honeyed words didn't have the same impact as they once had.

"But I can feel it." He pressed his fist to his heart, over which I'd held my sharpened blade a second before. "We were meant for each other. Don't you sense it?"

I shook my head. "Are you fucking crazy? Didn't you just hear me?"

"Do you dream of me as I dream of you?"

I flinched and moved farther away. Were the dreams some kind of vision? More than mere fantasy?

His tender smile sickened me. "You do dream of me." He shoved off the wall, stepping into my space. An unearthly force pulled at my core, like gravity drawing all things toward Thomas. I stood still, falling almost into a trance as he lifted a hand and cupped my jaw.

"You dream of me," he whispered with confidence, gaze roving my face, landing on my lips. "You must love me." When his thumb trailed across my cheek, I snapped from the strange icy hypnosis he'd held me in. Slapping his arm away, I sliced out with the other, nicking his sleeve. Then I walked backward toward the street entrance, not trusting this asshole at my back anymore.

Mira shrieked as she soared down the alley. Thomas glanced over his head just as she winged above him, then landed on my shoulder. The comfort of having her near grounded me, repelling his wintry aura. For these few minutes with Thomas,

I'd been spinning, lost in orbit. Mira brought me back to earth where I belonged, her protection a shield around me.

He stared at her, entranced, as most Flamma were when they first saw her. "She is your creation."

When my underlight glowed, so did Mira, shining like the beacon of light that she was.

Fortified by Mira's strength, I inhaled a deep breath and said with firm conviction so there would be no doubt of my feelings, "I do not love you, Thomas. I never will."

He swallowed hard. His Adam's apple bobbed, his jaw clenched.

"I understand now that killing you won't bring Jude back. But if you threaten those I love again—angel or not—I *will* kill you. Make no mistake about that. Do you understand?"

His chin dipped slowly. He closed his eyes in ascent for the briefest of moments. When he lifted his gaze to me, a flicker of raw emotion I'd never seen in his eyes sent my heart racing.

With a tight nod, he said, "I do." Then he sifted away in a blink.

Mira lifted off into the night. Needing to escape the confined and foul atmosphere of this alley, I immediately stepped away, jogging out of the alleyway and around the corner, literally bumping into Kat. She grabbed my shoulders to steady us both.

"Did you get him?" I asked.

"No. That bastard can't sift, but he's fast as hell and wily as a witch. What about the other guy?"

"Gone."

"What's wrong? You look like you've seen a ghost."

"Worse. An angel."

"No. Way. Thomas?"

I walked on. Kat fell in stride.

"So? What did the asshat have to say for himself?"

"Nothing worth repeating. Let's get out of here."

Before she could argue or ask me another aggravating question I didn't want to answer, I grabbed her hand and sifted us out, knowing Mira would instinctually follow us to Jude's home. She always knew where I was going. Our connection was constant and unbreakable.

As Kat and I tumbled through the Void, my mind kept drifting back to the glimpse of something primal in those glass-green eyes before Thomas had vanished. I couldn't name what I'd seen for a split-second there.

Only one word screamed at me when he quietly confirmed he understood my threat clearly. And it made no sense, for it was the opposite of what he'd said. In my mind, I heard only a defiant *no*.

7

After Kat had gone, I sifted across the ocean to the only place where I felt safe, where I felt closest to Jude. A blustery snowstorm whipped over the island. Once Mira and I were safely in the cottage, I barred the door tight and stuffed a towel under it to keep out the cold.

As I settled under a dozen quilts in the bed where I'd spent my wedding night in his strong arms, I listened to the gale winds howl and rattle the panes like some ominous warning of danger drawing closer.

I snuggled deep into my pillow, angry that I hadn't at least given Thomas a punch in the face. Leaving him with a bloody, broken nose would've made me feel better. After all this time waiting for the moment to show him what his betrayal had done to me, I couldn't lay a scratch on him when the time finally came. I'd nicked his shirt but hadn't cut to the skin.

What was wrong with me?

In his presence, I felt stifled, restricted somehow, my emotions jumbled, masking my anger. It wasn't that I forgave him. Because I didn't. It was pity…and compassion. I pretended his words meant nothing to me, but they did. I didn't return his sentiment of love, but I could certainly sympathize with his position.

He'd guarded me my whole life and had formed an attachment over time. He saw Jude for his flaws, his sins, not the remarkably selfless and loving man that I knew. Without a second thought, Jude had leaped into the arms of that wraithlike soul eater, knowing he would go into the pit of hell and possibly never return…for me.

Jude.

Jude.

Jude.

I burrowed deeper into the pillow, wishing with all my heart that I would see him again, that he would hold me in his arms and love me still. As grief threatened to pull me under, a warmth in my belly reminded me I wasn't alone. I smiled as I closed my eyes.

Soon, little one. We'll bring him home soon.

I WASN'T SURPRISED THE NEXT MORNING, WHILE SIPPING WARM tea and watching snow swirl on the cliff, to see George sift onto the hillside and march up to the cottage, lowering his head and pushing into the blustering island wind.

I'd awoken early and dressed before I'd eaten a bite. I hadn't even tried to connect with Jude across our invisible bond. A premonition that something was coming had me on edge. Armed and ready, I stood as George opened the cottage door, his expression grave. Our gazes locked, and I knew.

"It's time, isn't it? Uriel has what we need."

A sharp nod. He reached out his hand. "It's time."

Mira alighted from her perch on the chair onto my shoulder as George took my hand and guided me outside and beyond the wards. He sifted us a shorter distance than I expected, speeding us through the Void at a dizzying pace.

We arrived on a rolling hill of Dartmoor beneath the shadow of a boulder I recognized from our last visit here when we had a rather tense gathering with Prince Bamal and his lackeys.

A brutal wind cut across the moor, the sky rolling with white clouds, the sun zipping in and out of view. I wondered if it would be hot in hell, as mythology suggested.

I'd been in the Black Forest and Danté's castle before. The air was damp, tepid, dead. This time I was going where souls were kept and punished. I shivered at the yawning gulf of the unknown opening before me.

Standing in the stone's shadow were Kat and Uriel, waiting. Uriel stepped forward. He didn't use the cast of illusion outside the presence of other humans. I didn't think I'd ever quite get used to the aura of magnificent power and the sheer beauty of his glorious gold-tipped white wings.

He spoke to me as if it were commonplace to be having a covert meeting on an empty moor right before I went straight to hell. Feeling slightly manic, I tried not to laugh to myself as the lyrics of an old drinking song by Drivin' 'n' Cryin' popped into my head.

I'm goin' straight to hell, just like my momma said.

"You're smiling. That's unusual for one in your position," said Uriel when he reached me.

I waved a hand. "Just thinking of something totally ridiculous for a time like this. Nerves, I guess. But believe it or not, I am happy. Scared shitless, but happy. I'll be with Jude soon."

George came up next to us. "Be bloody sure you return, both of you, safe and sound."

"I will," I promised with sincerity, refusing to show any doubt.

Strange that I honestly had no doubt about finding him and bringing him back. Something inside me—my Vessel Sense or some higher power—sang through my bones that this was right. My doubts tended to leak in when I thought about what state Jude would be in when I did finally find him.

George sauntered over to Kat while Uriel spoke to me privately. He pulled from his jacket a small hourglass-shaped vial with a cork top. The liquid inside was clear glacier blue. Beautiful, yet not as fascinating as I'd expected.

"Hmph," I said.

"What is it?"

"I don't know. I guess I expected something more…heaven-like."

"Which would be…?"

I shrugged one shoulder. "I don't know. Glittery stardust or something?"

"You do realize we don't live in the clouds."

"Of course I do." I rubbed my forehead. "Don't be ridiculous."

Uriel smiled. When he did, my stomach fluttered. It had nothing to do with any infatuation-like feelings on my part. It was simply the fact he was stunning in every way. When he smiled, a girl's natural inclination was to lose her composure.

"This elixir will protect you from the veil. However, it has no power against the evil you will encounter there."

"Understood. Thank you." I took the vial, knowing this was for real now. "Is there enough that I can give some to Jude when I reach him?"

Stoic and serene, he answered with a directness I admired. "No. This potion does not restore memory. We will address Jude's ailments upon your return. Let us focus on step one first."

"Right. What about Mira?"

He studied the hawk on my shoulder, then stroked her head. "I'm not sure what effect the veil will have on an animal, even a divinely born one. Best give her a little as well."

"Okay. Good." I inhaled a deep breath and let it out. "I suppose that's it, then."

He placed a hand on my shoulder. A wave of power—all golden, bright, and exceedingly dangerous—jolted through my frame. His signature was off the charts.

"The power lies in you, Vessel of Light. You hold all you need for defense within you."

His electric-blue gaze dropped to my belly. He moved his hand to rest over my womb. I sucked in a sharp breath.

"You also carry a precious gift within you."

Mira clicked her beak together in agitation near my ear.

"How did you know?"

"I sense the child." His perfect brow pinched into a frown, then he removed his hand. "I am not sure why or how."

I diverted his attention to something else. "What happens after the veil?"

"When you cross Lethe's veil, you will find yourself among listless souls and demons who have wandered into her realm."

"How will I know if I've strayed out of her realm while looking for Jude?"

"Black rivers border each dominion." Rivers. Of course. The reason these creatures morphed from monsters into underworld waterways in Greek mythology.

A rumble of thunder in the distance drew our attention. Heavy, billowing clouds rolled in from the south, darkening the vast green moor to gray.

When Uriel turned back to me, his eyes had darkened with the storm. Strange. His expression hardened; the arches of his wings drew tighter against his back.

"What is it?"

"Just a reminder."

I frowned and glanced at the oncoming storm. "A reminder?"

"We are entering a darker age. The Flamma of Light and Dark will clash in battle on earth, bringing with them a storm like never before."

"On the night of the Blood Moon. That's when it will begin."

A deep nod. The wind before the storm blew his golden-blond hair across his forehead. Even so, nothing marred his appearance or aura of perfect power.

"What the prophecy doesn't mention is that not all Flamma will remain true to their cause. The war will be long. Light will become dark. Dark will become light. And there is no prophecy foretelling who will win in the end. If the end should ever come at all."

Uriel took a step back and gestured to the others. "No time to waste. Call the one you have struck a bargain with to take you to Lethe."

"How did you know I struck—oh, never mind. All-seeing archangel. I get it."

He smiled that serene smile as we ambled toward the others. "Not all-seeing, I'm afraid. That would be a great gift indeed."

When we joined Kat and George, who whispered with heads bowed together, I reached inside my pocket for the raven feather and lightly blew on the plume.

With a crackling snap, the well-dressed, heavily pierced, one-handed demon appeared in front of us.

Kat swung the black coat she held over her shoulder and crossed her arms. "You did *not* make a deal with him."

Dommiel crossed his arms too, mirroring her stance, and rolled his eyes.

"Yes. I did." I stood alongside Dommiel.

"He can't be trusted," said Kat.

"I've made an eternal blood oath with him. He can and *will* be trusted."

The demon hunter, the saint, and the archangel all stared in disbelief.

"Eternal?" George moved out of the shadow of the boulder, the dim light catching the edges of his chestnut hair, casting him in a golden halo. "You would put your faith and our fate in the likes of him?"

Dommiel puffed out his chest and scoffed. "Dude. What the fuck?"

I raised a hand, palm out, to silence Dommiel. True, he was a demon. One of the enemy. But he'd helped us in the past and had shown no signs of being untrustworthy. I'd learned in my short stint as a Vessel that the world was colored in myriad shades of gray rather than divided in resolute lines of black and white. Thomas was a prime example.

"My faith lies with my heart, which tells me to follow the right path toward the Light." I clenched my fist against my heart. "Everything in my being tells me to go to Jude, to save him. If that means taking steps that are slightly unorthodox for the almighty Dominus Daemonum, like swearing a blood oath with Dommiel, then so be it."

"Gen," said Kat, interrupting my tirade and pointing at my body.

My underlight glowed jewel-bright, my VS humming furiously through my veins, charging the air with stormy emotion.

George exchanged a knowing glance with Uriel. I hated it when they did that, sharing secrets with a look. But this was no secret. With every day that passed, I drew closer to my full awakening.

Uriel flared his magnificent wings, the tips catching the sunlight, sparkling like stardust in the darkest night.

"And so our Vessel must 'walk through darkness' to find her way to the Light. She knows her path, George. We won't interfere."

The prophecy. I'd not considered these obscure lines, thinking they had something to do with the eclipse. But no, the prophecy was already unfolding, even with every step I'd take into the underworld.

Kat lunged forward and gripped me in the tightest hug, the black coat she was holding bunched between us. "Be careful. Go kick some demon ass. And bring Jude back."

I squeezed her tight. "I will." I fought the tears welling inside, pretending I was fearless when I was scared out of my skin. "I promise."

"I brought this for you." She whipped out the coat that wasn't a coat at all, but a long, sleek cloak with a hood. The material was fine but not shimmery, falling against my skin like silk.

"This will hide that fair skin of yours and keep you under cover."

I'd already dressed in full black leather, according to her recommendation. Not for fashion, mind you, but because it was thick and could withstand an attack with claws or blades better than denim or cotton. And here I thought she always wore leather just because it made her look bad-ass.

"Thanks," I said with a smile as she hooked the cloak at my neck and adjusted the harness of my sword at my back so the hilt stuck out behind my neck at the perfect angle.

George said nothing. His earnest expression—a blend of determination, frustration, and admiration—was all I needed.

"Remember," said Uriel, his voice rumbling with restrained power, "you cannot save all the lost souls you will encounter, no matter that your human heart wants to do so. Your mission is clear—find Jude and bring him home. If you lose your way, trust your companion to be your guide."

Mira chirped in agreement next to my ear. I gave him a steady nod. "Yes. I understand."

"Take care, Vessel of Light. You carry many precious lives in your capable hands."

He spoke of the fate of the world, should I not return, but also of Jude and our child.

Wrangling my nerves before they splintered into a million pieces, I turned to Dommiel and held out my hand.

"Okay. I'm ready. Let's go to hell."

With a bored expression of indifference, he took my hand. "I thought you'd never ask."

"Hang on, Mira," I whispered to her at my shoulder. She clicked her beak and dug her talons in tighter. I was glad of the extra padding I'd sewn into the right shoulder.

We sifted into the midst of the Black Forest as I'd expected. Endless, starless night stretched above us. The damp chill seeped through leather to my skin. The eerie naked trees stood lifeless, like sentinels of a dead land, its inhabitants nothing but ghosts and memories and nightmares. But I knew better.

This dark woodland spread through the vast levels of hell, connecting one prince's realm to the next. And I knew whose realm we were in. I recognized this trail, this spot where we stood. Thomas had brought me here. We were in the realm of Damas, the prince who eluded us all but who seemed to be working behind the scenes at all times.

"This way," said Dommiel, his words echoing in the thick mist. "Stay close."

"Not a problem," I replied, my words a rippling echo. There was no telling if and when something might pop out and we'd have to make a run for it.

Dommiel, normally calm and cool, was antsy, glancing over his shoulder too often.

"Would you stop that? You're making me nervous."

"Do you have any idea what will happen to me if anyone finds out I brought you down here?"

"No," I answered honestly. He didn't reply. "What will happen?"

He faced forward and moved faster. "You don't want to know."

As crazy as it sounds, I hadn't thought about what it would mean for him. So wrapped up in my own selfish needs, I hadn't even stopped to wonder what demons might do to a traitor, for that was what he'd be considered for helping the Vessel of Light sneak into hell. I stepped faster to keep pace.

He led us along the same familiar path I'd trod about a month ago. Adrenaline pumped fast, quickening my gait even more, the memory of that day tightening my nerves into a knot.

"There is a place up ahead," said Dommiel. "I know that Damas has a sacred place near here. He's made some sort of bargain with Lethe to protect it. She will come when an intruder crosses there."

"I know."

He stopped in his tracks, his expression sharpened.

"Does this place have a tall, black monolith?" I asked.

He nodded.

"That's where Jude was taken."

Dommiel shook his head. "I don't know how he thought he'd get in and out safely in the first place." He walked on with me silently behind him.

I wasn't sure either, but I knew Thomas had set him up. I

balled my fists and swallowed the old anger wanting to rise to the surface. I needed to be calm and focused.

He stopped at the oak-like guardians, their craggy branches laced over the path—a twisted crown to mark the entrance.

"This is where I should leave you. I don't want Lethe expecting payment of me."

"Of course not."

I pulled the hourglass vial from my pants pocket, uncorked it, and dropped a little in the cup of my hand.

"Drink, Mira."

I held it up for her, and she drank without hesitation. I drank off the rest.

Cold fire poured down my throat and licked through my veins, igniting my VS. My skin tingled and burned bright. Even Mira gave off an effervescent glow.

"Wow."

"I'll say," said Dommiel.

I tucked the vial back into my pocket. "We're ready."

"So it appears," he said with a lopsided smile, the three studs in his bottom lip curling upward. "Follow this path into the clearing ahead."

"Right," I said, needing no instructions. I was only a few yards from my destination. I took a step, then held my hand out to the demon who'd risked much to help me. "Thank you, Dommiel. I won't forget this."

He took my hand in a firm grip. "For what it's worth, I hope you make it out. Even with your hunter, bastard that he is."

"Thanks," I replied with a smile and a squeeze of his hand before releasing. That was as close to a fond farewell as I would ever get from him.

Then he stunned me with a genuine, "Good luck, Vessel." And he meant it. He walked back up the path several yards, then sifted away, a swirl of ashy earth spinning in his wake.

"Okay, then." I wound my way along the path, rounding the bend toward the clearing drowned in ethereal blue mist. "Here we go, Mira."

She made a tiny squeak.

"Yeah. I'm nervous too."

I pulled her from my shoulder and tucked her into my jacket, zipping it and leaving space for her head to peek out between the sliding flaps of my cloak. She wiggled her tail feathers, tickling my ribs.

"Just be still. I know what I'm doing." *I hope.*

I walked into the circle closer to the stone monolith. The yellow parchment holding the centuries-old prophecy was no longer pinned to the stone.

The demon prince, Damas, must've heard we'd been here. I'm not sure why he'd move it now. We'd gotten the information we needed. Perhaps there were others still looking for it, like his brothers. Then why did he ever keep it here in the open, even if it was protected by Lethe, where demons could find it? It made no sense.

But I didn't have time to examine the inner workings of Damas. Not right now.

The air vibrated. A tremor shook the ring of bare trees, branches scraping. "Come on, you bitch," I mumbled, my words dying as sound drained from the atmosphere, the telltale sign of a soul eater's presence.

A flutter of movement at the center of the stone, a fragment of tattered gray billowing outward, the tails of her cloak preceding the ghastly body of Lethe. The hag with ratty hair and obsidian eyes floated into the clearing, her skeletal arms opening wide for my embrace.

Finally.

Her fleshless lips opened as if to moan or scream, but she made no sound at all. She was the essence of bleak nothingness, a promise to sorrow-filled souls who'd lost their way between heaven and hell.

She was also the monster in the dark, threatening to suck the unsuspecting into her desolate domain. She was the absence of life, of anything at all. She would make all of them forget, erase the memory of a world that loathed them. She was the balm to the weary, the bitter, the ones clinging to a mortal world that no longer knew they existed.

A thrill pumped my heart faster, for I'd waited to see her again all this time. But not to forget. Never to forget.

I sprinted toward the wicked fiend. Four steps, five, six, seven, then a giant leap into her spindly arms with one thought foremost on my mind and one name on my lips.

Jude.

8

Her cold, bony arms squeezed me breathless, then a soft pull drew me through a gauzy entry. Was that the veil?

I hovered midair, no solid ground beneath my feet. A damp cold seeped into my skin, then I fell like a rock. Hurtling through endless darkness, I flailed my arms for something to hold on to, to break my fall. Nothing.

It wasn't the same sensation as sifting through the Void, a purposeful movement toward a certain destination. It was a rocketing freefall—fast and hard—my hair and cloak whipping behind me, my lungs unable to suck in air. I crossed my arms over the bundle inside my jacket, though Mira had tucked her head under my arm.

Light up ahead. My eyes watered from the rush of wind blurring my vision. A faint gray glow drew closer. My descent slowed gradually, then suddenly, till I was merely floating, weightless and gentle above solid ground.

Setting one foot, then the other on hard earth, I glanced

ahead to a cave-like opening leading to open space. Blocking the exit was the origin of the gray light—a misty shroud of vapor, silvery light snaking in loops and whirls like a living substance. Lethe's veil.

"Okay, Mira. Here we go."

She popped out her head, orange eyes blazing bright. As soon as I stepped one foot into the veil, the rest of me was sucked inside. The vapor caressed my cheeks and hands like silken ribbons, a soft brush, a soothing pull forward. The veil wasn't thin but a barrier several yards thick.

Upon my second step, a seizing pressure wrapped my chest. I cried out at the sudden intrusion, the pressure increasing, moving up to my head. A crushing vise squeezed. I wrapped my hands around my head and stumbled forward, trying to get out. The pressure increased.

The tendrils of silver encircled my wrists, my chest. I launched myself the last few feet, stumbling out on the other side. Instantly, the pressure ceased; the veil let me go.

I spun around to see no malevolent thing coming after me out of the misty wall. The vapor swirled within the veil, silver ropes entwining and circling in a sinuous, benign pattern.

Mira wriggled out of my jacket to perch on my shoulder. I turned around to face Lethe's realm—a vast, bleak wasteland of black rock, craggy mountains and cliffs in the distance.

Lightning rolled over the mountains. No thunder. Only the *thump-thump, thump-thump-thump* of electricity beating in dark clouds, a storm trying to come to life. Though there was no sun or natural light other than the intermittent streak in the sky, the land was colored a murky gray, and I could see well enough.

No souls roamed the wasteland, but I could feel them—a drifting presence of humanity, absent of any emotion at all. Mira flapped and lifted up into the air.

"Not too far," I called after her.

Silent as a ghost, she soared higher but stayed above me. Reaching over my shoulder to the harness at my back, I unsheathed my katana and scanned the desolate landscape, wondering where to start.

I closed my eyes and reached out with my VS, hoping to find that connection with Jude. Nothing.

I inhaled a deep breath, blew it out, and started walking. The ground was solid rock, loose stones crunching under my feet. Rock formations jutted up out of nowhere. There was no rhyme or reason to this place. Mist might hover in one area only to evaporate a few yards away, showing nothing but miles of rock in the distance.

I walked and walked, finding not a sign of life anywhere.

After what seemed like an hour, I stopped and sat on one of the rock formations jutting out of the ground. Laying my sword across my lap, I pulled the flask of water from inside my jacket, remembering a conversation with George when I'd interrogated him on all he knew of the underworld.

"What about food and water? It may take me a long time to find Jude."

"You will need little. I'm not sure if you're aware of this, but you're a Flamma of Light."

Laughing, I'd said, "Yes, I'm quite aware of it."

"What you may not realize is that part of being ageless and in addition to the supernatural healing ability, you can go quite a long time without food or water. If you must."

"So, pack light."

"Yes. Bring something for nourishment, but more importantly, get in and out as quickly as possible."

"I plan to."

I laughed now as I swigged down the water, my throat parched after only a short time in this place. "I hope you're right, George," I whispered to the air.

A sound to my right. I jumped, swishing the water over the top, grabbing the handle of my sword as it slipped from my lap.

A woman rested against the rock. Dressed in an old gown, something I might've seen on a rerun of *Little House on the Prairie*, she stared up at me from wide, black eyes—no whites at all. She held up bony hands in a protective gesture over her head, trembling.

She was…afraid.

I don't know what I'd expected upon encountering souls here in this wasteland of the underworld. Ghostlike, waifish figures no more substantial than transparent figures floating about.

I hadn't expected them to appear as solid as me. Jude had been taken, body and soul. But most of Lethe's victims were souls wandering between death and the afterlife, lost souls Lethe found and fed upon before they could make their way to either heaven or hell. This place was its own kind of damnation—a limbo of nothingness.

After fumbling to screw the attached top back on my water flask, I shoved it back inside my jacket pocket. I lowered my sword but kept it at my side, raising a palm to show I meant no harm.

"Don't worry. I won't hurt you."

She smiled. Her front teeth broken, she was dirty, skin hanging from her bones, and yet somehow I could see she had once been beautiful. Fair skin smoothed over high cheekbones. Though her cheeks sank in too far, they would've been the envy of most women of her time when she was nourished and well cared for.

I knelt in front of her and realized she was around my age. Or had been at the time of her death.

"Hi."

Her eyes widened. Her throat moved as she tried to form a reply. A soft, ragged whisper came out. "Hello."

Her frail hand uncurled from her lap. She touched a crooked finger to the back of my hand where it rested on my knee. With her touch, a wave of infinite loss and hopelessness seared through my soul. It was a reflection of what resonated within her own. She dragged her finger over my knuckles, which glowed faintly with my underlight.

"Pretty." Her dark eyes met mine, then she curled her hand back into her lap as if remembering her manners. I was relieved, not wanting to feel what echoed in her sad soul.

"Can I ask you something?"

Mira landed with a *whoosh* onto the rock at the woman's back. The ghost woman jumped, cringing away.

"Whoa, whoa. It's okay. She's with me. She won't hurt you."

Mira stared down at the woman, twisting her head to the side like a curious dog in the way that always made me smile.

"Pretty," said the woman.

"Thank you," I said, accepting the compliment on Mira's behalf. Whether she was a damned soul or not, I'd still be polite. "Can you tell me where there are others? Like you?"

Her vacant eyes met mine again. She blinked twice as if trying to understand my question. She pointed her gnarled finger out toward the wasteland. "Everywhere."

"Yes. But I don't see them. Where do they go?"

"Away." She curled into a ball on her side and closed her eyes.

I didn't know if she told me that others went away or if she was telling me to go away. It didn't matter. She couldn't help me. I looked at Mira, who seemed completely unruffled that we were lost in hell. "Well, let's get going, then."

I walked on while Mira soared high above, my scout and lookout. As I made my way deeper into this desolate world, I passed other souls, hiding in nooks and crevices of rock.

All of them cowered if I approached, covering their heads with their hands. I wondered what or who they were afraid of. I'd not seen any malicious demons or creatures. Not yet anyway.

I'd sheathed my sword, having found no threat. As I traveled deeper, the black rock transformed into fine gray dust. The terrain began to change when I reached the foothills of the mountains I'd seen crossing through the veil.

The cliffs jutted high and far, and lightning licked the sky above. I craned my neck, unable to find the top where they vanished into the inky sky. As they had in the Black Forest, naked trees clustered along the base.

And still, I couldn't sense the bond with Jude. But I'd never give in to despair. I was here, and I knew he was here, too…somewhere.

I passed through a copse of trees, stopping short when I heard a scuffling and snarling, then sudden wailing.

Unsheathing my katana, I sprinted closer, concealing myself behind a thick trunk. Along the path was a ghastly site. Three hideous demons—two naked and scrawny and one bulky with three horns jutting out of his head—circled a young man, clothes torn and ragged. The two smaller demons were pot-bellied with long, skinny limbs, wide, fanged mouths and serpent-like red eyes. They held a net between them and tossed it over their cowering victim with a gleeful cackle.

"Bind him," said the big one, tossing a set of chains with ankle and arm cuffs onto the ground.

He held a wooden club in his clawed hand and wore a sleeve-less black tunic of a finer material. When he turned up the trail, a ratlike tail snaked behind him from the bottom of his tunic.

He stood on hooves, reminding me somewhat of the Fury I'd encountered in Jude's courtyard not long ago. But his domi-nant gait and clothing denoted him as someone with some power.

The cackling demon scuttled on all fours to the chains, apparently excited to do its master's bidding.

"No! No!" The man under the net kicked and fought, but it was certain he would be their prisoner.

Not if I could help it.

I stepped from behind the tree. "Three to one. Kind of unfair, don't you think?"

The smaller demons hissed. The one holding the net over the man lunged toward me as I'd hoped. With a swift sweep of the katana, I lopped off his head, and it rolled across the ashen ground.

The second, smaller demon shrieked and scampered toward me like a spider, fangs bared, spinning as he came. I swung, but my blade skimmed the creature's shoulder. It circled behind me.

I leaped closer to the trees, not wanting to give the big one my back. The cackling demon caught my leg and literally climbed me, claws digging into my leather pants. I gripped its throat as it snapped its jaws at my face.

"*Flamma intus.*" I squeezed its throat, my VS power zinging through my body straight down my arm and into the foul monster. Its red eyes flew wide. With a squeal, it exploded in a puff of ash and white sparks.

The leader of the trio stepped slowly around its captive, who stared out at the display through the netting.

"What are you?" asked the three-horned demon.

His voice was garbled by two yellow tusks protruding from his lower jaw.

Moving with wicked stealth for one on hooves, he circled. I countered the other direction, two-handing my katana, waiting for his attack.

"You are not a pet of Lethe's."

Pet? That was how he saw these poor souls wandering here for him to torture at will.

"No," I answered. "I'm not one of Lethe's."

"You are…different."

I'll say. I readied for his attack as his red eyes narrowed.

Suddenly, a wailing screech lifted our gazes to the sky. Mira dove like a bomb into the clearing, swooping with talons extended. Before the demon could swing his club, Mira clawed his arm, blue-white fire licking up from the wound.

The demon stumbled backward, screaming and flailing as fey fire crawled up his arm, over his face and down his torso until it consumed his entire body and he could scream no more. With a whirlpool of wind, white flames and ash twisted into a tornado, then vanished into the ether.

Slack-jawed, I stared at Mira, who now perched calmly on a branch above the smoking bones, hooves, and horns.

"Is there something you forgot to tell me?"

She opened one wing and scratched an itch with her beak, then settled back into place, giving me this laissez-faire look as if clawing a demon and burning him to ash was normal.

Okay. So my spawn had power of her own. Good to know.

I moved to the edge of the net and lifted. The man crawled out on all fours and rolled to his back, holding his arms above his head. No, not a man. A boy, possibly mid-teens.

Shriveled with wrinkles, his emaciated face and body aged him considerably. His eyes were hollow and black, though the whites of his eyes still shone bright. His teeth and fingernails were gritted with filth. His clothes were dingy and soiled with God knew what, but I could see the unmistakable outline of Spider-Man on his T-shirt underneath the grime.

The modern icon and the spark clinging to his eyes told me he hadn't been in the underworld long. I didn't even want to consider what manner of death had brought this teen here.

"Don't take me to him. *Please*, don't—don't take me to him." He stuttered and stammered like a frightened boy.

Sliding my sword back in its place, I tried for the universal sign of *I mean no harm*, holding my palms out as I had to the other woman on the plane.

"Look"—I pointed to the skeletal corpse of the demon who had intended to drag him off as some sort of bounty—"he's dead. He can't hurt you anymore."

"N-n-not him. The master."

My VS lit to life, prompting me to take heed. This wasn't mindless babble. I squatted on my haunches, bracing my forearms on my knees.

"And where does the master live?"

With a tremulous hand, he pointed toward a peak just beyond

the trees. Soundless lightning lit the sky, revealing the silhouette of a fortress on a cliff's edge.

Having come so close to the mountainside, I could even see tiny pinpricks of hazy yellow light. Windows. A knowing swirled in my gut as I stood, peering over the naked tree line.

"That's where we must go, Mira." She chirped in agreement.

"No, no, no, no, no…" The boy scurried off in the opposite direction, slipping out the way we'd come.

I glanced at Mira. "No personal escort, I'm afraid."

I stepped over the ashen heap of demon and followed the path toward the fortress on the cliff. My underlight blazed bright with each step toward the mountain.

I mumbled the words to cast illusion, not wanting to forewarn demons on guard for this master. My illusion would hide my glow, but not me. I pulled up the hood of my mantle, covering as much skin as I could, wanting to blend with the bleak surroundings. Now that I'd encountered a gang of nasty demons, chances were there would be more about.

Another internal switch flipped on the second I stepped out of the shadow of the trees. The sensation buckled my knees and dropped me to the ground—the distinct signature of flickering flame and impenetrable iron washed over my entire body like the sweetest balm in the driest desert. I breathed in a ragged breath, a tear slipping down my cheek.

"Jude."

9

I sensed him, even from far below the fortress. My VS pulsed strong along the bond I shared with Jude. Mira swooped low and landed beside me, chirping with nervous agitation.

"I'm fine." I picked myself back up again. "He's there, Mira." I dusted off my knees and lunged into a jog, trying to reach the edge of the cliff, then almost tumbling into a giant chasm.

"Ah!" I caught myself, my toe slipping over the edge, knocking gravel loose.

A sprinkling splash revealed this wasn't a chasm. Lightning flashed again, revealing a wide, winding river, blacker than the earth, dividing me from the other side where the fortress stood on a mountain peak.

"Mira," I whispered, realizing we were about to cross the border into another soul eater's realm. She landed on my outstretched arm. "I'll need to sift across, but I need you to be my eyes. Go over and tell me if it's safe for crossing."

She clicked her beak and winged across, her faint glow shining on the water, shimmering like a diamond on black glass.

Sifting could only be done to a place you knew or could see and visualize plainly, as if you'd been there before. I only hoped there was no invisible veil marking the division of kingdoms. Uriel had said nothing about that.

Of course, Uriel had never been here. The information he transferred to me had been gathered from a captured demon long ago. I hadn't asked what devices had been used to extract such a secret. I knew by now the stereotype of angels in white robes singing on puffy clouds was false.

A few seconds later, Mira swooped back with her guttural chirp. With grim determination, I stared across the stygian water, barely able to see the bank on the other side.

Mira perched on something I couldn't make out from this side, her white glow in the darkness giving me a visual. Closing my eyes and saying a prayer, I sifted.

Two seconds later, I stood next to Mira, who perched on a jagged crag of the mountain. I glanced back and forth, wary of demons now that I knew they were out and about. The atmosphere on this side was heavier, denser, more sinister than the air in Lethe's realm. I put my hand to my chest.

"Can you feel it?" I whispered.

She clicked her beak, twisting her sharp hawk gaze in every

direction. I realized it would've been a huge mistake to leave Mira at home.

I needed her if I was going to make it through this alive. Lethe was a ghostly wasteland. Here, malevolence rippled in the air like a sentient being.

"Okay," I said softly. "I don't want to walk around too far in this place. I'll sift short lengths. You move ahead and let me know it's safe."

And so we traveled along the base of the mountain this way. Mira acted as my guide, flying ahead then stopping. I'd sift as far as I could see, perhaps fifty yards at a time. No encounters with damned souls or demons.

Not until we started moving up the mountainside.

Upon the third sift to a mountain ledge, I saw the flickering of flame throwing long shadows on a cavern wall. I peered around the cliff's edge where I'd landed to see an open space.

Five demons in black tunics sat around a fire roasting a leg of something on a spit. The rancid smell made my stomach churn and bile rise in my throat.

"This one'll be tasty," slurred a six-horned demon, ripping a piece of flesh from the roasting meat.

"Wait your turn!" A bigger one clawed his forearm.

That was enough for me. I caught sight of Mira circling another cliff's edge high above. This would be a long sift, but I needed to get out of there fast.

"Do you smell that?" grunted Six-horn, sniffing the air in my direction.

With that, I sifted out and up, up, up, landing in a crouch with my katana drawn and ready. Thankfully, Mira had scouted a safe spot behind a boulder.

Crouching down, I peeked around the rock, finally able to get a good look at the fortress I'd seen from far below.

Like something out of a medieval textbook, more like a medieval horror story or a fortress in Mordor, the fortress wasn't a separate structure but carved into the mountainside, all sharp angles, iron gates and barred windows.

But it wasn't the sight of the place that struck terror in my soul and shot ice through my veins. It was the screams emanating from within its walls. Even more, the beacon of Jude's signature burned strong and true. He was inside that ghastly place.

Two horned demons in matching black tunics stood outside the arched entrance. Just as I wondered who the hell would be trying to break in, besides me, a shrieking woman tore through the open gate past the guards.

One of the guards lifted a bow and nocked an arrow from a quiver at his back. The other grunted something with a wave of the hand and pulled a weapon from his belt—links of barbed chain. He flung them through the air with frightening speed.

The chains wrapped her legs at the knees, tripping her to the ground. The one who'd caught her grunted something unintelligible. Grabbing her by the hair, he dragged her back toward the fortress.

My gut clenched at her wailing cries as she flailed and kicked. Like an insect trying to wrestle a lion, it did her no good. He seemed unperturbed as he continued to drag her and disappeared through the gates.

"My God," I whispered to Mira on my shoulder, nuzzling close to my hood.

I couldn't form a coherent thought that expressed the heartsickness and despair seeping into my bones. The guards weren't to keep people out, but to keep them in.

This was hell. This fortress of pain, reeking of malice and torture. Now I knew why damned souls might prefer Lethe. Better a land of forgetfulness than a land where evil thrived, eager to inflict pain for eternity.

These demons weren't like Garzel, the one who was taken by the soul collector, Acheron. He'd been taken as a punishment for his misdeeds. The demons I'd encountered capturing that teenager in the forest, the ones on the cliff, and the ones guarding this gate were uniformed. They held allegiance for this "master" the boy spoke of.

The master ruling such a place with so many at his disposal must be a powerful being. A high demon.

I licked my dry lips, thinking of the best course of action.

"I need a distraction." Mira clicked once with her beak and opened her wings. "Yes, but wait," I hissed in a whisper. "He has arrows. Be careful and fly high."

I straightened to prepare myself for the fastest run I'd ever made in my life when she clenched her talons in my shoulder with three aggravated chirps.

I heaved out a sigh. "I *will* be careful." I pointed up toward a tower spiraling into the inky black. "Those windows have no bars. If you must check on me, come through there. But you'll do me more good if you wait out here until I return."

I wouldn't admit even to her that I feared I might not return.

"No more dawdling. *Go.*"

She shot up like a missile until I could see her no more. I waited, watching the bulky demon, his four horns silhouetted by a torch at his back.

A high-pitched shriek made my heart leap till I realized it was Mira. On the far side of the fortress where a woodland of black trees sprouted, she swooped and circled in a wild figure eight. The demon guard watched her, slowly edging away from his post.

Then Mira flapped her wings, dropping sparks of blue from her wing tips. I shook my head, amazed at this lovely creature of my own making. She had all kinds of tricks up her sleeves. Or wings, rather.

When the guard ventured beyond my sight, I wrapped my cloak tighter, covering my hands and face, and darted for the open gate. Adrenaline pumped my legs faster than ever before. As I passed under the iron gate into a torchlit corridor, I avoided the line of blood left from the woman who tried to escape, then I slipped along the wall to the first door.

Heartrate drumming, I scanned the small room. At its center stood a round grate and a fire pit. Some sort of meat roasted on three skewers crossing the open flame. I didn't look closely enough to identify the limb. I didn't want to know.

Sharpened spears, axes and weapons of every size and shape lined the walls. There was no one here.

I caught my breath and peered into the hall. The missing guard hadn't yet returned. I mumbled the words to cast illusion over and over again, knowing that some casts could be so strong, they'd render the Flamma practically invisible. Not truly invisible, but warded so well that an enemy might overlook them, thinking they'd seen something, only to look back and find no one there.

Screams deeper in the fortress skated over my skin. My instinct was to run away. But the lure of iron and fire called to me, singing along the bond we shared.

Katana in hand, I skimmed along the stone wall, moving quickly under the sconces of torchlight. I passed another door. Though the doors were closed, an open square window appeared at eye level. Women whimpered and cried from within. I had to look to be sure Jude wasn't being held inside. I wished with all my heart I hadn't.

A cluster of men and women—some black-eyed from the land of Lethe, some with their natural eye color still shining bright—were collared around their throats in a corner. Dark splotches of blood stained the stone floor and a torture rack with ankle and arm cuffs.

A throng of demons sharpened blades near a wall of weapons—horned beasts in tunics like others I'd seen since I'd crossed the black river.

Two demons cackled near a small forge, heating a branding iron, then plunging it into a pail of water. A sizzling hiss rose with the steam, causing the prisoners to squirm.

One of the demons was bigger than the rest. With a curving blade like a scimitar in hand, he ambled toward the chained prisoners, his long rat tail snaking to the floor from beneath his tunic.

I couldn't watch anymore. I ducked down and whispered a prayer for those poor souls, wishing I could help but knowing I couldn't. I didn't think anyone deserved an eternity of torture.

Demons cackled behind the door, obviously excited by the violence.

"Chain her," bellowed one of them.

I slid away from the door, pressing a hand to my abdomen. When a woman's howl of pain reverberated off the walls, ice chilled my blood. I froze, wanting to go back and save her more than anything. I had no doubt that I could, but I wasn't sure I'd ever make it to Jude without the cover of stealth and surprise if I made myself known now.

Uriel's warning rang in my mind. If I saved her, I'd have to flee at once. But I couldn't do nothing.

Sheathing my sword and wrapping the cloak tight, I peeked through the window again to find the demons enthralled, their attention riveted to the poor woman being bound to their torture table.

I eyed the bucket of water next to the small forge in the corner. There were only three torches in the room. I said a quick prayer, calling my VS to help me move as quickly as possible. I stared at my target and sifted right next to the bucket.

The stench of the creatures and the foul smell of rank blood stung my nostrils. I grabbed the bucket and sifted once, doused the torch, sifted to the second torch, then the third, throwing the room in utter darkness.

A howl flew up from the demons as they scuffled around. One roared in anger, probably the leader, as bodies slammed into each other, bumbling blindly like panicked ants.

I sifted outside of the room and dropped the bucket, fleeing down the corridor and hoping I could make it back in time to help those poor souls before the morons in charge could regroup. Swallowing the pain of seeing that woman's suffering, I moved on.

Many of the rooms I passed were steeped in pitch-black, though I heard chains rattling from occupants inside.

As I crossed a basement stairwell, the bond I shared with Jude snapped tight, as if a rope were tied to my waist and jerked me to a halt. When I peered down the stone staircase, the raucous cackles and shrieks of a horde of demons drifted up to me.

Jude was down there.

Sliding along the cavern-like wall, spiraling downward into the dark, I crept faster and faster, following the powerful signature that was unmistakably Jude. Flames and steel interwoven in a tapestry of unparalleled allure brushed against my senses. My VS awakened to another level.

I repeated the incantation for illusion over and over in my mind.

The sounds became more definite as I descended and drew closer to the basement floor.

Crack!

A sharp sound slapped me with bone-numbing dread. A roaring of jeers, hisses, and demonic laughter followed.

I stepped out onto the landing, realizing I'd entered an underground arena. An inner corridor circled a vast space. No one stood guard. A wide round arch opened into the area where wicked cries of glee mounted loud and strong, beating against my VS like a fist pounding my chest. Deep-rooted evil dwelled through that archway.

Crack!

I flinched. Another wave of sinister joy from a demonic audience.

I stepped closer, whispering the incantation for illusion so that I might remain unnoticed.

Through the archway lay a miniature coliseum, a tiered audience fifty rows high, packed to the ceiling with ghastly fiends —red-eyed, multi-horned, sharp-clawed, some bony, some bulky. And every one of them was riveted to the display on the black-stone arena floor.

My view was obstructed by the man standing at the center with his back to me—a beautiful line of male perfection, golden-hued and bare down to the black silk pajama pants he wore.

Recognition dawned with a sickening punch to my gut. His muscles flexed as he swung his arm in an overhead arc. A whip in hand—the black snaking length whistling through the air—he sliced his arm down hard, the lash hitting an unseen target.

Crack!

The golden-haired god of this torture den tossed his head back in triumph, raising his arms to his enthralled audience, his whip dangling and writhing like a living creature.

"Do you want more!" he bellowed. His clamoring fans answered with a roar, waving arms with frantic bloodlust, begging for more.

Fear lanced through me, rising with the bile in my throat. His voice hadn't changed from the last time I'd heard him, even though his head had been severed from his body.

Danté.

10

Danté, the demon prince who'd possessed my soul and who would've possessed all of me had Jude not come to my rescue. He was the master of this den of demons.

Without taking another step, I knew the object of Danté's malice and hatred, the savaged being half-concealed by the prince. I moved closer, still within the shadow of the rafters.

Danté marched around his victim, gloating with his perfect smile spread wide. But scars marked his pretty face—the gash I'd given him from ear to lip. And his neck… It had been sewn back together with some rudimentary material and poor stitching, the scar an ugly welt wrapping his throat.

He circled to the other side. My heart sank at the sight of his victim.

Jude. Naked on his knees, he was stretched over a stone bench, chest-down. His arms were shackled into a cross position. I could see nothing of his skin or the intricately inked tattoo of St. Michael the Archangel defeating the devil, which had spanned in complex beauty over the entirety of his back. From shoulder to waist, he was a mass of blood and gashes, red dripping onto the floor beneath his knees.

On the other side of Danté stood two iron rods with shackles the height of a man's ankles and wrists. A pool of crimson filled the area between the iron posts. Dark splatters and smears ran from the posts to the bench where Jude lay prone, facedown and nude, unmoving—beaten bloody for the entertainment of this demon horde and for Danté.

I trembled, trying not to fall into petrified shock.

"Yes?" the demon prince asked the crowd. Sadistic egotism filled his voice. "I believe he wants more."

Danté's arm rose again, swinging his whip above his head.

I couldn't think, couldn't rationalize a fucking thing, my brain not giving a shit that I was outnumbered by two or three hundred. Whipping off my cloak, I stormed into the circle of the arena with a resounding, "No!"

My voice reverberated to the domed ceiling. A hush fell over the horde as Danté twisted around slowly, the whip falling impotent at his side. His expression of astonishment transformed to sickening joy as I met him in the circle.

"Genevieve," he said, all pearly whites and sparkling blue eyes. "My sweet. You actually came."

Stunned by the fact he seemed to be expecting me, I stepped down into the arena pit, strode closer and stood between him and Jude. I didn't dare drop my gaze to Jude, knowing I might crumble at the bloody sight of him.

I kept my body alert and ready for attack, wishing with all my might that I could sift out of here. But I'd been told on more than one occasion that sifting out of the realm of the soul collectors was impossible. Sifting within the walls was apparently allowed, but sifting out of here was a different matter.

At present, I needed to focus on the obstacle standing in front of me.

On closer inspection, I saw the irregular stitching around his neck was a gruesome, Frankenstein-style job, purplish wounds swollen and seeping around each stitch.

He stepped toward me in his confident, slow gait, charming smile in place, though the scar I'd given him pulled tight on one side. Before he was within three feet of me, I whipped up my arm, sword pointed at his chest. He stopped only when his skin met the blade.

"Now, my sweet. We aren't going to do this dance again, are we? I thought we'd skip the foreplay and go straight to the bedroom. I have one prepared in the tower, though I spend most of my time down here. Playing with my new toy."

His gaze drifted down my body, then jerked to Jude on the floor behind me, his mouth twitching on one side.

"Are you absolutely insane?" was all I could manage. I vibrated with rage.

"No, darling. I knew you'd come, so I made sure the former object of your affection was rendered useless. And as you can see"—he gestured his whip-free hand to Jude—"his body is worthless to you now. His mind was already gone when I found him. There's nothing left."

"*No.*" I shook my head, hot tears spilling down my cheeks

despite my determination to show only strength, not weakness.

Had Lethe wiped his mind completely? I couldn't believe it. *Wouldn't* believe it.

"Oh yes," Danté whispered, low and intimate. "He is gone. But I am here, as I've always been. Waiting for you."

My hand trembled, the blade point scraping the surface of Danté's chest. A streak of black blood oozed. He didn't seem to care.

"Danté."

"Yes, my sweet."

"Even if this were true, there is nothing in this world or the next that would ever make me succumb to a twisted bastard like you."

With a swift move, I lunged forward, thrusting with my blade. In a frighteningly fast spin, he swiveled out of the way to my right.

He laughed deep in his throat, raising the hairs on the back of my neck. His followers hissed with laughter in the stands, apparently enjoying this new entertainment as much as the last.

"Actually, I'd kind of hoped you'd want to play rough. We have some unfinished business between us."

With a sharp snap of his arm, the whip's tail sailed out and cut my wrist, the force knocking my sword from my grip. Before the blade clanged to the stone floor, the whip flared out again and snaked around my waist, constricting like a serpent. I grabbed the rope, but it slithered of its own accord beneath my fingers.

This weapon held the essence of Danté, his own personal spawn-infected torture device. He tugged me toward him.

"Come closer, darling. We've been parted far too long."

Legs apart, I dug in my heels and pulled on the slithering rope. It writhed in my hands, but I kept a tight grip.

"I'm not the same woman you knew before, Danté."

"No?"

"No."

Pulling my power of Light forward, I shed my cast of illusion. My skin beamed star bright, shining a white halo in the dingy dungeon. Dozens of demons hissed; some skittered out of the stands, unable to withstand the touch of my light, fanning outward in the dome.

Danté's shoulders grew taut with strain as he gripped the handle of the whip with both hands. His eyes bled blue to red, the beast in him rising to the surface.

Gripping the rope tighter, I stared into the crimson eyes of the demon who was once my captor, my possessor, and now my love's abuser. Fueling my power into a tight orb of pulsating force inside my chest, I said to him, my voice a reverberating echo, "I don't need weapons anymore."

He bared fanged teeth, transforming into the beast that he was, and yanked on his evil-infused whip, which slithered more tightly around my waist.

I smiled. None of it would be enough. I whispered the words of destruction.

"Mors liberabit vos."

Death will free you.

Like a bullet from a gun, I shot a ball of flaming light, channeling it from my chest down the whip, incinerating it into ash as my power zipped up the line to the demon prince.

Danté opened his fanged mouth in a bellowing yell, howling like a desperate animal. The explosive impact of the orb hit his chest. The blast fried him into charred bits.

The echo of my power rippled in white light across the room and sent the rest of the demons scuttling through the archway, clambering over one another to escape. My light filled the entire cavity of the domed arena.

I stood, chest heaving, till the light dissipated and there was no sound but the distant din of screaming demons and Danté's hissing remains that littered the blood-smeared stone floor.

For the first time, I was truly happy to be a Vessel of Light, to have the innate will and power to wield death against an evil entity of darkness. If any creature deserved to be wiped from existence, it was Danté. And now he'd never haunt my days or nights. He'd never hurt anyone again, damned souls or free. He was good and truly gone.

I spun toward Jude and fell to my knees. His battered cheek rested on the stone where he'd been positioned for beating and torture. One eye had swollen shut. His lips were wrinkled and cracked from lack of moisture, his body drained of so much blood.

The tears streamed hot again, scalding my cheeks. His body was lean from abuse and lack of nourishment.

"Jude."

His one good eye rolled wide, full black and seeing nothing, before closing again. I reached out and put two shaking fingers on the pulse point on his neck. A faint beat, but it was there.

After unlocking the wrist shackles, I tried to lift him around the waist, my hands sliding on his blood-slicked skin. He was dead weight. His body slid off the bench and flipped onto his back.

He gasped in pain when his skin hit stone, but his eyes never opened. He slipped back into silence, fists clenched tight.

I gasped, covering my mouth with my hands. The razor-sharp whip had scored him hundreds of times, cutting long slashes into his skin. The Celtic cross tattoo that adorned his chest was indiscernible under the torn flesh and blood. Bruises and gashes covered his legs, probably from being dragged from one torture station to the next.

I bent over him, gently lifting his head.

"Jude," I whispered. "Can you hear me?"

Nothing. Not a flutter of eyelashes, not a twitch of his hand. I pressed my lips to his forehead—one of the few places unmarred—and wept for the pain inflicted upon him. I wondered how he could possibly recover from such brutal suffering.

Seething hatred welled up inside me till I could see nothing but red. I wished Danté were alive so I could kill him again. And again.

Swiping my tears away with the back of my hand, I inhaled a deep breath. "Get it together."

I set his head gently down and stood to pick up my katana and returned it to its sheath.

A shriek overhead. But one that made my heart soar with relief.

"Mira!"

She swooped down onto the bloody bench that had held Jude a moment before.

"I'm so glad to see you." Her mere presence made my heart lift a little.

I squatted beside Jude and pulled his upper body into a sitting position. He groaned in pain but never roused. I strained under his weight. To lift him was utterly impossible.

"Damn it. I need you to stand up, Jude."

No response. I could sift with him to get back across the realm, but there was no way I could lift him. Killing Danté had drained my strength. How was I possibly going to do this?

Mira chirped and fluttered closer to me till she perched on his opposite shoulder.

"No, *don't*. He's hurt."

She clicked her beak in defiance. She was gentle with her

talons, barely pinching his skin. A glow emanated from her chest, brightening into a silvery orb, the same as the bright light that burned out of my chest the day she came to me.

She shot me a sharp-eyed glare with her fiery gaze over Jude's shoulder. She willed me to understand. I tried again to lift him. This time, he was much lighter.

Mira tottered as I slowly got him to his feet, with my neck beneath his arm for support, gripping his waist and the arm I'd draped over my shoulder.

"What other secrets are you hiding?" I asked.

She chirped twice as if to fuss at me for stalling.

"Okay. I need you to go to the entrance where we came in. See if it's safe."

Instead of flying, she sifted herself away with a tiny crackle. I realized then that sifting rules applied to her as well. Seconds later, she reappeared with three high chirps. All was clear.

I imagined the corridor, the one where the shackled men and women were being kept. A millisecond later, I stood outside the door, Jude's body leaning heavily against me.

Mira perched on a craggy outcropping, one of many jutting from this disordered heap of stones. The corridor was empty, but I heard the distinct whimpering of women on the other side of the door. One cried out in a high-pitched scream. Dim torchlight from within proved they'd managed to get themselves back in order.

"When I open the door, Mira, do that thing you did before with the fire. Okay?"

She clicked her beak and opened her snowy wings at the ready. Using the wall to help me keep Jude upright, I stretched out my left arm, lifted the latch, and shoved the door open. I caught the angry grimace of a three-horned demon with a hammer-like weapon in hand. Mira swept inside.

A demon growled, then a flash of blue-white light. Monstrous snarls and female screams filled the room as a burst of white flashed out into the dark corridor a second, third, and fourth time.

I couldn't lean forward or I'd lose my grip on Jude, but I heard the clamoring wails, then thunderous footsteps. *Thud, thud, thud* before the gargantuan leader collapsed in the doorway, burned down to a skeleton but still twitching and smoking. I dared one step forward with Jude's heavy weight leaning precariously against me.

Silence but for a repetitive tinkling sound and sparkle of light. I struggled to keep Jude up as I peered inside to discover the source of the sound. Mira pecked at the chains that bound the prisoners to the wall. They stared wide-eyed at the white bird who'd saved them from eternal torture.

"Come, Mira. They must make it on their own from here."

One of the men was already up and hauling another skinny girl to her feet. I couldn't take these poor souls out of hell, but I was glad to free them from the likes of this place. Better they dwell unmolested in some dark cavern in Lethe's realm than here.

Mira flapped into the corridor, then sifted away. Seconds later, she was back with a friendly chirp. As before, I'd follow her lead, sifting to the spot I'd used as a target on the way here.

Back down the mountain, holding Jude up, I skipped the ledge where the man-eating demons camped, then sifted across the black river into the misty realm of Lethe. Then I sifted through the naked-limbed forest where I'd helped the teenage boy, across the open plain where Lethe's souls hid in crevices, and behind rocks to avoid any contact with another being. Finally, we stood at the cavernous doorway facing Lethe's veil.

Exhausted, I let Jude slide to the ground, helping him gently onto his back. He made no sound or movement, his body slack except for his balled fists.

I checked his pulse again. Faint but beating. I pulled my flask from inside my jacket and unscrewed the top. Lifting his head from my lap, I pressed the rim to his lips. Most of the water seeped into the dusty earth, but, then Jude's throat worked, and two swallows made their way down before he coughed and spluttered.

"Jude. Jude," my whisper was broken and quivering. "Can you hear me?"

No sign of consciousness left me chilled to the bone. A cold mist draped Lethe's lair. Jude's naked and beaten form lay there unmoving, his wounds still seeping blood. I feared he would never recover, even if we made it out of here. The reality of what awaited back home fell like a heavy stone to the pit of my stomach.

Those lips, cut and bruised, had whispered a hundred passionate words of love to me. Those hands, scraped to the bone, had touched me countless times, reminding me again and again who owned my heart. This body, torn to shreds by a sadist's whip, had shown me the power and pleasure a man can give a woman when she succumbs to her desire.

Helpless and half-alive, he was no less the man I knew and loved, but the heartbreak of what he suffered crippled me with fear.

Mira chirped and clicked with impatience.

I wiped the dampness from my eyes with my sleeve. "Yes. I *know*. It's time to get out of here."

Though I'd been told it was impossible, I lifted Jude's upper body onto my lap, gripped his biceps and tried to sift. My skin prickled with the sensation of moving toward another dimension. Then nothing. We never budged. Whatever force field blocked the passage from sifting, it was strong and held firm.

I'd been considering possible means of escape ever since Dommiel had agreed to bring me here. I'd interrogated George several times. I remember standing in his high-rise apartment in London overlooking the Thames.

"I've told you this before, Genevieve. No soul collector will ever willingly give up one of the souls he or she has collected. It just can't be done." He'd combed a hand through his chestnut locks in frustration, tousling his hair in an uncharacteristic manner for the ever-calm Saint George.

He had meant to convince me to give up my idea of going to the soul eater's realm for Jude. Not that he didn't care. Hell, Jude was his best friend. But George truly didn't believe I'd come back. That was when it hit me. His words resonated with the answer I needed the whole time.

I'd gripped him by the shoulder with a gentle hand and smiled. "Have faith in me. I'll bring him home. I'll bring us both back, safe and sound. I promise."

That was the moment I knew there was only one way. Jude had summoned Acheron and fed him Garzel when the demon refused to give up information. He'd bargained with the banshee-like soul eater Cocytus to gain entrance to Dante's castle in order to save me in exchange for the body and soul of the foul prince.

I'd deduced the best way to get out was to make my own deal. My only fear was that a soul collector wouldn't want to wait for payment of fee, that he would demand it then and there.

It was finally time to see if my plan would work.

"Mira, stay close to me."

Hands firm on Jude's shoulders, I called to my VS and whispered to the air, *"Acherontis…adeo mihi…Acherontis…adeo mihi."*

Nothing happened. Mira twisted her head in my direction and chirped once, wedging herself between my outstretched leg and Jude's torso.

"I'll try again."

Closing my eyes, I channeled my supernatural power, calling to Acheron, envisioning his dark form, sweeping out with my Vessel Sense.

"Acherontis…"

The veil of vapor and silver light shivered like a drop in a pond, waves rolling out from a central point. The pinpoint at the center cracked, the tendrils of light shifting to the outer reaches of the veil. The sliver ripped up the entire length of the veil, a dark jagged line breaking the ethereal entity. Black-boned fingers wrapped the edges from inside, pulling the veil apart. An eerie aura of blue drifted from within, shading Lethe's bleak gray world an otherworldly hue.

Acheron stepped from a domain of pitch-darkness. The folds of his sable mantle rolled and billowed. His hood slipped, revealing a shiny black skull atop a spiny neck. Liquid pools of red with pinpoint pupils gazed from deep-set sockets—eyes that held the darkest secrets of the darkest souls.

When I'd formulated this idea, I'd counted on the fact that soul eaters could wander into any realm, even those of their brothers and sisters. In all other ways, they were creatures unbound by any rules. Apparently, my gamble had paid off.

There was no sound in this place. Even the slightest whisper of the faint breeze swirling the mist died. There was only the cracking boom of his voice.

"*Acherontis pabulum.*" The unearthly creature pointed a skeletal index finger at Jude.

"No." I shook my head. "I have better food for Acheron."

It tilted its ghastly head, observing me with keen scarlet eyes.

"I want to make a bargain."

The fey wind pushed his cloak open. A screaming well of woe washed over me. I winced at the scorching sorrow and bitter pain resonating from the souls he'd devoured.

"Hear me," I begged, palm out. "We request safe passage to the world above. In return, I can give you a soul worth a thousand human souls. It will feed you well."

The inhuman creature stared, waiting.

"I will give you the soul of a demon prince. If you come to me on the night of the Blood Moon, I will deliver Prince Bamal to you." I summoned my Vessel underlight, beaming brighter. "I have the power to deliver him to you."

The soul eater continued to watch for a painfully long moment. I thought perhaps he didn't understand. He spoke only in Latin. Recalling my Latin lessons last semester, I tried again.

"*In supremae nocte—*" *On the night*, I said, when he waved a bone-black hand in the air, silencing me.

His spidery fingers threaded in the air as he raised a hand to the sky, though here there was no real sky in hell, only a blanket of darkness smothering us from above.

"*In supremae nocte luna in sanguine…*" *On the night of the blood moon*, his voice crackled. "*Volo princeps…Aut leporem citus uenator.*"

His chilling gaze found Jude.

I want the prince…or the hunter, he'd told me with menacing finality.

I choked back the fear welling inside, a tidal wave threatening to swallow me and pull me to muddy depths. Of course, the only substitute he would take was one equal to a demon prince, the first Dominus Daemonum to walk the earth.

I couldn't allow doubt to take root and fester into a monster that controlled my will. I had no choice. I knew my course. And I would not fail.

"Yes," I said with a tight nod. "On the night of the Blood Moon. It is my vow. My payment for passage out of this realm."

Unable to wrap my arms around Jude for fear of hurting his torn and battered skin, I gripped him by the shoulders. His head rested in my lap, his body unmoving.

Please, please, please, I begged in my mind. I dreaded that the collector would reject my bargain on a whim and send us to some other horrific corner of the underworld, perhaps his own domain, which must be close by.

As I glared at the soul eater's bloody gaze, the silvery light of the veil at his back silhouetted him in stark black. Acheron dropped his dark head, the sable hood sliding forward.

The distinct pull at my core shot a bolt of adrenaline through my body. I almost cried, knowing the sensation before a sift all too well. I hooked my arms underneath Jude's arms, bracketing his body as close as I could.

Then we were gone, sliding through the Void, gray shapes ghosting past us. Mira clawed her way up my sleeve to my shoulder as we flew, Jude's heavy weight tugging us toward oblivion.

There was no way on earth I'd let him go. My arm would have to break and fall off before I'd let that happen.

The sift was long and rough, foul winds twisting around us before we were finally dumped onto solid ground.

Jude and I fell into a heap in some unknown forest. Not the Black Forest. The grass beneath our feet, the cold air in my lungs, the leafy trees waving in the breeze, but mostly the clear, starry night hanging above us told me we were back home, back in our world.

I sobbed with relief and pulled Jude back into my lap. "Mira," I snapped, "go to George. Bring him to Arran. We'll meet you back home."

Home. Yes, I was finally bringing Jude home.

11

I sifted onto the hillside where Jude always did before walking through the wards. I had to drag his body across, then was able to sift him into the cottage and lay him on our bed.

A painful ache gripped me as I placed his cut-up feet at the end of the bed and finally got a good look at his naked, bleeding form—bruised and lean from lack of food. Vulnerable. Broken. Alone.

My poor love.

He still hadn't wakened or shown any signs that he would. Refusing to give in to despair, I fetched a bowl from the kitchen and filled it with warm water, hands shaking. With a washcloth in hand, I started a methodical cleansing of his entire body, beginning from the feet up.

I stopped at his knees and sobbed. The blood and gore hid the depth of his wounds. He'd been thrown onto his knees many times for the skin to be scraped to the cartilage cap. I could hardly stand to imagine the amount of pain he'd suffered at the hands of sadistic Danté.

"Jude," I cried, tears rolling down my cheeks. "I'm so sorry."

Rinsing the towel, I wiped the grime from his forehead, his square jaw and cheekbones, more angular than usual, then from his cleft chin. I remembered how I'd kiss my forefinger and press a kiss there sometimes and how he'd smile.

"Jude, please wake up."

By now I'd cleaned his face thoroughly and pushed his dirty hair off his cut cheeks and bruised forehead. I had him home, and yet I wasn't sure if he could ever recover from this.

Even if his body healed, would his soul? I didn't know what they'd done to him in the underworld for nearly a month, but the evidence was staggering and heartbreaking.

The front door opened and slammed. A second later, George stood, breathing hard at my side, bringing with him the cold night air.

"Christ almighty," he said as he came up beside me.

George checked for his pulse.

"He's alive. But barely…I think."

"Go, get another bowl of hot water. We'll do this together." He jerked his jacket from his body, unbuttoning, and rolling up his expensive white shirt. "Go," he said more firmly when I didn't move swiftly enough.

After I'd dumped the bloody water, refilled a fresh bowl and returned, George was whispering to Jude as he slowly examined each bone down one arm, then the other. When I came up on him, he was mumbling nonsense to Jude as if Jude could hear him.

"You really did it this time, didn't you? Always wanting to prove how tough you are." He couldn't check his ribcage, for his skin was so lacerated with whip marks. "Ever the mighty hunter, determined to prove yourself the bravest of us all. Well, now you've gone and done it."

He continued to mumble accusations at Jude as if they were having one of their little skirmishes over breakfast, while he continued down one leg, feeling for fractures. When he gripped Jude's left ankle, the foot twitched at the slightest touch. Jude's brow pinched together in pain, though he never opened his eyes.

"Is it broken?" I asked.

"Possibly. Maybe a sprain, but we won't know right now."

He pointed to the smeared blood on the mattress by his torso. "Does that mean his back is as bad as his chest?"

"Yes," I managed to say on a fast breath.

"What happened to him?"

George's sharp aquamarine gaze narrowed on me, his anger seething for whomever had done this to Jude.

"It was Danté."

"Danté?"

"But I finished him. For good."

"What do you mean?" he asked, pulling the sheet up to Jude's waist. I think George was uncomfortable, not with Jude's nudity but with the sheer vulnerability of the strongest man he'd probably ever known. To be exposed in such a way—frail, weak, lifeless…

"I mean I killed him. Like I did that demon back at Glastonbury."

Shaking his head in disbelief and giving me a crooked smile, he said, "It's about bloody time. That's one less wanker we'll have to deal with come doomsday."

"George, if this is your idea of levity in a time of mourning, I don't think—"

"No more thinking, darling. Time for action. Give me the rag." He took it from me and gave me a sympathetic smile. "And don't fall apart on me now."

He began to wipe Jude's chest clean with a rougher hand that I ever would have.

"Be careful! You'll hurt him."

"Darling, he's hurt quite enough already. We need to get him clean and sterilized and sewn up so he can heal. He's a Dominus Daemonum, made by Uriel himself, which means he carries healing power in his blood. But he won't mend with open gashes all over his body. So snap to, girl."

I stopped staring all weepy-eyed and jumped back into action. George was right. I was overthinking to the point of becoming useless.

I ran to the bathroom and rummaged around till I found Jude's first aid kit. His job warranted being prepared. And he always was.

I brought it back and opened it on the bed next to Jude. George stood on the other side, having cleaned nearly all the excess dried blood. While George searched for antiseptic, I twisted my hands together, unsure what to do next.

"How can I help?"

"You're doing fine right there."

"No, George. Tell me how I can help. Give me something to do. *Please.*"

He paused and lifted his stern gaze to mine. "He'll need some sustenance of some kind, preferably broth, something we can get down his throat, if that's even possible."

"Right."

I dashed to the kitchen and found the cabinet of canned vegetables and soups. I'd seen a few cans of beef broth. Mira perched on a chair, cleaning under her wing as if we hadn't just traveled to hell and back.

I opened the can and poured the broth into pan then set it on the old wood stove, taking several minutes to get the stove lit and burning hot. As soon as the beefy aroma warmed and the smell wafted up, my stomach growled.

Dizzying nausea swept over me all at once, buckling my knees, though I caught myself.

I needed to eat before I took one more step. I hoped, with tears stinging my eyes and a shaky smile on my face, that the child in my womb would eventually meet her amazing father.

I unwrapped a loaf of bread, tore off a piece, then dipped a few bites in the bowl, soaking up the broth.

What if Jude never returned? What if his mind was gone for good even if his body did heal?

Shaking dismal thoughts away, I poured a bowl of broth and joined George in the bedroom. George had cleaned Jude's upper body and was now opening one of his clenched fists. A frown marred George's face as he glanced up at me.

"What's wrong?" I set the bowl on the dresser by the window.

"He has something in his hand. His fist is clenched tight. Strange. The rest of his body is relaxed, but somehow he's managed to keep his fist closed."

I moved around and peered over the bed as George opened his fingers, one by one, pulling something from his palm I never thought to see again.

"My necklace!"

Actually, the chain was gone. But Jude had somehow found my opal pendant—his first gift to me—and kept it hidden within his clenched fist. I lifted it from his unfurled fingers, which finally relaxed. I quickly flipped over the opal to read the inscription on the back.

Mea luna in tenebris.

My moon in the darkness.

I choked on a half laugh, half sob. "How in the world did he find it?"

"Where was it last?" George's stern tone and gaze darkened as he stared at the object.

"In the Void. The chain broke. I thought it was gone forever."

"Jude found it. And managed to train his body not to let go. He must've been holding it the whole time."

"But how?"

"Give it to me."

I frowned, wanting to pull away and refuse, but something in George's manner told me not to disobey. I handed it to him.

He flipped it over to examine the opal, whose bluish-purple markings mirrored that of the moon. A hairline crack divided the opal in half. I didn't care that it was damaged. I was so happy to have it back, but now George's odd silence had the hairs standing up on the back of my neck.

"What's wrong?"

"There is essence of evil in this object. Entity spawn."

"Entity spawn?"

I couldn't believe it. This was the most subtle of demon creations, but in my mind the most sinister. It could work it's dark magic on humans without anyone ever knowing, not even the one infected by the spawn.

Face drawn tight, he asked, "This is from Jude, you say?"

"Yes. And it's definitely mine. The inscription on the back proves it."

"I need to take it with me. I'll have Uriel take a look and see if he can identify who might've put their essence here. Sometimes spawn leaves a trail or aura that we can follow."

"But why would a demon put their essence in an object floating in the Void?"

George didn't answer, his full focus on the opal as he rubbed his thumb over the fissure dividing it.

"I'll try to get more answers. In the meantime, you don't want it near you or him until it's been purged of the essence and cleansed."

He was right, of course, though some part of me wanted to reach out and snatch it away from him. I'd just gotten it back, and my heart had broken the day I'd lost it, tumbling through the Void with Thomas.

"How could a demon's essence get inside it?" I couldn't understand how my beloved possession was lost, only to find it in the palm of Jude's hands. And now to discover it had an entity spawn tainting it.

"It's been floating through the Void," said George. "No telling who picked it up. I'll bring it back to you," he said, tucking the object into the pocket of his coat hanging over the back of a chair. "But for now"—he rolled his sleeves up higher and pulled the first aid kit closer—"we have more important work to do."

I stood closer to help George in any way I could, but my thoughts drifted back to the opal I'd lost the night I'd made the mistake of kissing Thomas. I never thought to get that beloved possession back. Refocusing my attention on Jude, I decided I'd worry about that tomorrow.

Right now, Jude needed me. And I needed him. The rest of the world could wait.

"Try to get some rest," said George, winding up the stitching thread and placing it back into Jude's first aid kit.

Not your typical kit. Rather than Band-Aids and aspirin, there were such things as stitching needles and casting plaster. George closed it, and we both looked at his patient.

It had taken hours for him to meticulously stitch every gash too large or wide to heal on its own. He wanted me to leave and rest in the front room by the fire, but I couldn't.

Though Jude had never fluttered an eyelid or twitched a finger, I couldn't leave his side for a second. I think George didn't want me watching. I'd seen where parts of Jude's flesh had been ripped out altogether. The stitches puckered the skin tight. I knew there would be many ugly scars on his body, and I didn't care.

The most difficult feat was changing the bloody sheets, which Jude's seeping wounds had soiled. Flipping him to one side, then the other, George and I managed to get the job done without too much difficulty. It was worth it to rid myself of the shocking evidence of his suffering.

Seeing him now, covered to his waist, the lamplight casting a soft glow on George's handiwork, Jude seemed at peace. George had matched the lines of the Celtic cross tattoo as best he could. Entwined by thorny vines and now slashed with scars, Jude's flesh was an example of the true pain of sacrifice.

He'd sacrificed himself for me. And look what had become of him. It should've been me. I'd be dead by now if I'd been in Danté's hands. Truly dead. Wiped from the existence of any and all dimensions.

"Genevieve."

I snapped my attention to George.

He picked up his designer trench coat and slipped into it, combing a hand through his disheveled hair before piercing me with a look. "Get some sleep. That's an order."

I gave him my best version of a smile. "I'll try."

He glanced at his silver watch. "It'll be morning soon anyway. I'll be back midday." He walked around the bed and took me by the shoulders. "You did it." The gratitude shining in his eyes made me want to cry again. He pulled me into a tight hug. "Good girl. Please rest. If he wakes, contact me immediately."

"I will," I muttered into the shoulder of his coat.

He pulled away and gazed at Jude's still figure one last time before he marched through the front room, opened the door and banged it closed. Though Jude had been away for some time, the wards he'd mounted around our little cottage still held so strong, not a soul could sift in or out.

I ambled to the door and bolted it tight, tucking the little towel at the bottom to keep the blistering cold from seeping in.

After stoking the fire in the den and adding another peat log, I stroked the top of Mira's head. Her eyes closed. She never moved, accustomed to my quiet attentiveness. Making my way back into the bedroom, I added two peat logs to the fire, and returned to Jude's side.

Flat on his back, unmoving, the only hint he was still alive was the slow rise and fall of his bruised and stitched chest. I bit my lip, refusing to have another breakdown. Though I finally had him safe in our cottage, he was still so very far away.

I pulled the layer of quilts up over his chest and tucked the covers around his torso, letting his arms lay atop the quilt. I brushed his black hair away from his face.

"Jude…please open your eyes."

Yearning for him to look at me with that familiar spark of fire in his golden gaze, I touched his face again, brushing my fingertips across his high cheekbone, trailing down the sharp angle of his jaw, drifting to the cleft in his chin. I kissed my forefinger's tip and pressed it to the dimple there as I so often had done in the past, a playful gesture he endured only from me.

Jude wasn't the playful kind of guy. Too much darkness in his world. But when we were alone, he often let his carefree spirit rise to the surface. I wanted to see that man again—strong, courageous, and ready to conquer the world.

"Rest now," I said. "Tomorrow, perhaps."

I'd have to find a way to wash his hair for him tomorrow. It was dirty and matted where the whip must have caught him on the back of the skull—dried blood proved the wound had closed on its own. I wanted to wipe away as much of that dismal place as I could. One eye was still swollen shut, one cheek still purple and bruised.

I walked over to the dresser and pulled out a pair of flannel pajama pants, opened another drawer and pulled out one of his T-shirts. From habit, I put it to my face and inhaled his scent—faint but still there—then slipped it on before climbing into bed next to him.

Not wanting to hurt him but yearning to be near, I rolled onto my side and wrapped my hand gently over his bicep. Warm. His body was so warm.

Gazing at his sharp profile in the lamplight, I wished with all my heart that he'd roll over and tease me for worrying so much or be angry at me for risking harm by going after him, or that he'd love me to sleep and whisper in my ear that I owned his heart. I wished that he'd hold me tight until I fell into a deep, dreamless sleep and awoke to him cooking me breakfast in the morning, saying sexy remarks that would make me blush.

But he didn't. Wherever he dwelled inside his mind, he wasn't aware of where he was now, that he was safe. I curled my fingers around his arm a little more and lay my cheek against his shoulder. He never moved.

"Please wake up, Jude. We just found each other, and I can't..." A tear slipped. "I can't do this alone."

No movement. No sign of life whatsoever.

"I'm a selfish coward, really, if you want to know the truth. Yes, I went to hell and back to get you...but it's because I'm incapable of going on without you. And now there's—"

I remembered an article I'd read that coma patients can still hear what's going on around them, and thought better of the confession that nearly slipped from my lips. I wanted him conscious for the news that he was going to be a father.

"There's something important I need to tell you." I burrowed my cheek into the pillow, pressing my lips to his shoulder. "Please come back to me, Jude. Please."

Unable to hold it in any longer, I wept silently. The heartache, like a gaping wound inside of me, reopened as if I'd just watched him leap into Lethe's arms. I had his body, but had Danté already destroyed his soul? The fear that I'd been too late, that I'd condemned him to this comatose state forever because I'd listened to the lies of Thomas, stabbed me in the heart.

Thomas. Did he know Jude could and probably would be found and taken prisoner by Danté in the underworld? Was that his plan the whole time?

Fury, bright and hot, lanced through me. I loosened my grip when I realized my fingers dug into Jude's bicep. Not that he responded to my touch. Another slap in the face. Jude had made me feel like the only woman on earth, the way he responded to my touch. With a deep groan or heavy sigh, he'd pull me tighter and make me feel as if nothing else mattered. But that Jude was still gone, no matter that I'd brought him back from that den of torture. He was still gone from me.

I forced my eyes closed. George was right. I needed to rest. Jude needed me strong and alert. I couldn't be the weak girl seeking his constant protection as I had been in the beginning. I needed to be the one to protect *him*, to nurture and help him heal. He was a lost ship wandering a wide, distant sea. I needed to be his lighthouse in the dark, to guide him home.

"Don't worry, Jude," I said, pressing another kiss to his shoulder. "I'll be stronger than ever. For both of us."

It's funny what paths change the course of your life. Take one, and you might be just fine, drifting through the world with a normal job and a normal life, dreaming your normal dreams of a blissful future. But take another, where a man with fire in his eyes and steel in his touch leads you down a perilous path with him, and the world is exactly as it always should've been.

Come hell or demons or death or the end of the fucking world, I wouldn't have had it any other way. He *was* my world. And the grief and pain and loss churning in my breast for what had happened to him, to us, would never make me regret choosing him.

Never.

I'd hardly slept for thirty minutes at a time until I finally pulled myself out of bed before dawn. Stoking the fires, which had died down to glowing embers, I busied myself as best I could.

I carefully inspected Jude's dressings and stitches. George had covered a horribly mutilated part of his back with patches of gauze over his crisscross hatching of stitches. A normal human would've needed skin grafts to help this wound heal faster, as some of the flesh had been taken off. Danté had severely abused the part of his full-back tattoo bearing the face of St. Michael the Archangel.

The second my mind drifted to a vision of Jude bound between the iron posts being whipped and beaten relentlessly under the hate-filled lashes of Danté, I wanted to vomit.

"Oh, no." I rushed to the bathroom and did just that, emptying my stomach in the toilet.

Morning sickness plus that nightmarish memory didn't sit well. I'd worry about feeding myself later.

After washing my face and brushing my teeth, I took a bowl of warm water and shampoo to the bed so I could wash Jude's hair.

In order to keep the sheets somewhat dry and clean, I propped his neck up with a rolled towel and an empty bowl underneath his head. I shampooed and rinsed half of his head at a time. It took forever.

I combed through his dark locks, then set about shaving the shaggy beard that had grown in his time away. Once the job was carefully done, I admired his beautiful face. Though more stark and lean, it was the face I knew and loved.

He still gave no sign he was aware of my presence. I tried not to think what that might mean. At least he was breathing.

I set about making myself some breakfast. Mira had gone out for her own along the beach. I'd taken my shower and dressed in jeans and a Loyola University sweatshirt, then slipped on my black-and-gold fuzzy Saints socks and was brewing a pot of coffee when the door swung open.

In stepped George, Kat, and Uriel and a whirl of blustering snow. A frigid storm of ice and snow had swept up on the island overnight.

"Good morning," said George.

Kat bounded across the small room and wrapped me in her arms. "Thank God you're okay."

I hugged her too, knowing how much she'd worried I'd never

return. She pulled back and scanned my face and neck. "You didn't get a scratch, did you?"

"I'm fine."

Uriel—all golden-hued, his glorious wings tucked against his back—greeted me with a nod. "I'm glad to see you safe, Vessel. I'd like to check on our patient."

His manners were like something out of a fairy-tale book, yet at the same time, I knew he was no Prince Charming. The power vibrating off him was more akin to that of a potent and dangerous villain.

"Of course." I gestured toward the bedroom. "Thank you. He's in here."

With a regal bow of the head, he swept into the next room, the tips of his wings brushing the floor. I followed with Kat and George behind me.

Uriel walked around to the head of the bed and placed his broad hand on Jude's forehead. "Has he stirred at all?"

"No," I replied. "Not yet." Dread sank like an iron anchor in the pit of my stomach.

Head down in concentration, Uriel's skin beneath a gray sweater and black slacks began to glow, filling the room with a golden hue. A responding light, tinted toward the color of flames, emitted from Jude's scarred skin.

A vibration shook the room. The comb on the nightstand rattled to the edge until it fell off onto the wooden floor. Jude's chest rose, his neck arched, and his mouth opened in a soundless sigh before he lowered back into his lifeless state once again.

The aura of light and rippling Flamma power diffused until it dissipated altogether. I found myself breathing faster and having no idea why. The sheer intensity of the energy in the room vibrated through my chest, zinging my underlight to a supernova glow.

Uriel removed his hand and turned to us, his handsome face fixed in an expression of indifference.

"Well?" I asked. "How is he?"

He rubbed the pads of his fingers and thumbs together in a slow movement, his brow quirking in concentration. "He isn't dead inside."

My gut clenched. The idea that there might have been nothing left of Jude to bring back sent a chill down my spine.

"But?" George prompted him to continue, for the angel's gaze fell back to Jude.

"I sense him within, but he is weak. Some of his Flamma power has died altogether."

"What! How can that be possible?"

Uriel's eyes transformed to a stormy midnight blue. Some sort of aftereffect of his power, perhaps? His mouth tightened to a line as he turned his gaze back to the still form of Jude, his profile a perfect silhouette of masculine beauty.

"Think of the body as a generator. The body isn't the source of the power. The mind, the heart, the soul is. The body keeps the power charged and primed for use."

I tucked my hands into my hoodie pockets to keep from

fidgeting nervously. "So when the body is weakened, the power stops flowing."

"Exactly." Uriel turned away from Jude, rolling his shoulders, then lifting his wings before tightening them once more to his back.

"You made him. Can't you give him his power back? Maybe that's all he needs to wake up."

"No," said George, stepping up next to me. "He's fragile, Genevieve. The power of making could crush what will to live he has left."

"Precisely," agreed Uriel. "And also he—"

The sharp pause created palpable tension I could've cut with my katana.

"And he what?" I asked, stepping forward and gripping a foot post of the antique bed.

Uriel cleared his throat, wiping his expression clean of any anxiety, making me think I'd probably just imagined it.

"The truth is, Jude's soul is alive and well. But he's burrowed himself so deep within his own mind, I'm not sure he will ever come up to the surface. I'm not sure he even wants to."

"No," I whispered, afraid to admit the possibility even to myself.

Uriel's midnight gaze fell on me. "And you must prepare yourself for the reality that he may not come back to us at all."

I wanted to punch something, scream till my throat bled, cry till there was nothing left of me that was sane or coherent. If

Jude never came back, I'd be lost. Alone. Kat stared in silent grief, as did George, neither wanting to admit defeat.

Rather than do any of those fury-filled things trembling through my frame, I moved around Uriel and placed my hand on Jude's head. No response.

"He will come back," I said.

"If he does," Uriel rumbled softly, more for me than anyone else in the room "it is up to you to bring him back."

"I know."

After a stifling, uncomfortable moment, George shifted toward the next room. "Why don't we come in here and discuss the other matter?"

I glanced up.

What other matter?

We filed into the cozy den. Mira had made her way back from the outdoors and perched on her favorite chair back, gazing out at the whirling snow.

"Would anyone like coffee?"

"I would," said Kat.

George and Uriel, standing near the hearth, shook their heads. After pouring and handing Kat a sugared-and-creamed cup of coffee, I brought my own and settled in the old, comfy chair Jude used to occupy.

"This is about the necklace, I presume." I took a sip of the warm coffee. "What did you discover?"

Uriel reached into his pocket and pulled from it my opal

pendant. He handed it over to me. The stone was remarkably cooler than usual. Perhaps from the weather? I doubted that. My VS hummed, approving of the change in the object.

"You removed the dark essence?"

"Yes," said Uriel. He paced closer, a grave expression in place. "I also identified whose essence I believe was residing there."

I straightened and perched on the edge of the chair. "Well?"

"Yeah. Come on, stop stalling," said Kat, sounding more like herself than the mournful woman who'd walked in here a while ago.

"Just as every Flamma carries an aura and emits a signature that is all his or her own, so does the spawn of every Flamma."

"I know this already," I snapped, my nerves threadbare. "I mean, I'm sorry. Please…go on."

Uriel arched a dark blond brow at me but didn't chastise me for my impatience. "It appears that Damas has paid you a visit while you were unaware."

"Damas!" screeched Kat, tipping her coffee over and sloshing half of it onto the floor. "Oh shit." She stood up. "I'm sorry."

"Don't worry about it," I said, setting my own down, grabbing a kitchen towel and wiping the floor.

"I'll do it," she said, trembling, eyes darting.

She needed something to do to hide her anxiety at the mention of his name. And I knew all too well why.

"Why would Damas inject his essence into the opal after it was lost in the Void? That makes no sense. There's no guarantee I'd ever get it back. Did he use Jude to try to get to me or something?"

The idea sent a primal fear shivering up my spine. Had Damas set his sights on me and I had no idea?

With his back to the fireplace, Uriel stood, feet set apart in a stance that exuded both strength and calm. Hands clasped in front of him, he said, "I'm not sure if you understand, Genevieve." He never said my name. This was serious. He had my full attention. "Damas put the essence there before it was taken into the Void."

I flinched. "What? But that's impossible."

"No. It's certain."

"When? How? I've never met him. And when would he have gotten the chance?"

"Where did you keep it?" asked George.

"At my apartment, which is cast in serious wards by Jude."

"Did you ever leave it somewhere outside the wards?" asked Uriel.

"No. Never. It was either in my apartment or around my neck."

"Genevieve, this is important." I'd seen charming George, battle George, and worried George, but this was entirely new. The expression of fear he tried to suppress made my heartbeat slam a bit harder inside my ribcage. "I want you to take some time and write down everywhere you went with the necklace, what happened in those events, and who you came in contact with."

I nodded, my throat thick with a new horror, that Damas had found a way into my life without me ever noticing. They all called him the prince of deception. And the cleverest of them all. About that I now had no doubt. An adversary I'd never laid eyes on, and yet he'd managed to taint my prized possession with his evil.

Kat folded the kitchen napkin and set it on the coffee table, recoiling back into herself. I hated that the mere mention of Damas shut her down. But I also understood why.

"More importantly," said Uriel, taking a step away from the fireplace toward the door, "strengthen yourself for the eclipse. The Blood Moon will rise in a mere ten days. I understand you will remain here and tend to Jude. This is the best course, as you are well protected at this cottage. I will cast my own wards to ensure your safety."

"Thank you," I said, feeling humbled by his generosity and kindness.

"Right. Let's let Genevieve have a little peace, then, shall we?" said Kat, leading the way to the door. Kat hugged me in silence and slipped out into the blistering cold behind Uriel.

George turned, his hand on the edge of the door. "Glad to see you made it back safe and sound."

"Thank you."

He quirked a brow. "How *did* you get back, by the way?"

I smiled, having already come up with an easy explanation. "Mira has many gifts."

He glanced back inside. "Hmm. Good to know."

I'd decided not to tell him or anyone else of the pact I'd made with Acheron, because there was nothing that could be done to change it. I'd made the bargain, and I planned to see it through.

He reached over and brushed a peck on my cheek. "If anyone can bring him back, Genevieve darling, it's you."

I smiled, swallowing the lump that suddenly appeared in my throat. Then they were gone.

Over the next two days, while the gale howled and snow poured down on our little cottage, I cleaned the place from top to bottom, trying to keep myself busy. I cleared the living space and moved through the kata my father had first taught me when I was a mere five years old. The rhythm and focus required to perform the movements with sharp precision kept me from going mad in those moments when I wanted to scream my frustration to the world.

I'd sent texts to both Mindy and to Dad, assuring them that I was settling in my dorm room and life was amazing in London. What a joke.

I'd become the queen of liars since all this began on my twentieth birthday, hiding the world of angels and demons to protect those I loved from the terrifying reality. A reality I knew we couldn't ignore forever.

Mindy had demanded pictures, so one morning I'd had to

bundle up tight and sift to Trafalgar Square, Piccadilly Circle, and Buckingham Palace to take selfies in recognizable places.

After I sent those pics to both Mindy and Dad, they texted that they were happy I was having such a wonderful time. I tried not to cry.

The outing had taken me all of an hour, but I was in anxiety-ridden agony the entire time. What if Jude had woken up and needed me? I'd forced Mira to stand watch and let me know if anything happened.

When I'd returned, she'd remained fixed in the bedroom, dozing near the fire. And Jude remained unchanged.

It was late afternoon of the second day as I finished up an hour of exercise routines and was heading for the shower when a piercing jolt pounded me in place, rattling my bones. My underlight snapped on in a millisecond.

I was being summoned by Dommiel, his signature screaming through my senses.

"Mira!"

She flapped into the living area from the bedroom and perched on her favorite chair as I sat and slipped on the boots I'd just taken off.

"Go find Kat and bring her to me immediately. I don't care what she's doing. She needs to meet me in New Orleans, and then you come back here and watch over Jude. This is very important. Do you understand?"

I think my bird rolled her orange eyes at me before she sifted away. The fact that I had a snarky bird didn't surprise me. After all, she was mine.

I strapped on my back harness for my katana and slipped another dagger into my boot sheath. Leaving Jude for any reason was like a stab to the chest, but the call zinging down my spine was unavoidable.

My blood bond with Dommiel was stronger than I'd imagined.

I ran out of the cottage beyond the wards, still wondering how Mira managed to defy this barrier, and sifted onto the street corner of Toulouse, one block down from The Dungeon.

The drunken crowd of a Friday night whooped and hollered down Bourbon Street, but this club appeared abandoned. No demon bouncer waited at the door. Just before I stepped into the darkened corridor, an electric snap sounded on my right, and someone grabbed my shoulder. I spun and deflected the arm to find Kat beside me and Mira on her shoulder.

"Whoa, chickadee! What the hell is going on? Mira swooped in while I was in conference with Dorian, grabbed me by the shoulder, and brought me here. He's going to be all pissy with me leaving like that."

Mira had landed on the sign for The Dungeon hanging above the door.

"Mira, go back home to Jude," I told her.

She chirped then disappeared.

"So why am I here?"

"Dommiel needs me." I eyed the strangely empty entrance to his lair. "And something is definitely wrong."

Crowds strolled the well-lit strip of Bourbon Street a block down the road, but here, all was dark and empty. It was as if even the tourists detected something not quite right in this direction. Kat and I stared down the corridor, where nothing and no one moved.

"Well, it's certainly odd not to hear their screeching nails-on-chalkboard music," Kat said, whipping out a thin twelve-inch rapier. "Let's go."

I led the way, following the blood-bond beacon flashing its SOS like a potion of dread pouring through my veins. Our boots echoed in the narrow corridor. When we stepped through the wide entrance beyond the courtyard, a wave of sulfur smashed into us, the residual burn-off when demons were expelled back to hell.

"Damn," whispered Kat. "Some serious demon activity."

I hardly noticed the smell anymore when dealing with a demon or two, but this had been more than one. Seeing as none of Dommiel's faithful red-eyed followers greeted us, I could guess who'd been cast out. But by whom? And why?

Two dead bodies lay on the floor, either human hosts who'd been carrying lower demons or humans serving Dommiel. A girl sniveled in wide-eyed terror under a bar-top table. Kat and I stood perfectly still, listening with weapons in hand.

My VS hummed, casting the dark room with a luminescent glow. Just as I took one step toward a stairwell, an ear-splitting bellow penetrated the walls.

Kat and I instantly looked at each other.

"His office," I whispered.

We raced through the club and leapt an overturned table in the hallway toward Dommiel's office. The door hung off its hinges, two dead demon hosts on the floor at the entrance.

Pale light fell into the corridor, a supernatural aura reeking with malevolent power. Whoever or whatever was in there was no lower demon. He was of the highest order. A prince, I was sure of it. All my instincts coalesced into this one thought, my VS rippling through my frame like an electric waterfall, preparing me for battle.

I glanced at Kat—her face contorting with flashes of fear—before I nudged her with my sword arm. "Now."

"No, Gen! It's—"

I was already hurdling over the thugs in the doorway, unable to process why she might want me to stop as I launched into the room. A tall, skinny, red-eyed demon met me with a punch to the chest.

I knew him, the one who'd gotten away that day we chased Bleed and his gangly ugly-ass crony. I sensed Kat at my back grappling with another demon. With two swings of my blade, I impaled the skinny one, his face registering he was a goner a split second before I incinerated him into ash.

Spinning, I found myself facing two situations that jarred me into frozen shock. One was Kat on her knees, facing me, with Bleed's hand fisted in her hair and his blade at her throat, a maniacal grin creasing his face. I'd never seen Kat bested by anyone. Ever.

The second was the gruesome scene of Dommiel staked to his office wall behind the desk, crucifixion style, pinned through his wrists and ankles. One of his eye sockets was empty, dark blood dripping down his face. His call for help still resonated in my veins, a plea to save him, free him.

But the most puzzling and horrifying thing of all that had me motionless and silent was the man who stood in front of Dommiel—a dagger poised in his hand to cut out the demon's second eye.

Only now did his signature reach my senses above the miasma of sulfur and black blood scenting the air—white winter and deep woods. His mask of serenity and compassion had fallen away, revealing his angelic perfection in an uglier, ruddier light.

"Thomas?"

Kat groaned—a deep, heartrending sound—before she choked and coughed.

"What's happening to her!"

I lurched toward Kat—bewildered and terrified. None of this made sense. Bleed pressed his blade just under her chin. A droplet of red slid down the column of her white throat.

"Drop your weapon, Vessel," demanded Bleed.

"Thomas, what's going on? That's Kat, my friend. Tell him to let her go."

"Drop the sword, Genevieve," he said, his own blade still fisted in his white-knuckled grip.

"You're working for the demons?" I asked, unable to comprehend how far his betrayal had gone, how far he'd fallen.

Bleed cackled and shook his head as if chastising a child, his purple hair sliding over his shoulders like silk.

Thomas smiled, his signature filling the room with cold dominance. "No, sweetheart. I'm not working for the demons."

The condescending blade of his voice cut me. Horrorstruck and hyperventilating, Kat riveted her attention on Thomas. Something was so terribly off.

"Kat—" I started forward but Bleed stopped me again by tightening his grip on my friend.

"Drop your sword," said Thomas, his words rolling deep and guttural, like chains on rock.

I dropped it to the floor, my VS burning through my body. A warning, fire bright.

"What have you done to her?" I trembled with the knowledge that I'd been missing a key element all along. Even as I watched Thomas round the desk with sensual grace, I knew, deep down, I'd been terribly wrong all along…about him.

He stepped up to Kat and gently cupped her chin in his hands, lifting her gaze to his. Tears streamed down her cheeks, fear choking her silent.

"Hello, my darling Katherine." He brushed the pad of his thumb along her quivering lower lip. "I've missed you so."

"What the fuck are you doing!" I reached out to snatch Thomas away from her, only to have him shoot out his arm and grab me, viper swift.

With a jarring snap, I stood in the cold rain, watching the entrance of Jude's home in the French Quarter. I saw the memory through Thomas's eyes. Someone walked up the pavement—Danté, gold locks slick against his head. He shook himself as he strode toward the alcove, transforming into the likeness of Jude. It was the day he'd bitten and marked me.

Why hadn't Thomas saved me that day? His memory drained away into another...

I was at the masquerade, watching the masked dancers twirl across the ballroom floor, that asshole Nathaniel leading Mindy in a waltz, her pretty head tossed back in laughter. Through his eyes, I saw my true self weaving toward the far side of the ballroom. A tall figure wearing a black mask slipped his arm around my waist from behind and pulled me into a private chamber behind a red velvet curtain...

His next memory...standing in the shadow of woods, I saw a giant beast of a dragon blowing streams of fire at George. Glastonbury Abbey. The clanging of swords sounded behind him where Jude and Bellock were engaged in a heated battle. My true self was flattened to the wall of the abbey's cathedral, where lower demons crept closer. Thomas was there and hadn't come to my aid then either...

Gone again into another memory. I strode into the dark corridor of the opera house—the Phantom and Christine screaming their love for each other in song. I saw my true self meet him there. The urgent yearning to take what was his drove him mad with violent need until his lips were on mine. These were all the thoughts of Thomas...or so I believed, until the last memory filtered in from so very long ago...

I stood in a room of stone and walked past a canopied bed to meet the beautiful, naked woman chained to my wall. My wall. The woman lifted her head with imploring eyes.

"Please," she begged. Despair marked every line of her face, yet lust still burned in her eyes.

"You are so fond of that word, my lovely slave." I lifted her by the thighs, her wrist chains rattling. "One more time, then." She moaned as I shoved inside her slick body with a powerful thrust...

"No!" I jerked so violently from the memory I stumbled back

against the office wall. The truth slapped me so hard, I couldn't breathe.

Thomas stared in serene calm, knowing the truth had finally dawned. "No…not Thomas," I whispered.

"No," he said with a dip of the chin.

"Damas." I exhaled his name on a hiss.

"Damas." He spread his arms. "At your service."

"But—how… I don't understand… Thomas—"

"You did have a guardian angel named Thomas. Once upon a time."

Yes, Jude had discovered he'd stopped reporting to his superiors about ten years ago. Ten years ago, when my mother died. My mother who had been a Vessel.

"You killed my real guardian angel," I said in disbelief.

"He's not truly dead. I don't have the gift of destruction as you do. But he is still somewhere in the bowels of Acheron."

"You fed my guardian angel to a soul eater?"

How? How had I been lured in by this heinous creature with a face of marble and a heart of stone?

"He wouldn't have protected you from the likes of my brothers. Bamal was lurking around your mother, but I knew"—he stepped forward with, heaven forbid, adoration in his glass-green eyes—"I knew you were special. I didn't lie, Genevieve. I've watched you all your life, kept vigil when others might've let you come to harm. But then that damned friend of yours had to take you to Tartarus for your twentieth birthday. Of all places and of all birthdays. It was as if—"

He bit off whatever he was going to say, so I finished the thought for him.

"It was as if fate wanted me there."

His mask hardened, washed with a grim light.

I smiled. "That's because it was fate. The Flamma of Light wanted me to meet Jude. Fate guided me to where a true guardian would find me. Where I'd meet a man who would become more than my protector."

He tapped his fingers in an agitated fashion against his pants leg, smeared with black blood from Dommiel, who still hung on the wall in utter silence.

"I can't believe you jeopardized yourself to save that filthy beast from the underworld."

"Of course you can't, Thomas…" I smiled bitterly at my slip of the tongue. "I mean, Damas. You couldn't fathom sacrificing yourself, possibly even your own life, for the one you loved."

"I would do it for you, Genevieve."

"Cut the shit, Damas. King of Deception. Master of Lies. I've been hearing about you from the start of all this, and never had I imagined that I'd fall prey to you. That I'd already fallen prey to you." I laughed at myself. "I thought I was too smart, too strong."

He stepped forward, closing the distance between us. I didn't care. The closer he came, the more easily I could kill him.

"But you weren't. And you know why? Because we were meant to be, as I've always told you. I've protected you, because I knew one day you'd become this remarkable woman that you are. You were the partner I was meant to have—an equal in power and beauty. I do love you."

"And I thought your brother, Danté, was delusional."

"My brother," he said with a derogatory sneer. "He knew nothing of love. Only selfish gain and violent lust."

"Yes. And you never prevented him from taking me. Yet you say you love me."

"The hunter had already inserted himself in your life," he said with a shrug, as if that answered everything.

"You're afraid of him."

"Afraid? No, dear heart."

He spoke with conviction but there was an edge of doubt I didn't miss. He moved within a foot of me, lifting his hand and brushing the backs of his knuckles along my cheek.

His signature slammed against mine—chilling cold, dark night. Though once his touch held some allure, now I felt only disgust, shame, and hatred. His otherworldly eyes traced the lines of my face, falling to my lips as always. He was mad if he thought to kiss me.

Another realization hit me like a bomb. The opal pendant. I remembered him looking at me just that way the night Kat and I went to that bar in the bayou to find Bleed. He'd held my opal in his hand and had admired it. But that wasn't what he was doing at all.

"You injected your essence into my necklace, the one I lost that night." No need to elaborate on which night. The one where I'd woken up from a dream and realized I was making a terrible mistake. "Oh my God. It was the essence all along. My necklace. I wore it everywhere. And you were in my head."

He'd also filled my nights, my dreams, seducing me there. Even while I loved only Jude during the daytime, Damas haunted me by night. His spawn had been infecting me. I wore it that night of the play. The violent need to let him kiss me, and more, had beaten within my breast so fiercely, there was nothing I wouldn't have done that night.

My VS had slapped me awake, and I'd taken us through the Void. My necklace had broken free, then we landed in the park... "I couldn't understand how I'd let myself go so far. When the truth is...you were controlling me all along."

His fingertips slid into my hair as he cupped my cheek. "You wanted me, sweetheart. You always wanted me. The essence simply tipped the scales so that you didn't have to feel damned human guilt over letting go. I can give you that freedom again. I can make all your fantasies come true." He drew closer, his body brushing against mine.

I placed my hand over his cupping my cheek. He smiled, and for a brief second, I remembered how I'd felt once as the object of his affection, as the reason for the heart-stopping smile of Thomas, my guardian angel. It was all a lie. All of it.

I curled my fingers around his hand, nails digging into his palm, and called my VS to the forefront, chanting in a repeated whisper, *"Flamma intus, flamma intus, flamma intus."*

His serene expression contorted to fury, then fear as my VS

channeled through my body down my arm, hand, fingers and into him. Black veins webbed across his perfect porcelain face and lit up with the brilliance of a burning star.

He jerked free of me with a cry and staggered back, his lit-up veins fading back behind the pretty mask.

I stalked forward. "You will die for what you did to me, to Jude, to Kat, to every poor soul who had the misfortune of being led astray by you."

The truth hit home. He spun and lunged in one bound toward Bleed.

"No!" I lurched forward and grabbed Kat, afraid he'd try to take her.

In a flash of ice-cold wind, Damas took his minion and disappeared. Kat crumpled onto all fours, heaving with desperate sobs. I dropped to my knees and pulled her into my arms, letting her cry out all her anger and fear.

"It's okay. Next time, I *will* kill him. And now he knows it."

"George," she whispered. "Please take me to George."

"Vessel," came Dommiel's raspy call.

I stood and rushed to Dommiel while Kat pulled herself together. Staring at the daggers piercing his body and holding him in place against the wall, I swallowed the bile rising in my throat.

"This will hurt," I said with regret.

"No more than I am already."

The vacant eye socket was a ghastly sight. I focused on the

task at hand and pulled out the daggers pierced through his ankles first, then his left wrist, then his right. He rolled into a ball on the floor, chest heaving.

"Dommiel, why would he do this to you?"

"Isn't it obvious?" he gasped out, curling his injured arms against his chest. "I helped you get into Lethe's realm. I'm branded a traitor now."

He turned his face into the floor, avoiding the sight of me.

He'd helped me, and I'd not only saved Jude, but I'd killed one of the seven demon princes. News had traveled, and those responsible were sought out and punished. I had no idea how they figured out it was Dommiel, but my St. George medal lying on the desk was proof enough.

"Kat. I can't leave him here. He has no protection."

She didn't tell me I was crazy and that we didn't protect demons. Dommiel and I shared a blood bond. I couldn't leave him alone. The next demon who found him would finish him off and take over as lord of New Orleans. He was injured and alone, ripe for the picking by the next predator who came along. And we were guardians of the defenseless.

Having regained her composure, though her eyes were red-rimmed, Kat came around and squatted next to him. "Give me your hand," she said to the wounded and bleeding demon.

Without looking at her, he reached out his one hand, the hooked arm still tucked by his middle. Kat reached out her other hand to me. "George. He will know what to do."

We sifted onto the lovely, clean street in Chelsea, hauling a bloody, battered demon up the moonlit steps. Within a minute, we were up the elevator and entering George's posh seven-thousand-square-foot flat overlooking the Thames. Dommiel's knees buckled, and we gently lowered him to the sleek parquet wood floor.

"What in the bloody hell?" George rushed from the bedroom wing, wearing only a pair of gray boxer briefs, his chestnut hair in more disarray than normal.

George always hid his chiseled body beneath fine, tailored clothes, but he definitely had a body built for battle.

"It was Damas," I said, holding Dommiel's head as he coughed up black blood.

George grew rigid at the name.

"He did this to Dommiel for helping me. I couldn't leave him."

George knelt at Dommiel's side. "Move, Genevieve. Both of you, back away."

"What are you going to do?" I asked, fearing the anger hardening George's expression.

"I'm going to bring him to someone who can help him." George lifted him and threw him over his shoulder. He was stronger than he looked.

All the while, Kat leaned against the wall and watched George, saying nothing, despair reeking from her.

George walked toward the exit. He'd have to get outside his own wards to sift.

"Don't you want to put some clothes on?" asked Kat.

"It's dark enough, and he lives alone," was his terse reply.

The door slammed shut. Kat pushed herself off the wall and walked into the den, then sank onto the sleek gray sofa with her head in her hands.

I followed, adrenaline still pumping hard at the crushing realization that I'd put my trust in the hands of a demon prince. Of course he used me to send Jude to hell. I was such a fool.

"Stop beating yourself up," said Kat, watching me pace the floor in front of her.

"Why should I? I was the one to put Jude's life in danger, and now…now I know if he never comes back to me, it will certainly be my own stupidity to blame."

"Damas knows how to beguile better than any of them. He studied you. He knew what to do, what to say to lure you into his web. Just as he did with me."

I paced to the wall of windows overlooking the Thames, which rippled under the starry night. "And now he wants revenge." Against Dommiel for helping me save Jude. And certainly against me.

Oh no!

I spun to Kat. "He'll want revenge against me, Kat. My dad! Mindy!"

I rushed across the den. Kat caught my arm. "No. Wait, Gen."

The door slammed. George reentered, black blood smeared on his arms and bare chest. "What now?"

"Damas will go after my dad next. Maybe even Mindy. I have to go to them."

He halted me with a hand in the air and swept his cell from the charger on the marble countertop. He texted a message, then set the phone down.

"Alexander and Tarquin will be here soon. I'll assign them guardian detail to your father and friend."

"But I can't let them—"

"Can't let them what? Put their lives in danger? It's what we do. Tarquin and Alexander are fitter for the job than you are, as you'll only make a prime target of yourself. Besides, you can't guard both at once, and Jude needs you by his side."

I leaned over, hands on my knees, catching my breath, not having realized I was near hyperventilating with fear.

"Calm down," said Kat, rubbing my back. "George is right."

An opening and slamming of George's door. I stood upright as the fierce, hard warrior, Tarquin, stepped into the room with Xander following, dressed in a black-on-gray tuxedo.

"You rang?" asked Xander in his casual tone. "Oh, we're having a party and no one told me."

"You're a bit overdressed," teased Kat, having shed her earlier anguish.

"It seems George is a bit underdressed. Ladies, I believe he has the right idea. Shall we shed some of these clothes together for a real party?"

"No time for this," snapped George. "Damas is on the prowl."

Both Tarquin and Xander straightened with tension at the sound of his name. Xander's playful expression vanished at once.

"Who was his target?" asked Tarquin, his rough voice matching the rugged exterior.

"A demon in New Orleans, the one who helped Genevieve retrieve Jude from Lethe's realm. We believe he will strike at her loved ones next. Alexander, you will guard her father. Tarquin, you will guard her best friend and roommate. There are wards in place, but neither of these individuals knows of the reality around them."

The reality that demons were lurking and on the hunt…for me, and possibly for them because of who I am and what I've done.

"You'll need to be discreet. Come," said George, "I'll provide you the details so you can be on your way."

As Tarquin passed, I stopped him with a hand on his arm. "Thank you. For doing this for me. I can't thank you enough."

The man of stone dipped his chin. "It is our duty to protect the innocent. No need to thank me." He walked on.

Xander paused before me and lifted my hand, brushing a quick kiss across my knuckles, all masculine grace and finesse. "Never fear, lady. We will watch out for them. We are all in this together. The burden cannot fall to one person alone."

He was right. For the briefest of moments, my heart lightened for the fact that I was not alone—that *we* were not alone.

"Jude." I walked toward the door and stopped by Kat. "He's alone. I need to get back." I hugged her tight. "Thank you. And I'm sorry for…for him."

I wished she hadn't had to encounter Damas again, after all she'd been through with him. Kat pulled away, her gaze finding George in the kitchen talking in hushed tones to the demon hunters who would now play guardian to Dad and Mindy.

"Don't be sorry. It's not your fault." She swallowed hard and licked her lips. "All my fear and guilt is mine alone."

"But you don't have to bear it alone," I said, squeezing her hand. "George loves you, you know."

Her sharp green eyes swiveled to me. A sad smile quirked her mouth. "I know."

I left with a new weight hanging heavy on my shoulders. I wondered if I'd ever be able to shed the monumental guilt from my heart, now that I'd brought Damas front and center, back between George and Kat.

Too weary to think about it anymore, I turned away from thoughts of the evil prince who'd ruined so many lives and thought instead about the man who put my heart at peace.

Even though Jude had not yet wakened from his deep sleep, hope wouldn't allow me to let go. And never would.

15

I'd taken a hot shower after returning from George's penthouse in Chelsea. I never did ask where he'd taken Dommiel. He and Jude knew all kinds of sentinels, typically monks, who were healers and messengers for the Flamma of Light.

I couldn't get the vision out of my head of that moment when George laid eyes on Kat and I told him that Thomas, my alleged guardian angel, was in fact Damas and we'd encountered him at Dommiel's club. I'd never seen that expression of blinding fear and fury warring on a man's face.

No, that wasn't true. I'd seen Jude look very much the same the night he'd saved me from Danté.

I was relieved to be back at the safety of the cottage, watching over my charge. After washing the long night's events from my body and my thoughts, I dried off and fumbled through the drawers in the bedroom. After pulling on a Union Jack T-shirt and a pair of white cotton panties, I jerked up a pair of sweatpants, eager to finally lie down and relax. And then my nail caught.

"Ow. Damn it." The nail had torn at the quick. As I stood there, my sweatpants having fallen to my ankles, the air in the room changed, became charged with electric heat. I glanced up.

Jude was staring at me. My heart dropped right out of my chest into my stomach. He still lay as I'd left him, but he tilted his head in my direction. His eyes—heaven help me—gazed vacantly. His irises were full black, the whites a murky gray, swirling with the mist of Lethe's lair.

"Jude?" No response.

I jerked on the sweatpants and ran around to his side, picking up his hand and squeezing it between mine. His focus followed me. And though he stared fixedly into my eyes, there was no recognition, no spark of light, nothing. He didn't resist when I took his hand. He didn't move at all.

I brushed the hair away from his eyes. "Jude. Baby, can you hear me?"

His brow pinched together in a frown at my touch. He turned his head to the side, his vacant stare settling on the window, where snow drifted down in fat flakes.

"Can you hear me?"

Nothing. For minutes, I simply held his hand and wondered what to do next.

"Okay. Maybe you're hungry. Maybe you'll eat something for me now."

I rushed into the kitchen and heated the stove at once. In the few days he'd been home, I'd managed to get him to swallow only a few spoonfuls of broth. Very few.

Knowing his system was still weak, I heated a bowl of tomato soup, adding just a dash of Tabasco the way he liked it. The way he used to like it, anyway.

I couldn't imagine how happy watching him take every spoonful would make me. He continued to stare out the window, but when I touched the spoon to his lips and coaxed him, he opened and swallowed.

"Good. This is good. Your body needs food, sustenance."

I put the straw that was in the glass of cold water up to his lips, which were still dry but no longer cracked and bleeding. To my surprise, he drank half the glass, taking in long, deep gulps.

"Okay. What would you like to do now, Jude?"

I pulled his heavy hand between mine and pressed my lips to his knuckles, doing my damnedest not to cry at this paltry improvement. Still no response.

"That's fine. You don't have to say anything." As if he would. "How about I just tell you what's been going on in the world since you left?"

I had no intention of mentioning demons or hell or the Blood Moon. Nor would I tell him about the backlash of riots in France since the terrorist bombing at the Eiffel Tower, or how Europe was in a violent uproar at the prospect of future terrorist attacks.

Sadly, no one had any idea that something far worse than a

war on terrorism was coming. I'd not fill his mind with any of that negative shit, so I tried to think of trivial things to fill the silence and let him know I was here.

"Well, Kat and George aren't fighting as much as usual. They seem to have come to some kind of truce. It seems, though of course, Kat won't talk about any of it with me. For someone who's as open as she is, she sure doesn't talk about her love life."

His gaze remained on the window. He blinked slowly, making no sign that he heard me.

"And Uriel is pretty cool. He's taking a more active role in things. He's changing my mind slightly on what I thought about angels and their stuck-up ways. I suppose it does require a lot of time to prepare for—" I stopped my rambling thoughts, realizing I was venturing into the topic of war. "And there's someone I'd like you to meet. Mira!"

She chirped from the next room and flew in, flapping her wings for a messy landing on the bed. I slipped on my leather jacket and held out my arm. She hopped across the blue, black, and green tartan lying on top of the quilts and climbed onto my leather-protected arm.

"Jude. This is Mira."

Mira made a sort of purring-chirp. She rarely made this sound, for it didn't sound like a bird as much as a contented cat. Jude's eyes shifted from the window to my snowy companion.

The swelling on his eye was gone. The bruising had transformed from deep purple to a mottled green. His cheek had only a small scratch left and a purplish splotch where the blood rose to the surface of his skin.

"Jump right here, Mira."

I guided her onto the bed at his side and picked up his arm, sliding his hand over her sleek feathers.

"She loves to be petted. Can you imagine where I got her?" No response, of course. "She came to me the night..." I cleared my throat. "She came to me one night. I was very sad. I was missing you, and this beautiful orb of light rose up out of my chest, and out came Mira. Can you believe it? Sounds ridiculous when I say it out loud."

Mira chirped once, her eyes sliding closed as I continued to pet her with Jude's broad hand.

"I couldn't believe it myself at first. The whole experience scared me to death, but I have to tell you, Mira is quite skilled in fighting, which comes in pretty handy. But she's a little spoiled." I whispered the last.

Mira chirped twice in her fussy tone but never opened her eyes.

"It's true, Mira, and you know it. How many hawks do you know who have a plush nest inside a warm cottage?"

Neither one of them answered me. Unable to hold his arm up any longer, I laid it back down by his side. Mira nestled onto the tartan at Jude's waist and fell into a deeper sleep.

"Looks like you have a new friend, Jude. She likes you. But I suppose most females do, don't they?"

His gaze had wandered back to the open window. I hopped up and stoked the fire, shifting the logs till sparks popped and the blaze grew brighter. After closing the grate, I turned to find Jude asleep again, Mira still cuddled into his side.

But something was different about him. I couldn't place my finger on exactly what it was. If I'd called George or Kat to come, they wouldn't see any change in him. Other than the fact his wounds were healing remarkably quickly—some of the stitches already dissolving after only a few days since George had stitched him up—to the average person, he wouldn't have appeared to change at all.

But I saw the difference. And I felt it. The tightness around his mouth had loosened. The strain of his brow had softened. The tension of his body had slackened into the pile of pillows and blankets. He no longer had the look of a haunted man wandering his tortured mind.

If I could put my finger on the emotion swirling in the room—the fireplace casting warm light on the bed and walls, the white blanket of snow coming down outside, the sweet bird nuzzled next to the man I loved with all my heart and soul—the one word that came to mind was *serenity*.

I crawled onto the bed and wrapped my arm around his waist, watching Jude and waiting, hoping he'd wake again soon.

"You'll come back to me, won't you, Jude?"

The fire crackled and spit up a spark in the grate. Before long, I drifted off into the most peaceful sleep since the day he'd been taken away. A warm throbbing cocooned my heart in the promise that my love would come back to me. I didn't care what Uriel had said. I'd find a way to dispel Lethe's dark mist shrouding Jude's mind and soul. I'd find a way to bring him back to me. To us.

16

We'd fallen into a pattern where Jude would wake and stare out the window, sometimes at the fire, sometimes at Mira as she perched on the foot of the bed frame. And every now and then, he'd stare at me, but there was no sign that the lights were on inside, so to speak. His irises remained full black; the misty vapor still swirled in his eyes.

I'd taken to using the iPad my dad had given me as an early Christmas present before I left to download and play Jude's favorite movies. I refused to play the Tarantino flicks, still afraid violence might not be the best way to coax him from his shell.

I didn't know if he actually watched the movies, as his eyes kept their glazed look while he stared at the screen I propped on his lap with a pillow. *Rio Bravo* had just ended, so I removed the iPad.

I'd recently picked up my historical romance, *The Captain's Captive*, which I'd stopped reading during our honeymoon and left on the mantel in the bedroom. Though I knew without a doubt that Jude would never in a million years read a romance novel, I'd decided to read aloud to him anyway.

Captain Sparr and his lady, Viola, had finally found a safe and warm cottage in the wilderness where they'd washed ashore. The cabin was conveniently abandoned and well stocked, so they lingered there before they sought out civilization where society would prevent an unmarried woman from being alone with a roguish man the likes of the captain. Captain Sparr had gone hunting for small game and returned in today's reading.

"Captain Sparr opened the door and froze at the sight of Viola standing before the fire. The golden glow silhouetted the soft curves of her voluptuous hips and breasts. Slamming the door shut and dropping the satchel of hare he'd caught in his traps, the captain strode across the room in three strides, then took Viola into his arms. She gasped as he pulled her close, her full breasts pressing against his hard chest. 'Oh, Captain. We mustn't.' His heated gaze seared her, drinking in her luscious parted lips. 'It's about time you called me James.' Gripping his taut shoulders for balance and to try to resist the deep yearning spreading through her body, Viola whispered, 'Why—why should I?' A wicked smile cracked his rugged face as his lips descended. 'Because a woman should cry out the first name of her lover when he pleasures her.'"

I paused, feeling a shocking flush of heat crawl up my neck. Glancing at Jude, I snapped the book shut. I'd read quite a few romances, but never aloud. And here I was, spiraling headfirst into a hot sex scene while my own lover remained catatonic before me and didn't even know my name.

"Maybe that's enough reading for the day." Inwardly laughing at myself, I'd been trying so hard to get to the part where Viola and Captain Sparr—no wait, James—finally got down and dirty. But when I read it aloud, my pulse had picked up a feverish pace and I realized how much I'd missed my own lover giving me pleasure.

I found my gaze wandering to Jude's lips—now smooth and healed—and imagined those lips on my mouth, on my skin. Perhaps reading the captain's seduction of Lady Viola wasn't such a good idea.

I tossed the book on the nightstand and found the broom. "I will say this, though," I rambled, "that captain sure knows how to get into a girl's pants. Or skirt, I guess, in this case."

I swept around the hearth where soot had gathered and yammered to break the constant silence.

"I just wish we could get Netflix out here on Arran so we could watch some of the cool new shows. This one called *Peaky Blinders* looks awesome, Jude. I think you'd like the no-nonsense kind of guy Cillian Murphy plays—"

The sound of movement jerked my attention to the bed. Jude was sitting up on his own and gazing out the window. I didn't know when he'd awoken. Barefoot and shirtless, I was glad George and I had managed to dress him in black workout pants when George popped in to check on him yesterday.

Though Jude was much leaner of brawn than usual, he still weighed a ton for me to lift and dress on my own.

While he was here, George had said little to nothing the entire visit. I wasn't anywhere near ready to have a conversation about Damas. That could wait, as far as I was concerned.

"Jude?"

He shoved himself off the mattress and took a labored step forward, seeming as if he might fall at any minute. I dropped the broom and ran to his side.

When I took his arm to help him, he flinched away and shot me a fierce look, his brow furrowed.

Palms out in a gentle gesture, I said in a soft tone, "Let me help you."

He still didn't know who I was it seemed. Rather than let the sting of that reality send me into a pit of despair, I reminded myself that this step of him moving around was a good sign, a sign his body was healing, even if his mind didn't seem to be recovering as quickly.

The second time I lifted his arm to drape it over my shoulder, he let me align my body next to his, though I felt him shiver and shift away at my touch. I guided him to the window. We shuffled forward till we were at the sill. He pulled away. Though I wanted his touch more than anything in the world, I stepped to the side and gave him his space.

He braced his hands on the sill. His knuckles were mostly healed from the abrasions pocking each one. I'd often wondered how he'd gotten them in Danté's keep, because it looked like he'd punched a brick wall over and over.

His back seemed to be healing as well as his front, even though Danté's malicious abuse had mostly been heaped on his back. The whiplashes zigzagged in thin red welts. The stitches had nearly all dissolved, and I could make out the grimace of the devil being defeated by St. Michael the Archangel.

I dragged my eyes away from his wounds and leaned on the

window frame next to him. He gazed through the pane. The heavy gale had passed last night, leaving a dusting of snow on the ground and a gray but clear day. Mira swooped in circles out over the sea.

"Would you…would you like to go outside?"

He turned his head toward me without saying a word, but I knew that was what he wanted.

"Okay. Good. Great." I smiled, my pulse pounding. This was an excellent sign. "You come and sit here and let me help you get dressed."

He let me guide him to the chair propped in front of the fire —the one where I'd snuggled in his lap during our honeymoon as we kissed and whispered our love to one another.

Push it away, Gen.

If I let myself think of the way things used to be for even a second, I'd tumble back into the abyss of despair. This black-eyed man saw me as a stranger. But at least a friendly one.

I found a white T-shirt and slipped it over his head. He helped me get it through his arms, so at least he wasn't a vegetable. He remembered how to put clothes on, though his body was still too weak to do it on his own.

I found his charcoal-gray cable sweater and slipped it on him. A quiet tension filled the room as I knelt on the floor with his foot in my lap and tied the laces of his boots. When I looked up to find him watching me with intense concentration, I almost thought he remembered me.

"Jude?"

He blinked once, meeting my gaze, but still made no sign of recognition.

With a smile, I stood and said, "Okay, then. Wait here."

After scurrying to slip on my thick coat because the temperature was somewhere around ten degrees, I bolted outside with one of the wooden kitchen chairs. Within five minutes, I had Jude through the door and out in the frigid air. Well, certainly frigid to me. He'd always loved the climate here.

I remember once standing on the cliff's edge with him, shivering till my teeth chattered, while he wore nothing but a long-sleeved shirt and a bright smile on his face as if we were basking on a sunny beach somewhere. I wanted to find that smile again. I needed to find it again.

Once he was settled, I ran back inside and brought out the green, black, and blue tartan, the one from his descendants, the Campbell clan. I wrapped it over his lap and made sure his hands were tucked underneath, then stood back and watched him watch the sky.

Mira loved to soar in the blustery clouds right off the beach. She looped down, then up, then did figure eights, came closer, then swooped back out over the sea again.

"She's showing off," I said, knowing I'd get no response. "To be honest, I think this is her way of flirting with you."

He made no sign that he heard me, but I could see his eyes following her every move. There was life in those eyes. That was the important thing.

WHEN I AWOKE THE FOLLOWING MORNING, I FOUND HIM seated in his comfy chair by the fire, his hands clasped in his lap. When I scrambled out of bed to check on him, his gaze flitted from the fire to me, resting a moment, then swiveled back to the glowing coals. If he were his old self, he would've conjured fire with the snap of his fingers to warm the room. But he either couldn't do it or didn't know he had this power.

Still, he was out of the coma, and that was enough to make me giddy as a schoolgirl. I refrained from jumping up and down with glee for fear of scaring him to death, but inside I was doing celebratory cartwheels.

"How about some breakfast?"

Knowing he wouldn't answer, I went ahead to the kitchen, quickly lit the stove and scrambled some eggs. We'd not yet tried solid food, but the man needed protein.

With the plate of fluffy eggs in hand, I settled on a stool close to him and forked a bite. As I raised the fork toward his mouth, Jude lifted his hand and wrapped it around mine, stopping me in midair.

My heart kicked into fifth gear. This was the first time he'd touched me. Oh, I'd touched him often while dressing him or helping him sit up or walk outside, but this was the first time he'd initiated contact.

His gaze was less bleak, less desolate, less empty. The mist didn't move as quickly behind his eyes. As a matter of fact, the vapor seemed to clear for a moment, though his irises were still dark as pitch.

His lips parted on a rusty request. "Let me."

He slid the fork from my hand and slowly picked up the plate from my lap. I let out a short laugh, a tear sliding down my face. I swiped it away quickly before he thought I'd gone insane. To hear that voice—though broken and hoarse—my heart soared.

"Jude?"

He looked up from his plate, chewing. Okay, he recognized his name. Good.

"Do you know who I am?"

His brow pinched together in concentration, then his gaze roved over my face, down my neck, and over my body. As if he'd been caught doing or thinking something naughty, his gaze flicked back to his plate as he stabbed a giant hunk of scrambled eggs. Hearty appetite. Excellent sign.

I thought he wouldn't answer, but he said, "You are the woman who takes care of me."

"Yes," I said with another laugh, unable to contain the glee lighting me up on the inside like a firefly. "I am the woman who takes care of you." It wasn't the answer I wanted, but it was enough for now.

I didn't care that he didn't know me yet. At least, that was what I told myself. He was healing at a remarkable rate. His stitches were entirely dissolved. The redness of his wounds had lightened to those of someone who'd been healing for months. I wouldn't doubt if Uriel hadn't added some of his angel mojo to help him heal even faster than a Dominus Daemonum when he laid hands on him the other day.

Jude finished his plate, set it down and stood, arching his

spine and stretching his back. I jumped to my feet, ready to help him if he toppled over. His body stiffened at my swift movement.

"Sorry. I-I just want to help you if you need it."

He gestured behind me toward the bathroom. He wanted me to move so he could go to the bathroom on his own.

"Oh! Sure. Of course."

I stepped aside. He walked into the bathroom, favoring his right leg more than the other. George hadn't found any broken bones, but there must've been some injury we couldn't determine without X-rays.

George had refused to take him to a hospital. There would be no way of explaining how he'd become so severely injured without the staff calling the local police and asking questions we couldn't answer. And he'd heal too fast for a normal human, drawing more questions.

I sat on the stool, my crossed leg bouncing, and waited for him to finish, when something dawned on me. He'd known where the bathroom was. The door had been closed, so he couldn't see that it was a bathroom from where he was sitting. Did he assume it must be a bathroom? Or did he know it was there because a part of him remembered this place?

A burst of excited butterflies flitted around in my stomach. Instincts told me he remembered.

When he opened the door, he looked through the open doorway into the next room. "May I have some water?" Though still hoarse, his voice sounded smoother than before. No longer stilted or hesitant, he spoke like the man I knew.

"Yes." I snapped to attention and hurried to the next room. "Of course."

He followed me. I grabbed a glass from the cabinet and poured water from one of the many jugs of filtered water I'd stocked. He took the glass, leaning on the dining table for support, his dark gaze keen and watching, then he tilted his head back and guzzled. When finished, he handed me the empty glass.

"More please."

I poured another. He drank, and I poured another. I'd been forcing small sips down his throat these past few days as he lay in bed. Now that he was conscious and able, he finally quenched his thirst from the long days in hell, where surely he'd been given nothing to sustain him.

"Um. Are you still hungry?"

He shook his head, scanning the room and taking in his surroundings.

"Do you know this room? I mean, do you remember this room?"

After another shake of the head, he walked to the mantel and picked up a white sheep figurine I'd noticed my first time here. With a creased brow, he lifted the ceramic figurine and said, "It's from Brodick."

"Yes," I said, delighted and trying not to frighten him with my enthusiastic reply. "At least, I think it probably is. You bought it. This is your cottage."

He's remembering.

With an expression of deep concentration, he said, "I didn't buy this cottage."

"No. You didn't. You built it. Many years ago."

He slid his hand across the mantel, his fingers smoothing over the detail of an oak-leaf design at the edge. "I don't remember."

Swallowing the lump in my throat, I said, "It's okay. You will. Would you like to go outside today?"

He set the white sheep back in place next to the black one. With a nod, he turned back to me, studying me with such intensity, it reminded me of the first day I'd met him. Those dark eyes missed nothing. The gray mist was less than before but still there, swirling in a haze.

"Good," I said. "Well, let's get our coats on. I'd like to take you somewhere I think you'll like."

And hopefully remember.

17

We stepped onto the wooded trail where he'd first taken me during our honeymoon. The same heavy silence pressed down from tall, gnarled trees. Leafless, the branches webbed together, a dusting of snow on the boughs. The wind no longer howled across the island like a fierce beast, but breathed softly, whispering that all was well.

Jude paused at the entrance, a menacing scowl marking his face. I glanced back into the woods, darker than the open air, but sensed no danger. I reached out with my VS, scanning for Flamma with deep concentration. Nothing.

What caused the alarm was likely the similarity in appearance to the naked trees in Lethe's realm. But there, the air was bleak, weighed down by sorrow and regret. Here, the woods were clean, draped in a gentle beauty all their own.

"It's all right," I called back to him from several yards within the canopy.

An expression of wonder flickered over the hard planes of his face. His cheeks were still too thin, cutting a sharp angle to a square jaw.

My VS beamed bright white through the line of exposed skin between glove and jacket.

"Oh."

My face must be glowing, which would explain this look of awe and fear skittering across his face. Rather than force my VS to behave and dim the illusory glow that appeared any time I used my power, I let it shine.

"I'm a Flamma of Light," I said. The fact that I had to explain something he'd once told me for the first time was ludicrous.

He stepped farther along the trail, closing the distance between us.

I pulled one glove off to show him my hand. "This is my underlight. It shines when I'm seeking danger or using my power in other ways."

Like destroying a demon prince for what he did to you.

Jude stopped in front of me, lifted his hand hesitantly and glanced at me from under heavy lashes before taking my shaking hand. My palm rested on his. He brushed his thumb over my knuckles, observing closely. My underlight brightened with his touch. My hand trembled more.

"You're cold," he said, white air puffing out as he spoke.

"A little," I admitted.

"You're shaking."

"Yes," I said, my voice as tremulous as my hand.

He started to pull his hand away, but I closed my fingers around his, aching to feel his touch a moment longer, unable to say a word as my breath came out in a white cloud between us and adrenaline shot through my body.

Rather than flinch away, his fingers curled slowly, enveloping the back of my hand. I wanted to close my eyes and drown in this moment. Palpable energy sparked between us, sure and strong as it had ever been before Lethe had taken him and scraped away his memory of me.

Somewhere inside, he must know there was nothing to fear from me, that this was natural between us, that we belonged together. His chest rose and fell as quickly as mine, his gaze melting from wary to smoldering, his gaze dropping to my lips.

I thought I'd fall down in a faint on the spot when he brushed his thumb once more before dropping my hand, his scowl back in place.

"Shall we walk on?" he asked.

Gathering my wits, which were strewn all over the forest floor, I inhaled a deep breath and turned up the path. "You know, if we're quiet, we might see some wildlife."

I heard him, felt him right on my heels, keeping close to me.

"There are red deer in these woods," he said with conviction.

An aching smile split my face. "Yes." I glanced over my shoulder to find his gait stronger, his posture taller. "There are. We've seen them here before, you and I."

He didn't ask me why I used the term "we," though I could see I'd puzzled him. I didn't care. I planned to push him as far as I could till Jude surfaced all the way to the top and remembered me, remembered us.

We walked on in silence…comfortable silence, which made my heart swell with hope till I thought it would burst.

Our arms brushed once, and he didn't pull away, only glanced at me. I smiled. Though he didn't smile in return, his expression had lost the look of fear and anxiety that so often marked his brow since he woke.

I wanted to take him to Glenashdale Falls or even to the standing stones on a moor not so far away, which he'd showed me on our honeymoon, but in order to do that, we'd have to sift. And I wasn't sure how he'd react to that.

Did he remember what sifting was? Or would he freak out and jerk loose from my hold while in the Void? Though he'd lost the thick ropes of muscle while in the underworld, he'd not lost all his strength. I couldn't take the chance of losing him. Not again.

But there was no need. He didn't appear bored with a walk through the woods. We never saw a deer, but we saw a red-eared squirrel zip from branch to branch above our heads.

Mira joined us on our walk back, scaring the squirrels into hiding for good. Jude didn't seem to mind that either, his dark gaze following her as she swooped to a branch, panned the tops of the trees, then swooped onto another.

By the time we made it back to the cottage, we were both exhausted. Jude lay on top of the quilts and fell asleep on his side, the way he always had before. I couldn't help but crawl up next to him and drift off as well, content and warm.

AN EAR-SPLITTING SCREAM JARRED ME AWAKE.

Before I could shoot up into a sitting position, Jude rolled on top of me, straddling my waist, pinning me down with his bulk, his hands wrapped around my throat.

Though his eyes were open, he didn't see me, his face a mask of rage, blood vessels popping out along his temples and forehead, his lips drawn tight over gritted teeth.

"No," I choked out before he closed my throat for good.

He didn't hear me. Beating him was useless. His hands were brutal bands, squeezing off the airflow like cinching a sack. Rather than panic, I placed my hands on his cheeks and called my VS.

An aura of white filled the darkened room. The sun had fallen while we slept. I pulled a ball of power into my chest and guided it through my arms and hands, sending him a jolt —not to harm, only to push away.

The jolt pushed his torso back, lifting his weight from me and his hands from my throat. The Flamma power didn't hurt him but served to punch him into consciousness. His eyes cleared at once, the misty vapor that had enveloped him draining away like water through a sieve.

The rage transformed to shock, then fear.

"I-I'm so sorry." He jerked off me and jumped out of the bed, pressing his back against the wall, chest heaving.

I coughed and turned on my side, sucking in air. One hand went immediately to my belly as I reached out with my VS to be sure my baby was all right. Reassured with the steady inner pulse that connected me to my child, I pushed into a sitting position.

"It's okay." I coughed again, then slid off the bed in front of him. "You were having a nightmare."

"I hurt you." He stared at my throat, which surely was ringed with red.

"I'm okay." I touched my fingers to my neck, the skin already sore and raw.

He rocked from one foot to another, like a frightened child. "You take care of me…and I hurt you. I could've killed you."

"I wouldn't have let you," I said with a smile. "I'm stronger than you think."

It was true my power was growing by the day. I felt it like a pot percolating to the perfect moment. My awakening drew closer, and I knew exactly when that moment would be. But there was time to worry about that later.

"I'm fine. Really." I stepped closer.

Then something extraordinary happened. One side of his mouth quirked up into a smile. And my heart, my poor, miserable heart, just fell right off her shelf onto the floor. As I gazed into his smiling face, I thought I'd never break free long enough to pick it up and put it back where it belonged.

"Can I—" I stammered, my voice breaking, heart aching.

"Yes? Can I get you something? Does it hurt?"

I shook my head, reveling in the sound of his deep voice rumbling with concern for me.

"What can I do for you?" he asked, worry shining in his eyes.

"Can I…please…hold you?"

His smile faded, and I was sure he would push me away. Again. Instead, he opened his arms. On a heavy sigh, I melted into him, wrapping my arms around his waist.

I simply stood there, lost in the warmth of his embrace, in the fluttering of his pulse where my cheek pressed to his neck, in the utter joy of being where I belonged most in the world. He said nothing and never pushed me away, just let me hold him with his hands placed at a respectful height on my back. I wanted more, so much more, but for now, this was enough.

I'd sent Mira to bring George back to the cottage. After our all too brief hug, Jude had become agitated. The night terror was proof that his memories were buoying to the surface, and the horror he'd experienced at the hands of Danté and his minions threatened to push him over the edge into rage-filled madness.

It wasn't something he could convey in words, but I sensed it all the same. Whether it was my Vessel Sense or women's intuition, I knew this to be true.

Jude sat before the fire, tapping his foot on the ground, his knee bouncing twice per second.

"They'll be here soon. I'm sure of it."

"And these men, you say I know them?"

"Yes."

He'd finally come to grips that there was a lifetime of memories he couldn't remember. I wouldn't even try to explain that his lifetime extended for centuries. It was too much to try to make him understand.

"They are Flamma of Light. Like me. Like you."

If he didn't stop frowning, he'd have a permanent dent right in the middle of his forehead.

A gentle knock on the door—three raps—then it opened.

Jude shot to his feet, as did I. George entered the room first, Mira on his shoulder, with Uriel behind him, the cold air whooshing in. No one said a word, but I watched the exchange between Uriel and Jude as the angel stepped farther inside.

Jude's frown smoothed, his lips sliding apart in wonder and…recognition.

"I've met you before."

"Of course you have, Jude Delacroix. I made you what you are."

By now, Uriel stood directly in front of an awestruck Jude. He wasn't surprised that a beautiful man with white-gold wings stepped into the cottage. He wasn't alarmed by George's presence either. There was a knowing of the soul that transpired beyond the mind's memory.

Again, for about the hundredth time, a dagger slid into my heart and cut out another piece, for he hadn't yet remembered me. I put my own selfish thoughts away.

Mira flapped her wings and flew up to her coverlet nest on top of the kitchen cabinet. I twisted my hands together, anxiety riding me like a lightning bolt.

"I need you to remove your sweater and lie down for what I must do," commanded Uriel.

"And what is it you plan to do?" asked Jude.

"Make you again. The fire I gave you once is all but a few dying embers. I must feed you the burn to purge away the darkness and bring you back to the Light as you were before."

Jude gripped the bottom of his sweater and lifted it over his head, tossing it onto the dining room table. No matter that thin scars—fully healed in a remarkable few days—slashed his chest and back with white ribbons across the black ink, the sight of this shirtless man nearly brought me to my knees.

I loved him so, wanted him every second of every day. His dark gaze flicked to mine. Did he feel the heat of my ogling? Embarrassed, I looked away and moved around behind the sofa.

Frown back in place, Jude lay back, probably realizing he was literally putting himself in a vulnerable position, which I'm sure didn't sit well with his instincts. This took a great deal of trust. I smiled at him for reassurance. His chest and abdomen —flexed tight—relaxed as Uriel knelt on the floor beside him. I stood behind the sofa near his head, where he could see me if he needed.

Uriel splayed his large hands on Jude's chest and abdomen. In a booming voice that shook the panes in their casements, Uriel said in Latin, "*The fire of heaven come to me.*"

I cried out and flinched back as a brilliant golden light flared to life, gold-orange flames licking up from Uriel's hand and Jude's chest, a fire that didn't burn the flesh, perhaps only the soul.

Eyes squeezed shut, mouth agape in agony, Jude arched his back as if he were being lashed all over again. I stepped forward, wanting to reach out and touch him, take his hand.

"No." George gripped my arm and watched the display as if it were perfectly normal to witness an angel set another man on fire.

Who was I kidding? This *was* normal for them. My VS pumped a steady beacon from within, telling me to be calm, that all was well.

Reminding myself that these flames would burn away the evil smothering Jude's soul, I gripped the edge of the sofa, heat pouring from the supernatural flames rising higher and higher, spreading down Jude's legs, up his neck to his head. I bit my lip so hard, the metallic taste of blood filled my mouth.

"Light up the dark. Set him free."

With the last word, Uriel lifted his hands, straightened his arms, and clapped them together over his head. The flames snuffed out in a blink. One second, the room was filled with a hallowed fire purging Jude's soul; the next, it was all gone, the air cool again. Only static electricity in the air marked the room as any different from before.

Jude was once again unconscious. "Is he okay?" I asked.

"Yes." George wrapped his arm around my shoulder.

"What?" I asked, fear taking hold. "What's wrong?"

"Nothing," he said, giving me a tight squeeze before circling the sofa to Uriel's side. "All is well, actually. I believe Jude will be all right. When he awakens."

Uriel had his hands on his thighs as he knelt on the floor, his head bowed, shoulders rising and falling with the deep breaths he sucked into his lungs. The arch of his wings drooped, the edges sagging.

"Uriel? Are you okay?"

I'd never seen the mighty angel appear so exhausted, so weak. Finally, he lifted his head. I hitched in a breath at the sight of the intense brilliance of his crystal-blue eyes, sparking with a fire all their own.

"Your eyes."

"A side effect of using the fire of making," said George.

Uriel lifted to his feet. Without a word, he planted his hand on Jude's shoulder and sifted out with him.

"No! Where'd they go? Where'd he take him?" My pulse pounded in utter terror to have Jude taken from me again, even by someone I knew.

"In here," said Uriel, walking out of the bedroom to rejoin us. "I wasn't about to carry him after I spent all that energy."

"He's okay, then. How long will he be out?"

"Hard to say. That'll be up to him, I'm afraid. Let him rest. Hopefully, when he wakes, he'll have more of his memory. It still may come back in stages, but he didn't fear us. He knew us right away, though he wasn't quite sure how. His trust was a good sign."

I walked them to the door. George gave me a quick kiss on the cheek. "Alert us when he wakes again."

"I will. And George?"

"Yes?"

"How's Dommiel doing?"

His brow bunched into a frown. "Quite well. He'll recover."

"Thank you. I know it's not exactly protocol to help a demon, but I appreciate it."

"Of course."

"And"—I bit my lip in hesitation—"how is Kat?"

When I'd left her at his flat, she was standing on the balcony, staring at the Thames with a look so distant and full of regret, I'd slipped away with a sad heart. There was nothing I could say to take away what Damas had done to her. And though it had happened long ago, the scars had never healed.

Grim-faced, George said, "She's fine…now. But we will have to have a conversation about the repercussions of your inter-action with Damas."

To clarify, my mistake of accepting the power to sift from a demon might bring me to harm in some way we hadn't yet determined. I'd been told long ago that only angels held and could share the power to sift. Of course, I kept forgetting that high demons were once angels—the fallen. If it wasn't so grave a mistake, I'd laugh at my stupidity.

"Not now," I said to George. "Please." I could handle only so much anxiety in one day.

"Not now," he said with a smile, giving my shoulder a squeeze before slipping out into the cold night.

The archangel stepped forward, weariness in his slumping

shoulders and drooping head. He appeared so frail and brittle.

Jude had once told me that angels rarely shared their power because it depleted their own strength. I wasn't exactly sure what had transpired in this rekindling of the fire within Jude, but it held the essence of Uriel. The event had cost him on some level.

"Uriel?" I stopped him as he passed through the doorway. "Why do your eyes change color? I thought they were green the first time we met in Jackson Square. But they change to all manner of shades of blue too."

He chuckled. "When my mood changes, so do my eyes."

"Wow. Cool, but…unusual."

"Windows to the soul, Vessel." He looked out at the night, the moon smudged behind a wispy sweep of clouds. "Angels are more akin to the spiritual realm than the human. It shows in such ways." He turned to face me, his smile slipping to a grave expression, all levity drained from him. "You've done a fine job. With Jude."

"Have I? He still has no clue who I am." I tried to keep the bitterness from my words, but it was impossible.

Uriel cupped my cheek. The tactile sensation of his hand on my skin sent my VS into orbit, energy pulsing from him to me at an alarming speed.

"Do not doubt his love for you, Genevieve." His deep voice had dropped to a sonorous melody, the hypnotic tones of an angel. "He will remember. And he owes everything—his body, his heart, his soul—entirely to your courage and faith."

"Not entirely," I whispered. "I couldn't restore his power as you did."

"I could never have done so had you not gone into the pit of hell and dragged him out again. Never forget that, Vessel of Light. You braved the darkest reaches of the world with faith and hope that could buoy a legion of sinking ships. You could've certainly doomed yourself—and the precious one you carry—to bring him back again."

A tear slid down my cheek. Uriel brushed it away with his thumb, still holding his palm against my skin.

"It is the kind of love that moves mountains. The kind that wages war against evil…and wins."

As he slipped back into the night, crunching across the snow and crossing the wards to sift away with George, the heavy boulder I'd been carrying from the moment Lethe stole my love from me chipped away into dust, until finally I could breathe again.

Hope. Faith.

Yes, I'd clasped them and held on tight, never allowing despair to convince me Jude was lost for good. Once I was past the grief, I needed these two companions to keep me going. And they'd not let me down. Not then. Not now. Not ever.

19

He didn't wake the next morning, nor did he have any more nightmares. Silent. Still. Nothing. I left Mira at his bedside and sifted into Brodick to pick up dinner. I wanted food that I didn't have to cook. Funny the little things you miss when secluded on an isolated island.

A McDonald's quarter pounder with cheese and salty fries would've been perfect right about now, but I refused to go anywhere too public, where I might be discovered.

I stepped into The Brodick Bar and Brasserie. Jude and I had dined here a few weeks ago, before my world had gone to shit. Their food was delicious. The sound of Christmas music greeted me. A string of lights lined the bar.

In the corner of the room sat a short, fat Christmas tree, its multicolored lights blinking cheerily. The place was near empty but for a little old man hunched over the bar with his brown wool coat and flat cap still on. He was here the last time I'd been here, sitting on the same corner stool.

I scanned the chalkboard menu, finding what I wanted right away.

"Are you okay there?"

It was the rosy-cheeked waitress with strawberry-blonde hair who'd waited on us last time. She peered over my shoulder before settling a disappointed smile on me. She was looking for Jude probably who'd been with me last time.

"Table for one, or are you expecting someone else?" she asked.

"I'd like to order something to go, please."

"Sure, then. What'll you have?"

"The grilled sirloin steak with parsley butter and chips. Oh, and a piece of the chocolate torte, please."

"How'd you like your steak?"

"Medium rare."

I craved red meat and chocolate. My stomach growled just thinking about it.

"It won't be long. You can have a seat in the bar while you wait."

"Thank you."

Hands tucked in my jacket pockets, I ambled into the bar and sat on a stool, my only company the old gentleman two stools down, who nursed a pint of dark beer.

"What can I get you?" asked the bartender, a rough-looking guy with kind eyes.

"Um, just a cup of tea please. Waiting on takeout."

With a nod, he disappeared for two minutes and returned with the tea, placing it on the bar along with packets of sugar and a tiny jug of milk. "Here you are."

"Thank you."

He went back to stacking the rack of clean bar glasses. I stirred the milk and sugar in the coffee, then took a sip. Not the same as café au lait but still nice and warm.

"You closing up early?" I asked.

"We sure are. For Christmas and all."

Christmas? I frowned and pulled out the phone I'd tucked in my jacket before leaving the cottage. Wow. It was December 25th, and it had never dawned on me.

I had two missed calls. I listened to the messages from Mindy and Dad, wishing me a merry Christmas. How had it never even dawned on me what day it was?

A year ago, I would've been curled up by our big tree in the living room, listening to Bing Crosby with Dad and making s'mores by the fire—carefree, happy, and oblivious to the angel/demon world.

That was also before Jude—the love of my life who didn't even know me anymore. I shook my head at my sad state.

"Not keeping Christmas with your family?" asked the old guy next to me with a thick Scottish accent.

Shocked out of my self-pity, I glanced over with a small smile. "Afraid not."

"You're American. Traveling the world on your own, are you?"

"Yeah. Sort of."

"A bit young to be doing such a thing, in my opinion."

If he only knew the places I'd traveled already. Sure, I was a bit young. But I'd grown decades in the past few months. My happy little life of college and clubbing had come to an abrupt halt on my twentieth birthday. With the Great War pressing ever closer, I'd been slapped into a reality that required mature focus and a very adult outlook.

"I suppose I am," I agreed.

"Don't look happy about it."

Was I that transparent? Even to a stranger? Probably.

"Just a little homesick, I guess."

"Aye. I'd say it's more than that."

He angled his body to get a better look at me, then reached out his hand for a shake. I took it in mine—well-worn but strong.

"My name's Murdoch."

"Nice to meet you. I'm Genevieve."

"Genevieve. Lovely name for a lovely girl. And a lonely girl, I'd say."

I smiled at the way *girl* was drawn out with rolling r's like "gurrel."

"Yes, I suppose I am. I'm missing someone. Terribly."

"Aye. Your man, I'd bet."

"Are you a psychic or something?"

He chuckled. "No. Just old. I've seen enough heartbroken women to know what one looks like."

"Break a few hearts yourself?" I asked, teasing.

"I did. Quite a few. In my time," he said with a wink, draining the last of his beer. He knocked his knuckles on the bar. "One more, Hamish. For the road."

The bartender turned from his cleaning and nodded.

"I hope you're not driving," I said, suddenly worried about the old guy. "The weather seems to be getting worse." And no telling how many beers he'd had.

The bartender set another pint glass in front of him. "Don't worry about him, lass. He lives about a mile away. Always walks."

"Convenient too," said Murdoch. "The wife can't complain when I get my exercise. Two miles a day for an old man's good for the lungs and heart."

He took a deep gulp. Hamish turned back to his duties, disappearing into the kitchen.

"Won't your wife be wanting you home? On Christmas?"

"Oh aye. She'll be nipping my head by the time I make my way home. But that's nothing new. The family comes tomorrow from the mainland, and I'd rather be out of her way with the cleaning and all."

I finished my tea and pushed the cup away. I was happy for

him, imagining him celebrating with his family on Christmas, the normal joys of life.

"There goes that sad look again. You're too young, Genevieve, for such distress. Has this man broken your heart for good? Or is he smart enough to return to ye?"

My stomach flip-flopped at his question. "I'm hoping he'll return."

"I'm sure you don't want advice from an old man, but I'd like to give it to ye all the same."

"I'd like to hear it."

For the majority of the conversation, he'd stared ahead or at his ale, glancing at me here and there. Now, he swiveled on his stool to face me properly.

"There are few things in this world that truly make us content. There's a difference between happy and content, did ya know?"

I shook my head, having never given the idea much thought.

"Happy is what you are when you buy yourself a new hat, when you look on something grand for the first time, when a lad surprises his lass with roses. But content is different entirely. A content person feels that all is right with the world even when tragedy strikes, even when loss weighs the spirit down. They're still at ease within themselves, no matter what calamity breaks their heart. Do you see?"

I did. I nodded, though I wasn't quite sure where all this was going.

He gulped down two swallows of beer. "Just so, a person can

be depressed or sad. The depressed person feels the blow of some misfortune—loss of a job, a pet dies, a car accident. With time, depression goes away. But the sad one…" He shakes his head, leveling his gaze on me. "The sad one allows misfortune to darken the spirit, to smother any hope left inside. The sad one doesn't live long."

"What do you mean? You can't die from sadness."

"Even if the body's breathin', that don't mean you're livin', lass."

He swallowed the last of his beer and stood back from the bar, tossing a ten-pound note on the bar. "Good night, Hamish," he said. The bartender waved with his back to us, still tending to closing duties.

"Night, Murdoch."

"And good night to ye, Genevieve. Shake that sadness off, lass. Every day is precious." He tipped his flat cap to me. "Merry Christmas." Then he ambled out into the evening.

When I returned to the cottage, I settled before the fire with my steak dinner and chocolate torte. Jude lay on his back, his head tilted to the side in peaceful repose. Mira hopped off the bedpost to the arm of my chair.

"I know. I'm going to share with you."

I cut a few pieces of the pinkest part and set it on the hearthstone. She chirped brightly and set to gobbling her meal. I pondered Murdoch's words of wisdom. The snow fell softly outside the window. The firelight illumined the room with a soft glow.

With my plate balanced on my lap, I pulled my phone from

my pocket and scrolled through my music, finding an old playlist I'd made for Dad and me, then pressed Play.

Bing Crosby crooned "Silent Night" as I forked the first tender bite into my mouth. I was warm. I was safe. The man I loved was warm and safe with me.

Murdoch was right. Every day was precious. Even with an apocalypse closing in on me, I believed this to the heart.

Mira finished her meal and peered up at me, orange eyes bright and pleading. I placed a few more bites in front of her. She chirped again, a sound of thanksgiving.

I laid my hand over my belly and whispered, "Merry Christmas," to all three of my loved ones in the room.

Close to noon a few days later and after eating a late breakfast of homemade biscuits, sausage, and eggs—as my appetite increased daily—I spent the rest of the afternoon going through routines with my katana, watching Mira soar gracefully in the clouds over the sea, and finishing my romance novel.

I did *not* read it aloud. I mooned over the happily-ever-after ending, dreaming of my own. If only life could be more like books.

I glanced at Jude on the bed, flat on his back, before finally deciding to take a long, hot shower.

The steaming water streamed over my back while I mulled over what Kat had texted me today about violent protests breaking out in all parts of the US. Tension was rising, just as the demons had wanted. War was drawing closer. What she hadn't mentioned was our encounter with Damas. And I sure as hell wasn't going to bring it up.

The entire experience, and the revelation of my horrific mistake in ever trusting him, had me on edge every time I thought of it. The alternative was to ignore the issue as long as possible, which I planned to do.

I was scrubbing my shoulder with the shower scrunchie I'd brought from my own apartment—one of the many amenities I'd stockpiled before I'd gone after Jude—when a whoosh of cold air sucked the steam into a whirl over the shower rack. Someone had opened the door.

Through the transparent curtain, I could tell Jude stood there in the bathroom, facing me. The scrunchie fell from my hand as I whipped the curtain back with a jerk, just enough for my head. My heart slammed in my chest.

His eyes. Sparking fiery gold with an unnatural luster, no darkness whatsoever, they held a myriad of emotions all at once—desperation, fear, adoration, longing, and something so deep, my pulse tripped and fluttered. His bare chest heaved like a man who'd run the most desperate race of his life.

"Genevieve."

He said my name.

I froze, my head and shoulders poking out of the shower, steam drifting from the opening. "You…you know me?"

He took the two long strides needed to cross the bathroom, yanked the curtain aside, and pulled me into his arms.

"You know me?" I asked again in disbelief, trembling in his arms.

His voice grated with heartbreak and need. "My love, my

heart, my wife." His lips brushed my ear. "I know you. Yes, I know you."

I sobbed as I linked my arms around his neck and pulled him closer. "Jude." I could manage nothing else.

He pulled back and stared at me, raking greedy eyes over every line before he lowered his head and sealed his mouth to mine, pouring all the loss and loneliness and love into a searing kiss.

His tongue stroked deep, a groan rumbled in his chest and throat, his hands slid over my wet skin, caressing the curve of my waist, rounding over my hips. He kissed a trail over every inch of my face—cheeks, nose, brow, back to lips. The water streaming from the showerhead washed away my tears as quickly as they fell.

I said his name over and over, a yearning plea for more, more, everything. Our jubilant reunion transformed from intense joy to intense longing as soon as I skated my lips across his throat and bit down, his name leaving my lips in breathy supplication.

He backed me into the shower and pressed me into the wall. Mumbled and muffled, words were lost as our lips, mouths, and tongues brushed over and into each other, frenzied desire driving us into a heady, dazed place I'd never known before.

His hands slid lower till he cupped the backs of my thighs and lifted. Instantly, I opened for him, wrapping my legs around his waist, my core settling against his hard crotch, his soaked sweatpants the only thing between us.

"God, Genevieve," he whispered as I rocked against him.

"I've missed you, my heart." Another drag of his mouth along my skin. "Missed you."

A maniacal laugh slipped from my lips as I nipped the tight cords of his neck. He had no idea what those words did to me. "Jude…I need you…inside me." My voice trembled like my hands. Like his own.

With the weight of his body keeping me in place, he jerked the waistband of his pants down, and the head of his dick pushed into me with such swiftness, my brain hazed.

I cried out at the sensation of him easing all the way in.

"Genevieve." He nipped and sucked my neck, my jaw, my earlobe, my lips. "Genevieve." I couldn't get enough of his voice—rough and throaty—repeating my name with heartbreaking reverence.

Hot water slicked over our bodies as Jude thrust into me with a fierce need that shook me to the core. My body responded as he drove deeper, that lovely mounting sensation climbing. "Please…deeper. Harder!"

He stopped kissing me and locked his gaze to mine. His lips apart, breathing hard, he pumped a slow, steady rhythm, keeping me with him as control slipped away from me, my passion carried too high, too fast.

When I came, my head snapped back against the ceramic tile, my inner walls convulsing around his thick cock. Jude stilled while my body pulsed with the orgasm. Before it had even subsided, I was rocking my hips and sliding again, my juices making me slicker.

"Genevieve." My name was his mantra, like a prayer for the dead man he once was.

Every time he thrust inside me, hips moving in a languid roll, he felt more alive. I knew this, because I felt the same way. My heart had been splintered and cracked and so broken, I thought I'd never be whole again. Only now did the poor thing beat with hope for true healing, the shards sealing together with every brush of his lips, every roll of his hips, every slide of his hand, every whisper of breath hot on my skin.

I laced my fingers into his dark hair that fell over his brow, and nipped along his jaw till my lips grazed his ear. He quivered when I spoke. "I love you, Jude."

He froze, fire and gold holding me in his sight, his expression softening to sad longing. "As I love you, my heart. As I always have."

I wanted to weep, to have him fuck me all night, and never come up for air. For all that we'd suffered, for all the mistakes I'd made, for all the pain he'd endured…because of me. The intensity of the moment was too much.

As if he sensed my certain fall, with a swift movement, he pulled out of me. Lifting with one arm behind my knees, the other around my back, he cradled me in his arms and carried me to the bedroom.

Laying me on the bed, he covered me, both of us still wet, our bodies sliding skin on skin, the most beautiful sensation I'd ever known. His hard erection pressed against my thigh, but he made no move to ease his anguish.

He brushed the wet strands of hair away from my face,

observing every curve and line as he'd always done when I had his complete, singular attention. Jude oozed such focus when he looked at me this way, he made me feel like I was the only woman in the world. And I'd missed this so much.

I thought I'd break apart in this moment of beauty with Jude looming above me in the dark, the dim firelight capturing his stunning profile. This man owned me, body and soul. I'd never admitted to myself that had he not returned to me fully, I would have been lost to the darkness.

"What happened there?" he asked, nodding to my throat.

It had only been a day, but my VS had already wiped most of the bruising away. Still, he had seen the injury. And he didn't remember doing it. I wouldn't burden him with that.

"Nothing." I combed one hand into his hair. "I've missed you so much, Jude."

"I know, love."

"Do you remember…everything? Do you?"

"Shhh. Not yet." He pressed his lips to mine, coaxing them apart, stroking his tongue against mine before he pulled away to kiss up my jaw and whisper, "I'm not done yet. Talk…later."

A man on a mission. Far be it from me to disturb his determination.

I moaned as he worked his way lower, sucking at the hollow of my throat before descending. His mouth skated across my breast, his tongue flicking out at the taut peak of my nipple, still damp from the shower but tight from the cool air and unquenched desire.

"Please," I pleaded, one hand in his wet hair, pushing gently. He opened his mouth and sucked.

I thought I'd pass out from the pleasure, arching my back to get closer. He used teeth. I opened my thighs so his tight abdomen pressed against my core. He growled low and opened his mouth, hot and wet, over my other nipple, flicking his tongue in delicious torture.

"Jude…please." I tried to urge him up, wanting him inside me again.

He peered at me from under dark lashes, his scruffy chin abrading my breast, dark desire written in every line of his face. "No, my heart. I'm going to taste every inch of you tonight."

My stomach flipped inside out at his erotic words, heavy with intent, as he moved down my body and held my thighs open. He nuzzled my inner thigh with sweet caresses, hot breath tantalizing my senses as he pressed a wet kiss just beyond where I wanted his mouth.

I watched him nuzzle my thigh then slide his tongue through my slit. This man was my all, my everything. His hot love threatened to make my heart beat right out of my chest.

I watched his lips sweep so close to my clit, spots hazed my peripheral vision as I desperately wanted him to work me there with his mouth.

He slid his fingers along my slick slit in a slow, slow tempo, opening me farther. My knees fell wide on a moan, like the wanton I was when it came to Jude. His dark gaze held me in rapture as he circled my clit with a leisurely stroke of his tongue.

"Fuck," fell from my lips.

He grinned like a fiend before opening his mouth and showing me the true definition of erotic bliss. My head fell back onto the pillow. I couldn't watch him do what he was doing anymore.

Unable to keep from squirming—the sensation too heady, too intense—I rocked against his mouth as he stroked and licked and sucked with ravenous appetite. He pushed a finger inside me, then another, thrusting in the same languid rhythm as his mouth. Without warning, my body skyrocketed.

"Oh God! I'm coming again," I said, panting.

He withdrew his mouth and fingers and rose onto his knees. "No," he said, his rough timbre scraping so deep and low, it sounded more monster than man. "Not without me you're not."

His entire body was a rigid wall. He sank into me with an inhuman groan, thrusting once, so hard and deep, a flash of stars crossed my mind, my VS awakening to the pulse of Jude's body connecting with mine.

Needing to hold on, I reached above my head and gripped the wooden slats of the bed, knowing Jude wanted to drive at a hard pace. I remembered our honeymoon. He was gentle when I needed it. And now he needed hard and raw and unrestrained. I would give that to him.

"Go on," I said. "Don't hold back."

The recognition shone bright. He raised his torso above me, pelvis settling hard between my legs. I crossed my ankles at the small of his back, readying for the ride. He gripped my waist then drew out and slammed in once, holding himself in a rock-solid line, hissing out a vulgar epithet. Like I cared. He could curse to his heart's content. The fact that he wanted me this much made me pliant and willing to do anything for him.

His head fell back a little, his eyes slipped closed, and Jude took me the way he wanted. It wasn't a mindless thrusting, pistoning like a machine. No. It was a sensuous roll of his spine, pounding hard at the end, like the sensual beast he was.

He nudged his knees wider, stretching my thighs farther apart, and pumped with punishing speed. I gripped the slats harder to hold my body in place. Our bodies met with such force, I grunted with every thrust. So did Jude. A rivulet of sweat ran down the valley of his abdomen.

The bond that so often pulled us together tightened like twine being wound to a taut line. Our breaths quickened, hearts raced, and bodies met in a coalescence of sweat and heat and need. The union that was forged before he left, when we became man and wife, strengthened tenfold as I lay beneath him and let him show me with his body how desperately he needed me.

He shifted angles, lower and closer, so that his chest brushed against my nipples with each thrust and his pelvis rubbed deliciously against my clit as he slammed inside me. An unexpected peak built again.

Moaning louder, I reached for that bright spot once more.

"Yes, *mon coeur*…come with me," he whispered with the heavy French accent he used only when that term of endearment slipped from his lips. "Let me feel you come hard."

When I climaxed, I screamed loud enough that if we'd had neighbors, they would've thought someone had been murdered. Jude stilled, pressing his hips hard as he spent inside me. If I wasn't pregnant already, I would've been then.

Pregnant. He didn't know. Not yet.

He collapsed beside me, both of us just staring at each other and panting. He smiled—that great big Jude smile that made everything melt inside. He reached over and swept my hair off my face, brushing his thumb across my cheekbone.

"I've missed you too, *mon coeur*." Serious, grave, heavy words. "And I'll never let you go again." His amber-gold eyes sparked with new fire. "Never."

We lay there for a long time afterward, saying nothing, just staring at each other. And smiling.

"What happened when you woke up? Did you just…remember?" I asked, rolling onto my side and tucking a hand beneath my cheek.

"It was like I awoke from a long dream. I knew who I was, knew where I was. I remembered George and Uriel coming here. I knew them, and yet they were still strangers to me. I knew that it must be you in the shower, because we'd been here alone."

"And did you remember thinking me a stranger?"

He propped up on his elbow. With one finger, he swept a lock of my damp hair away from my face, trailing his finger down my cheek to my jaw. "I remember thinking you were beautiful and magnetic and somehow familiar to me. Also that I'd been somewhere horrible and ugly and shouldn't get too close to you."

I pushed up into a sitting position, bringing the covers with me. "Why not get close to me?"

"I don't know."

He sat up and swiveled out of bed, walking to the dresser, where he rummaged and found some gray sweatpants. He did know, but was evading the question. He thought himself dirty or soiled somehow from what had happened to him in the underworld.

I swallowed the lump forming in my throat and slipped out of bed. If he didn't want to face what happened there yet, I sure as hell wasn't going to force the issue.

"I'm hungry," I said, slipping on a pair of flannel pajama pants and a T-shirt. "Are you?"

"Definitely."

I was actually starving. I had made a chicken and sausage gumbo two weeks ago and frozen it in servings for two in hopes of Jude's return. I hadn't heated any yet, because I wanted to see the joy in his eyes when he recognized a favorite dish I'd made especially for him. Until today, he didn't know me or his life before.

I went about lighting the stove and plunking the frozen block into a pot. I stood over the stove and stirred the gumbo as it melted, the center still a frozen chunk. The rice was nearly done on the back burner.

Bare-chested but wearing sweatpants—dry ones, that was— Jude wrapped his arms around my waist, cradling me close as he nuzzled into my hair. I dropped the spoon, and it nearly disappeared into the gumbo, the silver edge just above the roux.

"Jude. I can't concentrate when you do that. Aren't you hungry?"

"Yes." Trailing his mouth down my neck, he kissed, then bit the sensitive skin.

I let my head fall back against his shoulder, reveling in the seductive power of this man. My man. My Jude had come back to me. Such a glorious feeling, I never wanted to do anything else but this.

One of his hands roamed down over my hip, squeezed, then slipped underneath my T-shirt, skimming over my ribs to cup my breast. He sucked on that tender spot I loved on the slope between shoulder and neck, making me needy for him again.

"I love it when you do that," I said.

"What? This?" He palmed my breast and squeezed my nipple gently between thumb and forefinger.

I exhaled on a sigh. That wasn't what I was referring to, but my mind fogged. "Yeah." I swear, I lost brain cells every time Jude touched me. I grabbed the wrist of his hand still flat against my abdomen and guided him under my T-shirt.

"Genevieve," he whispered with a groan, cupping both breasts and teasing my nipples into tight peaks. "I can't keep my hands off you."

Music to my ears. "Then don't." I arched my back, brushing my bum against his hard ridge. Then my stomach growled so loudly, Mira chirped from her bed atop the cabinet.

Jude slid his hands out of my shirt and turned me around. A scintillating smile creased his face. He brushed his lips against mine and planted a sweet kiss there. "Food," he said. "Then a shower."

"Yes. Maybe separate showers, so we can actually get clean."

He chuckled. "Or maybe a dirty shower, then a clean shower."

Teasing Jude was back. I laughed, my heart so full, I thought it would burst. "But you really need to do something about this." I brushed my fingertips along his scruffy chin. "This scruff has become more of a beard."

I hadn't shaved him again, not since that first night I'd brought him home. Whenever he woke up, I didn't think it wise to approach him with a razor, afraid he'd think I meant him harm.

"Whatever my queen commands."

"Stop it."

A sizzle and splat drew our attention back to the stove. The gumbo was bubbling. "I've got it. Go sit."

He sat in a dining room chair just as Mira hopped down from her little nest and landed on her favorite chair back. She clicked sweetly at Jude. I'd already scooped the rice and gumbo in two bowls and sliced a piece of French bread for us both.

As I carried the bowls over and set them down on the table, I watched Jude's unwavering gaze on Mira.

"You don't remember her, then?" I asked.

"Actually," he said, taking a small chunk of bread and holding it out to her. She nipped and gulped it down heartily, making a cooing sort of sound I hadn't heard before. Flirting. Go figure. "I do remember her. I even remember seeing her when I was in a dark place, in Erebus."

He must be gaining some memories of his time there. I didn't want to resurrect that ugliness. Not just yet.

"Do you remember me telling you who she is? How I got her?"

He glanced from Mira to me, then back to Mira. "She's your spawn, isn't she?"

I smiled and scooped a spoonful of gumbo into my mouth. I truly was starting to get light-headed and needed sustenance. Fast.

"When did she come to you?" he asked, turning his attention to his own bowl.

I took another bite before answering. "The night you were taken by Lethe."

I felt his attention rest heavily on me, but I dipped a piece of my bread in the dark roux and bit off a chunk. Then I paused.

"I was overwhelmed with grief, Jude. As you can imagine. And I wanted to be taken away, when I felt a warmth unlike any other. And she came right out of my chest, a burning orb of white before transforming into this magical creature. She has helped me so much since then. You just don't know."

Mira preened the feathers under one wing, then opened her snowy wings wide before flattening them again to her back.

Jude reached across and brushed his forefinger along my jaw with a sad smile. "You needed a companion to keep you buoyed up, so the Light sent her to you. It is the way of Flamma who have the gift of making. I never knew Vessels had this power."

Mira opened her wings and lifted off the table, then sifted straight through the wall. Going to find her own dinner, I imagined.

"She passes through the wards," he said in surprise.

"And walls," I added. "I don't know how."

I settled my attention back on my food, eager to fill my empty belly and feed my baby. The baby I needed to tell him about. Butterflies flitted around at the thought. "George said he didn't know how I'd made her either."

"Maybe that's because all Vessels have fallen to darkness or to death before they had the power to do so. But you're different. You're the one."

I scooped up the last spoonful, went to the fridge and removed the jug of distilled water. After pouring us both a glass and downing mine in one long draught, I wiped the back of my mouth and leveled my gaze on Jude.

"You weren't kidding when you said you were hungry, were you?" he asked in a whimsical tone.

I leaned back against the counter and crossed my arms, dead serious. "Jude. There's something I need to tell you."

His smile slipped. "What?"

"I don't know how to sugarcoat this or ease you into the news, so I'll just come out and say it."

"Genevieve." His alpha voice was back. "Tell me whatever it is."

"Okay." I took a deep breath. "I'm pregnant. I'm going to have your baby. Our baby."

Deafening silence. Blank, lost stare. Mouth slowly falling open.

"Did you hear me?"

He shook his head.

"No. You didn't hear me? Or, no, you don't want this baby?"

I never thought there would be a chance he might not want her. I was sure it was a girl. The idea crushed me to the core that he was disappointed. I wanted this child more than anything in my life. I pressed my lips together and blinked back the tears threatening to spill over. Something I found myself doing too often these days.

"I'm going to be a…a father?"

"Yes," I assured him, still gritting my teeth.

"How could that be? How could…?"

I glanced at the bedroom door. "Are you joking?"

My heart squeezed with a pang of hurt. I'd imagined a number of reactions, but this look of almost disappointment gutted me.

"You don't want the baby?" I managed to ask somehow.

He shook his head, still dumbfounded, and I thought I'd burst into tears.

"No, it's not that. I just can't believe this is possible."

Still upset, I snapped, "Well, you certainly know how to make them. Why is it so surprising you actually did?"

Unable to hide my stress, I got up and stormed past the table. Before I could step out of his reach, he grabbed my arm and pulled me into his lap. I went, reluctantly. He was laughing.

"Slow down, my heart." Whenever he used that pet name, I was putty in his hands, and he knew it. He cradled me close, pressing a kiss to my temple. "I just didn't know I was still capable. As a Dominus Daemonum, we are told the power to create life is forfeit."

"Well, I sure as hell haven't been sleeping with anyone else, if that's what you're implying."

Heat flushed my cheeks. I'd overreacted because I'd been so afraid for so long how he'd take it. Plus, pregnancy hormones.

"I know you haven't. I know you wouldn't." He nuzzled into my hair and kissed my cheek, sliding a hand to my lower abdomen. "It must be that we are both Flamma of Light. I don't know. I don't know what this means."

"It means we've got a baby coming in about eight months."

"Four weeks? I've been gone four weeks?"

"Nearly."

"Are you sure you're pregnant? That's not very far along."

"I'm sure. I took about ten pregnancy tests."

He smirked. "One wasn't enough?"

"No. I was in slight disbelief myself and needed convincing."

"Slight disbelief?"

"Mm-hmm."

His brow puckered into a frown. "What day is it?"

"December 28th. Which makes me somewhere around five weeks, not far along at all, actually. The gestation period is forty weeks, which is really ten months. That whole nine month thing is total bullshit."

He chuckled. "How do you know this?"

"I've been reading a few books on it."

"I'll bet you have." He rubbed his heavy palm back and forth on my belly.

"I've had some free time to Google lots of information. So ask me anything you need to know about pregnancy, and I'll tell you."

"How could you have possibly allowed me to do what I did last night? Won't that—"

I finally laughed, the tension falling away. The expression on his face was a mixture of horror and fascination. "Jude. Sex won't hurt a baby."

"I know that. But I was a little rough. Goddamn it, I'm so sorry. What if I—"

"You're being ridiculous. And don't damn my baby. I won't have it."

He smiled then, moving his hand from my belly to wrap my nape and draw me close. He pressed a tender kiss to my lips, slipping his tongue inside for a brief taste. "I love you, Genevieve. This is more than I could've ever dreamed possible. You fill my heart over and over again."

I brushed my fingers lightly over the wispy hair falling across his brow. "I was afraid you didn't want her."

"Her? You know already?"

"Well, no, not for sure. That would be impossible at this early stage. But I just feel like I'm having a girl. A strong one."

He shrugged, a smile quirking on one side. "Or a strapping son."

"Well, girl or boy, I don't care. I'm just glad you want her. Or him."

His face registered shock, his brow creasing into a frown. "Why would you ever think that? That I wouldn't want our child?"

"I don't know. You just seemed so shocked at first, I was afraid you—"

"Don't ever think that. There's nothing I'd love more in this world than to be a father to our child. The one thing that terrifies me is the prophecy still looming. Tell me what you and George have planned, because I know you haven't just been sitting idly by."

"Well, you know George. And Uriel has become much more involved."

He smiled. "Oh, is he living up to your expectations of an archangel now?"

"Yes. Finally," I teased with a smile.

Uriel had become quite the hero in my eyes for all he'd done for Jude.

"So fill me in. Tell me the plan, because I know George has a plan."

"Do you remember the prophecy? I mean, what it said."

His frown was back. "I only read it once before I was taken."

A heaviness settled between us. We hadn't spoken of Lethe or the underworld yet, and now it seemed unavoidable, hanging in the air like a noose swinging in the breeze.

"Genevieve, why were you there? In the Black Forest in hell. How had you even gotten there?"

While I'd thought Thomas had taken me there, it was Damas, a demon prince. How had I not figured out that an angel couldn't enter the underworld without a Flamma of Dark leading the way?

Even after Uriel had told me he couldn't help me on my journey to retrieve Jude, I still hadn't connected the dots that Thomas couldn't be an angel if he'd guided me there. All along, I'd been swept up and nearly seduced by a demon lord, and I never suspected that he was anything other than what he'd said. I was so stupid, I wanted to punch myself in the face.

I stood from Jude's lap and took our bowls to the sink.

"What are you avoiding telling me?"

His commanding voice rolled deep, his question hitting me like a death knell. Time to get it all out in the open.

"Let's get dressed and go into Brodick. There's more I need to tell you."

Jaw clenched, mouth set in a grim line, Jude looked as if he'd argue and force me to spill it. Instead he rose and headed to the bedroom.

"Dress quickly," he called over his shoulder.

Ever since my discovery of Damas, I'd dreaded this moment. To tell Jude I'd put my trust in a demon lord. No, *the* demon lord considered the most dangerous of them all. And I'd accepted the power to sift from him.

Through any transfer of power, there would be a connection of sorts. No telling what repercussions would come of that. And the worst was the knowledge that I hadn't just taken the power in a kiss. I'd let that dark kiss morph into a passionate meeting, one that could've doomed me to become his plaything. Like Kat had been.

When I remember Damas pinning me against the wall of the theatre, his mouth and hands wandering. *Shit.* Yes, his essence had been in my necklace pendant, twisting my mind and my body to a fever pitch of desire. I knew now that what Kat had endured was the most ghastly of tortures. He'd made her want him, yearn for him, beg for him. And the whole time she'd hated herself for it.

I knew because I hated myself too for that brief moment of betrayal against Jude.

"Hurry, Genevieve," Jude called from the next room.

Deep breath in. Time to face my mistakes and accept the consequences.

It was around nine o'clock when we sifted into Brodick. I'd sifted us into the alley close to The Brodick Bar and Brasserie. Just a few days ago, I'd come in for takeout and had that enlightening conversation with the old guy, Murdoch. He wasn't sitting on his regular stool when we walked into the place.

The Christmas lights were still strung up over the bar, creating a warm and cozy atmosphere. Jude and I ambled in. The little tree still stood in the corner, blinking brightly in blue, green, and gold.

Jude's stiff posture—shoulders tight, hands in pockets—told me he was preparing for bad news. And I sure as hell had some.

The pink-cheeked server popped up to the hostess area with a bright smile. "Come right this way. We have a table near the window."

"Near the back...please. Thank you," said Jude, his Scottish burr sliding back into place, though his tone was a tad gruff.

We followed her to the back corner. Only a few tables were taken.

"Here you are," she said cheerily, placing menus in front of us. "And would you like something to drink?"

"I'll have water with lemon, please."

"Whisky on ice," said Jude.

He pulled a chair out for me. I shrugged out of my coat and settled in. He took the seat with the back to the corner, where he could see the entire room, still vigilant in his defense.

"Will Glenfiddich do?" she asked, trying to coax a smile from him. No dice.

"Talisker, if you have it."

"I'll have that right away for you."

She swished off, leaving me alone with a super-tense Jude, a heavy scowl marking his brow. I pulled on the cuff of my sweater, playing with a loose thread. The buildup had taken too long. My nerves rattled around like mad.

"Tell me." Jude had stretched out one arm on the table—his knuckles nicked white with scars—drumming his fingers once before prompting me again. "I know whatever it is, it's bad. I know you well enough by now. That expression means guilt and regret. So you might as well just spill it. What happened while I was gone?"

"It wasn't anything that happened while you were gone."

The cheerful waitress bustled up to the table, setting down my glass of water and Jude's tumbler of whisky. "Would you like to order now?"

"This will be all for right now. Thank you," I said, realizing Jude's jaw was clenched so tight he couldn't open it to grit out the courtesy.

She ducked away, her pretty smile fading when Jude wasn't as cordial as he'd been the last time we were here.

No more stalling. It was time to cut the albatross from my neck, as long as it didn't strangle me in the process. I cleared my throat and sat up straighter.

"First, I should tell you that I was forced to make an oath with Dommiel in order to get me into the underworld. He was the only one I trusted well enough not to betray me."

"Dommiel, trustworthy? Really, Genevieve, I thought you'd learned by now none of them can be trusted."

"Well, that's where you're wrong. I made a blood oath with him, and he hasn't betrayed me."

"A blood oath? And George let this happen?"

"He had no choice. There was no one else. Anyway, that was never the problem. Dommiel kept his end of the bargain. In exchange, I promised to defend and protect his place as demon lord in New Orleans. You always said he was manage-able, obeying the rules for the most part, whereas other demon lords might prove more troublesome."

Jude gave me an agreeing nod. "Where is this leading? Some-how, I fear the worst is still to come."

Oh yes. It most definitely was.

"You remember Thomas?"

His forefinger stopped tapping. "How could I not? Though I've never had the pleasure of meeting him face-to-face as I'd hoped." His sardonic tone could've cut through marble.

"Actually…you have met him."

As always with Jude, whenever his emotions heightened, so did the aura of flame around him, swelling out to lap into my personal space. I'd missed the sheer intensity of this man. And though I preferred to feel his fiery aura when wrapped in the passionate storm of his embrace, I didn't dismiss the idea that it was fortunate I could feel this at all.

"Go on."

"After I brought you back from…you know, you were unresponsive. A few nights ago, I felt the urgent tug of Dommiel through the blood bond. He was in danger."

"You did not go alone." A sharp command not a question. "Tell me you didn't." Now more of a plea.

"No. Kat came with me while Mira stayed here with you. What we found was Dommiel's club piled with dead demons and a strong residue of sulfur."

Jude hadn't yet moved, still as a statue, awaiting the grenade I was about to toss him. Nothing left but to pull the pin.

"We found Dommiel staked to his office wall by none other than Thomas. Or so I'd thought he was Thomas. He wasn't my guardian angel at all."

Kat's fear-drenched expression popped to mind, paralyzing me all over again.

"Who is he, Genevieve?" His words rumbled out slowly, precisely. As if he knew the answer already. Perhaps he did.

Pulse pounding ninety miles an hour, I finally spit it out. "He's Damas."

Jude made no move at all, though his irises bled into black. A minute ticked by. Then another. I squirmed in my seat. "Jude?"

I was afraid he was going to slip back into oblivion. He knew that my "guardian angel" had saved me several times. He also knew I'd shared a kiss of power in order to sift. And he knew I'd let that kiss go a little too far.

I licked my dry lips as he still said nothing, his expression a stone mask.

"When I brought you back from the underworld, George and I found the opal pendant I'd lost clutched in your hand. You'd found it somewhere in the Void. We're not sure how. But George sensed the essence of evil within it. He…he brought it to Uriel, who told us it was the spawn of Damas. That's why I…why he was able to twist me so easily."

I stopped babbling, afraid of what else might spill from my mouth, like the fact that Damas had used his essence to lure me into his trust. So much so that I'd fallen into his seductive arms too easily.

I wondered if our sharing the kiss of power was how I'd had a recent dream of us as lovers. Or was that my subconscious telling me he wasn't Thomas at all? But the demon lord Damas who'd captured Kat and taken her into his realm. The truth had been staring me in the face all along.

I wanted to slap myself. Too late. I couldn't live with regret. I could only move forward and hope my strength was enough.

"Jude? Say something…please."

My heart hurt. My stomach hurt. I needed his reassurance. His forgiveness.

His fingers curled around the tumbler of whisky. He knocked it back with one gulp, then stood beside the table, pulled out his wallet, and tossed a large bill on the table. I knew he'd kept a box with all kinds of currency in his top dresser drawer.

I'd rummaged through it in the days I was so bored I thought I'd go mad. He must've remembered it was there. Apparently, George was wrong. He remembered everything as if he'd never left.

He held out his hand to me. "Let's go."

No anger rumbled in his tone. No. In fact, he sounded more like the Jude I'd first met—confident, strong, powerful, the epitome of masculinity.

I stood and shouldered into my coat, then took his hand. He pulled me swiftly through the tables and the bar, then out into the blistering cold. "Put your gloves on."

I didn't argue. Apparently, we weren't going home yet. I pulled my leather gloves from my pocket and slipped them on as we walked around the corner to the out-of-eyesight place we sifted in.

He pulled me into his arms, wrapping my waist, hands splayed across my back and pressing me close. Such an odd reaction. I'd expected fuming anger, a bunch of filthy words, maybe even his aura of flame to light up the night, the main reason I'd chosen to tell him in public. Perhaps cowardly, I avoided the wrath I'd thought would come of my confession.

He stared down at me, still not speaking of the bomb I'd dropped on him. This time, he initiated the sift. A few swift seconds in the Void, and we were back on solid ground under a canopy of stars. He released me.

We stood within the circle of standing stones where he'd taken me during that one glorious week of our honeymoon. He stepped away and leaned back against one, tucked his hands in his pockets and gazed up at the gibbous moon. The full moon drew closer.

I eased to the stone nearest him and mirrored his stance. My VS tingled under my skin when I leaned against the ancient stone, some part of them recognizing one another. This place spoke to me, resonating with my Flamma power, telling of times past, battles won, and lives lost within this primitive space.

Jude's gaze remained fixed on the night sky. The clouds had parted, revealing a dotted canvas of stars. This place was hallowed ground, majestic, beautiful. And yet all I could think about was the fear rotting in my gut that Jude's disappointment in me had pulled him further away.

"I'm sorry," I said shakily, having nothing but a paltry apology to offer him.

"Don't." One word—gentle, loving, kind. No fuming anger roiled off him at the thought of Damas's lips on mine.

I shivered from the cold and the heartbreak digging deeper. When I couldn't stand it a second longer, he finally spoke.

"Haven't you ever wondered how I've been able to cross into the underworld?"

Strange. But I hadn't. "You rode Cocytus into Dante's realm."

"No." He shifted his attention away from the stars to me. "I used Cocytus to get into his castle. But I've always been able to go into the underworld. The first time he soul-sifted you there, remember?"

Yes. He'd been waiting on the threshold on his knees, bloody fists pounding the door to get in. I could never forget that moment. "I remember. I'd assumed you had some sneaky demon hunter way to get in."

He didn't laugh. "No Flamma of Light can cross into the underworld without the aid of the Flamma of Dark. No one except me."

"But you had help that last time to find the prophecy. You told me that you'd fed Styx to travel there, right before…"

He shifted and leaned one shoulder against the stone so he could face me. "I used Styx to get within the sacred circle. Flamma of Dark use wards to keep us out just as we do to them. But I'd been hunting in the Black Forest for a while. When I couldn't find the prophecy anywhere on earth, I knew it must be somewhere down below."

"But Jude…you are Flamma of Light. Aren't you?" My heart hammered faster. He was about to confess something heavy, I could feel it.

"I am the first of the Dominus Daemonum. But before my making by Uriel, I was a creature of Damas. I'd fallen to the dark, long before I ever hoped to live in the light."

The humped moon above glazed the stones, Jude's hair and sharp profile in silver. I didn't understand what he was telling me, so I waited. And listened.

"When I came to this land as a slave, I was raised into a warrior. This I've told you before. I lived a simple life, growing stronger and fighting for my clan. One day, after I'd grown, a man came to our village. A foreigner." A derisive laugh escaped him as he remembered. "I had no idea how foreign he was. He was a fine, noble man, a Roman he looked to us—black hair, pale skin, fine clothes."

"Damas," I whispered.

Jude untucked his hands from his pockets and crossed his arms. "Damas. At the time, I knew nothing of this world of Light and Dark, only my very earthly existence. This man, who claimed his name was Titus, brought news from my home in France. He said that he'd been sent to find me by my grandfather, who'd been on his deathbed when he'd left."

He scratches his stubble, but I remained quiet and waited for him to go on.

"I doubted his words, of course, for my grandfather was an old peasant just as I was. What would this nobleman have to do with an old beggar? For that's surely what he'd become without the aid of my father or me to support him. He was my father's father and had lived with us before Octavius had come into our lives and ruined us all. Octavius, a grand name for the grand man he thought himself to be."

"I'm sorry. Who is Octavius?"

Jude dropped his chin and hunched his shoulder. "You know him by another name. Danté. I remember him as Octavius, the great Roman prefect who came and took over our village after the Romans had conquered our land. After my parents' death, my grandfather could do nothing to save me, an old man with little power and few friends once Oct—I mean, Danté had sunk his claws into the villagers. They'd all stood by and watched when Danté sold me to the Campbell clan."

"So your grandfather was still alive when you were taken away. Was Damas telling the truth?"

"Damas only ever tells the truth as it suits him. Why he'd targeted me, I'll never know. But he told me of how Danté had risen high, remaking our town into a Roman settlement, had had a son from the girl I—"

He cut himself off, glancing across the moor into the dark of his memory.

"What girl?" My stomach twisted with a new truth. That Jude had loved someone before me. "You loved her?"

"No. It wasn't love. I was still only twelve when I left. Melisende was fifteen. Beautiful brown hair, fair skin, lovely eyes. All the village boys wanted her. But she had chosen me to become her favorite friend, or so I'd thought. I would tell her of my troubles, of my family. How my father had become angry with my mother. How my mother wept at night, espe-cially after Danté had made a round through the village."

He crossed his arms, clenching his jaw at the memory.

"For every time he did so, he paid particular attention to her, offering her a position as a servant in his house. We all knew what that meant. For a peasant girl to serve in the prefect's house was as good as enslavement. I never knew my mother was a Vessel, not until Uriel made me into a hunter years later. Danté had wanted her from the first, knowing who and what she was. There would be no end to his torment of my family as he attempted to seduce her to his will."

I knew firsthand the agonizing torture of Danté's amorous attentions. I couldn't imagine having a husband who must stand by and watch a nobleman lust after his wife.

"Melisende comforted me with whispers that I could tell her anything, that she was my friend. And so I told her…" He paused, shaking his head at the memory. "I told her that we planned to leave, that the prefect was forcing us to run away and start a new life somewhere else. I actually wept in her lap, because I thought I loved the girl, and up to that point, leaving her was the greatest pain my young heart had known."

I ached for the young, brokenhearted Jude. I could see him, lying in the pretty girl's lap, weeping for what would never be as Melisende brushed his dark hair through her fair fingers.

"I didn't know that she'd already become his lover with the promise of being his wife. She was a peasant girl, you see. To become the wife of a Roman prefect would elevate her beyond any good marriage she could make among the villagers.

"But her worst betrayal was yet to come. One of the servants in the house of Danté told us that afternoon that he'd overheard Melisende telling their master this news and that Danté had ordered men to our home to retrieve my mother. My parents knew what would happen next. He'd kill my father and take my mother as a slave, which he'd been promising to do since the moment he stepped into our village. So…" Jude's gaze settled back on me. "You know how that story ends."

I swallowed the lump in my throat. "Your father bound your mother and drowned her in a pool, then killed himself. And you were sold into slavery."

A slow nod and heavy sigh. "And so Damas brings news that my grandfather died, and his dying wish was that I might avenge him for the wrongs done to our family." Jude laughed and shook his head. "Damas couldn't have said anything more tempting to a young warrior with bloody revenge on his heart. I didn't ask how he knew my grandfather. I didn't care. I wanted to kill. I wanted to slaughter everyone I ever knew from my past. No one had tried to save us. No one had tried to protect me from being sold like a dog. The entire village had trembled in fear and bowed down to the almighty Octavius." He combed a hand through his hair. "My clan brother Lauchlan and I set off with a band of warriors. My adoptive father understood and let us go."

"And Damas traveled with you?" I shivered from the cold, my teeth chattering when I spoke.

"Oh yes. Of course. He wanted to see me stir up trouble for his estranged demon brother, Danté."

Jude shoved away from the stone and stood in front of me, pulling me into the warmth of his arms. I burrowed my head under his chin.

"I wanted to come here, to remember in this place that reminded me of my clan. But you're too cold. Best get you home."

I didn't argue as he held me tight and sifted us home.

From her nest on top of the cabinet, Mira turned her orange-eyed gaze on us when we entered the cottage. She ruffled her tail feathers, then resettled and closed her eyes.

"The fire has gone down," I said, standing on the hearth, still shivering.

"No matter. I can take care of that."

Jude stacked fresh kindling on the coals, then rubbed the pads of his fingers against his thumb three times, making static electricity snap in the air. He gestured as if he tossed something onto the kindling, though his hands were empty. Instantly, a yellow flame ignited there. He knelt down and added a peat log. I'd always wondered how he could conjure fire. Now was the time to finally ask.

"Where did you get that power?" I settled on the sofa. "From Damas?"

"No." He sat next to me. "From Uriel."

That served me right to depend on stereotypes, thinking the demon had given him the power to conjure fire.

"Why?" I asked.

He shrugged. "It happened in the making, the initial transformation. Neither one of us knows why. One of those side effects, I suppose."

"Yeah. Just one of those side effects of becoming a kickass demon hunter. Happens all the time, I'm sure."

He smiled at my sarcasm.

I smiled back.

"I'm glad you're not mad at me."

He reached over and pulled me into his lap, just like he used to do before he'd been taken from me. My heart clenched. My Jude was truly, fully back.

"I didn't get to finish my story."

His expression was fixed in tight lines. This story had no happy ending, yet he needed to tell it. I would listen with no judgment at all, only open ears and open arms. So I wrapped my arms around his shoulder and snuggled close, both of us gazing into the fire as we often did on our honeymoon here.

"Tell me, Jude."

One of his hands sat gently atop my thigh. "On the journey to my village, I'd noticed that Damas wore a bronze cuff. It was beautifully made with intricate designs. At the center stood a fierce dragon. Of course, I didn't know it was a symbol of strength in his demon world. I'd admired it often, till one day while we were both abovedeck on the ship as it approached the shores of France, he removed the cuff and handed it to me. He said, 'A gift for you in the hope your inner dragon will defeat his foe.' It was a generous gift. We hadn't its equal in fine metal or craftsmanship in the clan."

Jude shifted beneath me so that I was perfectly cradled against him. He played with the loose strands of hair falling down my back.

"That first night I wore the cuff, I dreamed of Damas. An intimate dream." His tone fell to a guttural timbre. "I'd never dreamed or even thought of a man in such a way. I was surprised that I might lust after a man. I couldn't know that Damas wasn't a man at all, but a demon."

I bit my lip to keep from screaming the rage roiling inside of me. Damas had targeted Jude as a lover, just as he had done to me and Kat.

"But by the light of day, all was well. Normal. Even though my bond with Damas strengthened, I started to wonder about my feelings toward him. It puzzled me. I wanted to impress him and be close to him. He drew me in, would sometimes kiss me and touch me. Though I'd known men who preferred the company of other men, I'd never felt that desire. Until Damas."

He frowned. I rubbed a hand over his chest, soothing the ache of his memories.

"I though it all a simple infatuation with a man I'd admired, who'd promised to help me avenge my family, who *cared* about me." He scoffed. "Of course, then, I knew nothing of demons or their spawn or essence. You can guess now that he'd poured his black essence into the bronze cuff, planning on seducing me to his will. And he did."

Jude's hand grazed up and down my arm, both of us touching each other softly in the quiet of his confession.

"He promised me to make him his lover once I'd done as I vowed and avenged my family. My dreams became more passionate and erotic. So much that I started to want him even during the daytime. And by the time we reached the village of my home, I was glutted with malice and wrath, burning to kill and to slaughter. For myself. But also for him. Anyone who crossed my path that night was a dead man. Or woman."

He paused. The memory of his former self was a heavy burden.

"I killed Melisende. I killed her son by Danté, and I tried to kill the man, the demon, who'd started me on this path toward hatred. But of course, I didn't. I wasn't quite the swordsman I am now."

I lifted my head, remembering what he'd said about becoming a Dominus Daemonum. "You were mortally wounded."

"Yes. I would have been one of Damas's creatures in truth had Uriel and George not arrived that night."

"But you were the first hunter. Why did they come that night?"

"The Flamma of Light had begun to watch Danté and knew he'd gotten out of hand. Uriel, even then, was one of the few who interfered in mortal affairs. George had died a martyr and had been a warrior against evil in his life on earth. The two had paired up to monitor the demons, discovering their activities had extended well beyond the margin of Flamma rules. So that night, when I returned to my former home, the presence of two demon lords, bloody carnage, and a burning inferno was enough to attract their attention."

I gazed up at Jude. "I saw this vision of you attacking the village."

He turned his attention from the fire to me, his expression solemn. "You saw?" Vulnerability was written in every tight line of his face. "And yet…you don't cringe away." He shook his head. "How can you—"

"What the hell did you think? That I'd reject you with this story? That I'd leave you because you were seduced by evil?"

"Quite frankly, I thought you might."

"Jude Delacroix. I know the temptation of the Dark. I nearly fell to it myself."

That night of *The Phantom of the Opera*, when Damas had me in his clutches, burning me up with desire, I yearned for him. I nearly slipped over. I almost let him take me.

The truth that I'd been so close to the edge of the cliff was horrifying. Even now as I sat here in the lap of the one I loved most in the world, the thought that I could've been trapped, like Kat, sent a bone-chilling shiver down my spine.

He brushed a strand of hair behind my ear with a gentle hand. As always, his slightest touch warmed me to the core.

"I know you did, Genevieve. That is why I told you my story. When you said his essence was in the pendant, I understood your struggle to resist. No need to tell me the sordid details. I can't be angry with you for falling prey to the same demon I did. What I can't forgive was my own blindness." He clamped his jaw tight. A log shifted and popped in the grate. "You told me your visitor was your guardian angel, Thomas, and I believed you."

"Why wouldn't you? George confirmed that I had a guardian named Thomas. At one time." A pain throbbed in my chest for the angel I'd never met and who was now in Erebus somewhere, solely because he was the guardian for the wrong human.

"Yes, but knowing Thomas had severed ties with his superiors should've been a warning something was awry."

"Jude, you're too hard on yourself. If you recall, you demanded, in strict Jude fashion mind you, that I not entertain Thomas alone again."

He slid his fingers along my jaw and into my hairline, resting his palm against my cheek. "And you did it anyway."

No need to answer. When I'd sensed him at the theatre, I should've resisted. But I couldn't. I wanted the power to sift, and I wanted…him. There was no denying that anymore. Now, I just wanted to kill him. For what he'd done to Jude, to Kat, and to me. I owed Acheron payment, and I knew exactly whose soul I'd be feeding him come the Blood Moon.

I sat up straighter on his lap. "If you can forgive me, I can forgive you."

"There is nothing to forgive, my heart. I'm no priest or confessor." He chuckled. "Not even close."

No, he certainly wasn't a man of God, but he was a good man. I didn't like his self-deprecating tone, the way he diminished himself, his worth. He had no idea what he truly meant to me.

I stood from his lap and reached out my hand. "Come. Let's go to bed."

He held me in his dark gaze for a moment, then took my hand. I guided him to the bedroom, where I'd spent most my hours since he'd been gone. He stepped into the bathroom. I went about getting undressed.

Even though he was my husband and had seen me naked a number of times now, I was still shy. But I planned to make him forget all his worries tonight. I planned to show him that my love was unconditional, that his sins couldn't push me away.

Reaching into the back of my panties drawer, I pulled out the emerald silk nightie I'd bought on a whim back in New Orleans. In the days leading up to my descent into the underworld, I'd gathered all the necessities here to help Jude recover. Food, water, bandages, antiseptic. I knew his recovery would be slow. But I also hoped for the day he'd be fully healed, the day I'd want to show him how much I missed him.

He was still in the bathroom, the door ajar. I hurried and stripped, then slipped the nightie over my head, pulling the spaghetti straps into place. It hugged my breasts and fell midthigh. I thought I'd slide into bed and wait, but I could see Jude standing in front of the mirror.

I stepped up to the bathroom and peered inside. He stood shirtless, staring at his reflection, tracing the line of the thickest scar across his chest. Danté had lashed him good there. Repeatedly. The skin puckered in a diagonal slash across his pectoral, marring the once-perfect Celtic cross.

He stared at the wound, his face a mask to hide his thoughts. "He did a good job on me. I'm rather ugly now, aren't I?"

It dawned on me that this might've been Danté's very plan—to destroy Jude's beauty. But there was nothing, no whip or weapon of any kind that could erase the noble man he was or the love I had for him. Tears stung my eyes.

His steady examination of the marks on his flesh revealed a wounded man, soul-deep. It wasn't just the physical pain he endured while in the hands of Danté that had put this self-doubt in his voice, in his eyes. It was the enslavement, the humiliation, the breaking down of his spirit that had placed this expression of hopelessness where it didn't belong.

I stood behind him and brushed my hands over his broad shoulders. He shivered. I peered over one shoulder at his reflection.

"You are the most beautiful man I've ever known, Jude. Then. Now. Ever."

He said nothing, his silence telling me he couldn't or wouldn't believe me. I lifted my hand to the most gruesome mark and skimmed it with the pad of my index finger. He winced, watching our reflections.

"Do you know what this means?"

I trailed my fingers to the smaller marks nicked across his abdomen. He clamped his jaw tight. The ridges of his abdomen flexed under my touch.

"Every one of these is a reminder of your sacrifice…of your love for me. It should've been me taken by Lethe. It should've been me dragged into that abyss."

"I would never have let—" His voice was gravel and sand.

"I know," I interrupted him. "I know you would've never let me go into that darkness. So you went instead. You endured —" My throat caught on the word. I swallowed hard. "You endured torture so that I wouldn't. Every mark on your body is beautiful. It is sacrifice. It is love. So I *forbid* you to look down on yourself. If anything, I am the one who should be ashamed."

He turned, taking in the gift I'd bought and worn for him. Sliding his arms around my waist, he pulled me against his hard body, growing harder by the second. With his face buried in my neck, he whispered, "Don't be ashamed. I would do it again. I told you once I'd go to hell for you."

"I know," I said with a shaky smile. "So you did. And I went to bring you back." I wrapped my arms around his neck, molding my body to his. "I love you, Jude." I pressed a soft kiss to his lower neck. "Let me show you."

Backing out of his arms, I tugged him by the hand toward the bed. He followed, gaze dark. He let me push him back onto the bed. Never a brazen one when it came to my sexuality, I had to force my anxiety away.

I knelt over him and unbelted and unzipped his jeans. He helped me work them off. There was no need for me to be stressed. His desire for me was more than evident. Yet he remained still, waiting for me to make my move, to take control. I sensed his need to feel wanted, cherished, adored. And I planned to show him.

"Lie on your stomach."

His mouth ticked up on one side. He apparently remembered giving me the same command on our wedding night. He obeyed and rolled over. Even with the cross-hatching of scars, his physique was lovely. Perhaps I was biased, but he truly was an extraordinary specimen of man. Perhaps the scars made him even more endearing to me.

On all fours over his body, I leaned down and kissed the first slash across his shoulder blade. Jude's body tightened beneath my touch. I kissed every scar, every mark the lash had made, while gliding my hands softly down his back, over his well-muscled bum.

"Genevieve." A protest and plea in one.

"Be still."

I moved farther south, sweeping my lips over a hard gash on his upper thigh. Jude's deep moan into the pillow told me I was doing everything right. After one last feather-light kiss to the nick behind his left knee, I lifted up onto my knees.

"Other side."

He rolled onto his back, his heavy-lidded expression speaking volumes. I started from the bottom this time, finding the light white line above his kneecap, then the thicker slash on his upper left thigh.

I glanced up to find his eyes closed, the cords of his neck drawn tight, then I swept my mouth upward. I didn't neglect his engorged cock. I opened my mouth over the crown and sucked, then slid my lips down the length as far as I could go.

His inhuman groan of pleasure and his hand in my hair encouraged me. I licked and sucked till he was harder still.

"Fuck, yes, like that."

He encouraged me gently with a palm around the back of my skull, nudging me lower.

I whimpered and sucked him as good as I could till my jaw started to ache. When I popped off, making a rather sloppy sound, his half-lidded gaze held me. He traced my bottom lip with the pad of his thumb.

"Don't think I can get any closer to heaven with your sweet, wet mouth on my dick, love."

My thighs clenched at the dark rumble of his voice, all sex and dominance.

"But why don't you climb up here and see if we can find it together."

I lifted off and moved up his abdomen, pressing an open-mouthed kiss to the heavier scars as I went.

"Genevieve," he growled. "Enough."

I crawled over him, straddled his hips, and sank down, guiding him inside me. The glorious feel of him stretching me as I slid down his length made my underlight glow, humming through my blood like wildfire.

"Ah," I gasped as his thickness then closed my eyes. His hands slid up my thighs, under the silk fabric, gripping my hips, and guiding me up and down. I leaned slightly forward, hands on his chest for balance, and met his upward thrusts, riding him with the passion of a woman solely devoted.

He sat upright and edged the spaghetti straps off my shoulders. As he cupped one breast with a rough hand, his mouth found the other, licking and sucking my tight nub.

"Jude," I whispered.

Somehow in that moment, I remembered when he was taken from me, when I was curled in a ball on the cottage floor, mourning the loss of him, feeling my heart splinter and break into such miniscule pieces I thought it would never be whole again. But now, my love was home, in my bed, in my arms, adoring me with his hands, his mouth, his body.

I moaned louder, feeling my climax build. So fast. Too fast. I couldn't help it.

His thumb and forefinger gently rolled my nipple once more before his hand glided across my waist to my back and down to cup one cheek. Fingers curling tight around my ass, he guided me, flesh slapping.

His tongue and mouth continued to work one breast—kissing, nipping, sucking. I came with a loud cry, head falling back. A starburst broke across my mind. Jude held me still as my inner walls convulsed with an orgasm that made me light-headed.

I slumped forward onto his chest, having no strength to keep my body upright. He brushed my back with his fingers, still rock-solid inside me. No way was I taking my pleasure and leaving him unsatisfied.

I lifted my head and slanted my mouth over his, stroking my tongue along his, before pulling apart.

"Where do you want me?" I asked him.

He wasn't a man accustomed to relinquishing control. Yet, he'd allowed me to have it as long as I needed. Now I wanted him to take me in whatever way would bring him the pleasure he always gave me. He needed to wield his dominance for that to happen. I understood that.

"Lie on your side. Face the window."

I did, seeing nothing but the night through the panes. He molded himself to my back, pushing my top leg into a crooked position. Grazing my neck with heated breath, he kissed a line up to my ear. One hand glided over my hip and down to the slick cleft between my legs.

"Jude," I protested, that spot too sensitive now for touch. I rolled slightly away from him and closed my legs.

"No, my heart." He nuzzled my ear, biting the lobe. "Open for me."

Hesitantly, I crooked my knee up again, allowing him to slide two fingers up and down the sensitive line. I reached back and gripped his hip, clenching my other hand into the sheets. I was so wet as he stroked and stoked my desire hotter.

Before long, he had me rocking to the slow rhythm of his fingers. I picked up the pace, wanting him to press harder on my clit. On one backward rock, he thrust inside me from behind. I sank my fingernails into his hip, which he didn't seem to mind, grinding a slow, steady beat. He gentled me toward another climax.

"That's it, my love," he whispered, nipping at my neck. "Take me in. Let me fuck you like you're mine."

"I am yours," I panted.

"That's right." He thrust in a little harder but kept his slower pace. "Say it again."

"Yours…I'm yours," I murmured, laying my head on his bicep.

He curled that arm across my chest and nipped little bites with his teeth up my throat. And still, he was fucking me with slow languid rolls of his hips.

I wasn't sure if he was being tender because now he knew about the child or if he just wanted to drive me mad with his insanely slow fucking—in and out. To feel the heat of his hard body against my back and all the way down, his thigh pinning my bottom leg to the mattress, the other lifted for him as he demanded.

He reached let go of my breast and reached down, pressing harder on the my clit. "Come with me," he said on a hoarse cry, pumping deeper. "Need to feel you come again."

"Ahh!" I cried out and clenched my fists, surely hurting him as my nails dug deeper. He bit my neck harder than usual and stilled, his shaft pulsing inside me as he groaned through his release like a feral beast.

Both of us lay there panting for several moments before he finally pulled out. I couldn't move, my eyes sliding closed as I fell into utter bliss and exhaustion. I felt the covers drape over me and his arms wrap around to cradle me close.

I drifted swiftly into sleep, but not before I heard his deep voice whisper words that mended my fractured heart once more.

"I love you, *mon coeur*. My wife."

Sitting on the beach, my bum getting cold, I leaned back against a rock jutting out of the coarse gray sand and watched Jude holding Mira on his arm, saying something to her in a gentle whisper. Now *he* was flirting with her. I smiled at the two of them.

When she lifted off over the water and sifted away somewhere else, he walked back to me and sat on the rock. She did that from time to time, so I wasn't worried. I wasn't sure where she was going, but she always came back.

"I think my bird has traded me in for a handsome substitute."

"Oh, I don't think you have too much to fear," he said, nudging me gently with his knee. "She's your making, so of course she's attracted to me. She can't help it."

I narrowed a look up at him to find him grinning like a fiend. Yes, that was the Jude I missed—the confident-as-hell guy with swagger enough to melt a stadium of girls into mush. He laughed. Instant butterflies fluttered in my belly. I wondered if that feeling would ever go away. Somehow I doubted it.

His expression sobered. "We haven't discussed the prophecy yet."

"What's there to discuss?"

"Genevieve." A chastising tone. Not my favorite of his.

"We know the gathering will be held in three days, the night of the Blood Moon. Other than that, the prophecy was little to no help whatsoever. So happy you spent several weeks in hell for it."

"I believe you're wrong about that," he said, ignoring my sarcasm. "I didn't have time to digest it before. But I read it again this morning."

I'd seen him with his cell phone and that deep furrow in his brow and wondered why he was so pensive and broody.

"And what conclusions have you made?"

"Originally, we'd thought Bamal and Danté were the two demon princes mentioned in the prophecy."

I'd memorized the prophecy. I knew every line by heart. *Two great sons of Morning Star; divided, until death will mar. One will woo the warrior maid, one will cut her to a shade.*

I glanced up at Jude, his profile silhouetted against a gray twilight. "Who else would it be? They were the ones after me from the first."

"True. But I think not now. 'One will woo the warrior maid.' That would be Damas, not Danté."

I sat up straighter and turned so I could see him.

"I believe Danté was the one to cut you to a shade. I could never figure out the meaning behind that line. Not until this morning. I had a flash of memory of when I was in Danté's dungeon. I saw you, standing nearby, that infernal whip made of some hellacious spawn wrapped around your waist while you pulled and faced your enemy—Danté."

He tucked a piece of hair behind my ear absently.

"While your underlight burned bright, a ghostly halo of malice hovered all around you, seeking to find a way in. Danté had tainted your soul that night of the Masquerade. He'd cut a piece of your light away. You'd given in to wrath when you killed Nathaniel but somehow had rebuilt your coat of protection."

His voice grew soft and gentle.

"In that deepest pit of hell, when all darkness sought to swallow you, it couldn't penetrate the shield of light you'd created. He never did cut you to a shade, which is exactly what you would've been had you remained his slave in Erebus —a shade, a ghost of your former self."

"So, what you're saying is the prophecy is wrong?"

"Not wrong. Only that it's a prophecy. By definition, that means it's a prediction, a divination, a forecast of possible events."

"Possible, not probable."

"Probable but not definite is a more accurate interpretation."

I picked up a stone and rolled it between my fingers. The sky was bleak and heavy, promising rain or snow or both.

"So Bamal was trying to kill me in the beginning to remove me from the whole equation until he got hold of the rest of the prophecy. The lost piece."

"Yes. That appears to be so."

"And, of course, he backed off when he realized the prophecy demanded both me and his Vessel must be there on the night of the eclipse. That's when he just wanted to kidnap me until the time came."

"I'm sure he planned to warp you as best he could under his *gentle* care. The essence you described that Gorham had used on those girls in his nightclub, the House of Hercules. That is similar to Bamal's own gift. It's like a narcotic to numb the senses and the will. I'm sure he planned to infect you with it, to make you ready to sacrifice yourself at the gathering and ensure he held dominion once and for all."

I tossed my rock out toward the water, where it plunked in the shallows. The lapping waves washed ashore in a steady, even tempo. The sound was hypnotic in its soft, repetitive rhythm.

A memory flashed to mind. My mother holding my hand as we walked along the beach of Gulf Shores, Alabama, when I was a child. I saw something bone-white sticking out of the sand by my toes. I'd scooped it up and brushed off the grains of sand to find a sand dollar with a quarter of it missing.

"Why are you sad?" my mother had asked.

"Because it's broken," I'd replied.

She had knelt down beside me and peered down at the fractured sand dollar in my palm. *"But look at the beautiful lines here. Nature made this lovely work of art for us to cherish. Be grateful for such beauty in the world."* I remember peering into her crystal-blue eyes as she smiled sweetly, her sun-kissed golden hair blowing in the ocean breeze. *"Remember my sweet girl, even broken things can be beautiful."*

"Genevieve?"

I snapped out of my reverie.

"Are you okay?"

I stood up and brushed the cold sand from my jeans. "Yeah. Just a memory."

"A sad one," he said, wrapping his hand around my wrist and tugging me closer.

I let him pull me between his legs. I sat sideways on his knee and wrapped an arm around his shoulder.

He looked out at the sea, a content smile creasing his face, the lovely lines of his jaw, chin, nose, and brow standing in silhouette against the gray beach and gray sky. Yes, my mother was right. Even broken things can be beautiful. He turned to me with a curious expression.

"What is it?"

I smiled so as not to alarm him with my intense ogling. "Nothing. Just that I love you."

"That's not nothing." Sparks of gold lit up his eyes. He trailed the fingers of one hand along my jaw and combed them into my hair, wrapping my nape. "That's everything."

He pulled me down for a kiss. I went willingly, sinking into him with a sigh. A sweet kiss turned sensual in a heartbeat when he nudged my lips farther apart with his own, stroking in with his tongue. A soft moan hummed from my mouth into his. He gripped me tighter.

A snapping *whoosh* and the presence of electric energy sent us both jolting apart and upright into fighting stances. Sifting carried a very distinct sound and energy.

It was George and Uriel. I breathed a sigh of relief, then my heart clenched at the expressions of the commander and the maker of demon hunters as they gazed at Jude and clearly realized he was himself again.

George strode toward us, the breeze tousling his perfect chestnut hair. He didn't seem to mind. Jude met him with a masculine embrace. They said nothing, but the keen affection was evident.

Then Uriel stepped forward, his eyes the color of the sky today, his skin paler than usual, but his wings no less brilliant and beautiful. When they embraced, I heard Jude say, "Thank you."

"None needed, my friend."

Okay. So I hadn't realized that Uriel was really his friend. His maker, yes. His sort of super-boss, yes. But friend wasn't on my list of descriptors, till now.

"You didn't have to bring me back," said Jude.

Then I wanted to slap him. Why would he say such a thing?

"Yes. I did," said Uriel. "It's a small price to pay, believe me. I wouldn't do it for just anyone, but you… Yes, it was worth it."

George had told me the loss of power can be great for any Flamma when they share power. Using the power of making, especially on one as far gone as Jude was, must've had a serious impact on Uriel. As I stepped closer, I observed how his face seemed drawn tight around the mouth from pain or distress. His eyes lacked the luster I was accustomed to finding there.

"Well, darling, you could've told us he was up and about," said George as I edged next to him.

"I wanted him to myself for a little while."

"Yes, as we could see from the cliff top."

"That's a little stalkerish, George, even for you."

"We sifted in and knocked on the door. Finding no one home, we decided to walk along the cliff until you both returned. Naturally, we saw the lovely display below."

"Naturally."

Jude and Uriel turned back to us.

"Right," said Uriel, his serious game face back on. "As much as I'd love to reminisce and stroll down memory lane, we need to discuss the night of the Blood Moon, which is in three days' time."

"Do we know where the gathering will be held?" asked Jude.

"Dartmoor."

That seemed logical to me, as it was neutral ground for Flamma of Light and Dark gatherings of the past. It was where I'd laid eyes on Prince Bamal the first and last time. Seemed I'd be meeting him there again.

"The prophecy doesn't specify a time," said George. "But it appears an hour before the eclipse will bring us to—"

A bloodcurdling shriek pierced the darkening sky. All our eyes whipped upward. Jude and George drew weapons. My VS rippled through my blood like prickling needles as Mira dove straight to me, settling on my outstretched arm.

I nearly buckled under the weight of the evil pouring through me. Mira shrieked again, imploring me to follow her at once.

"Oh God. Something terrible has happened. Give me ten seconds!"

I sifted up to the hillside, sprinted to retrieve my katana, cursing at myself for leaving it anywhere but on my person outside the cottage, and sifted back to the men, who'd linked arms. Mira perched on Jude's shoulders.

"Take us, Mira. Now!" I yelled.

Without fail, Mira sifted us through the Void, a longer sift, so the danger lay abroad somewhere. The fear twisting my gut into knots brought the truth shattering home when we landed in the backwoods swamp of Bayou Sauvage within the shadows of the demon haunt where Kat and I had met Bleed.

It was also the place where Damas had held my opal in his hands, held it too long. Then, I thought it a flirtation. Now I knew better. That was when he must've poured his essence into my precious possession given to me by Jude. Damas must've enjoyed the irony. He used my love of Jude, knowing I'd wear the pendant often, to twist my mind to yearn for another. For him.

Heavy clouds billowed, swooping across the sky with the *thump-thump* of thunder and lightning streaking low, cranking up the electricity in the air. The raucous and sinister jeering of a demon horde sent stabbing chills down my spine.

We rounded the corner to find a mass of red-eyed lower demons within human hosts circling a display of some kind, their backs to us. A sword swung above the crowd within the center, then fell. It clanked against another blade with the rough grunt of someone wielding it in defense. We couldn't see who the swordsmen were, but a sinking sensation of dread fell like a hard stone in my gut.

Uriel stepped forward, a broadsword in hand, not bothering to cast illusion and hide who he was. "We sift into the center together. Ready?"

Jude took my arm. "Stay close," he whispered. His eyes had lost the golden spark, darkening to midnight.

"Go," commanded Uriel, his voice dripping with ancient power.

Both hands gripping my katana, I closed my eyes and sifted, Jude holding on to me. In a blink, we stood in the middle of a nightmare. The beast-like creature, Bellock, bore down on his opponent. Gray skin, black veins streaked beneath, powerful arms swinging his curved blade high and bearing the overwhelming signature of darkness itself. He wielded a scimitar, bringing it down on the fair-haired, charming Xander.

"Oh no," I mumbled. He was supposed to be guarding my —"Dad!"

Crumpled in a bloody heap on the far end of the pit behind Xander lay my father. All demons stopped watching the heated battle between angel hunter and demon hunter. Heads swiveled in our direction. Then all hell broke loose. Literally.

Jude stormed after Bellock, while George and Uriel turned on the mass of demons, spinning and slicing faster than my eyes could follow. Mira shrieked over the top of the horde, talons drawn. I sprinted for my father, cutting down a skinny red-eyed demon with one slice.

"Flamma intus!" The demon—both beast and human host—collapsed inward, then exploded in a cloud of ash.

I was in no mood to save the human hosts buried within. My dad lay as still as death, wearing his white gi, which was bloodied from cuts around his face and half ripped off his body. His black belt had been torn and tossed away. Demon after demon got in my way, no matter how many I killed with one stroke of my blade.

"Fuck this." I sifted across the maddening crowd in front of my father. Just as I knelt down, a thin rope circled my wrist, then the other, yanking me back. "What the—" A hard jerk on my sword arm sent my katana falling to the dirt.

A white-misted dome suddenly covered me, blurring the sound of fighting. I glanced down at my wrist to see a crystalline web wrapping my wrists and my ankles, keeping me pinned in place. The tendrils snaked up my arms till I couldn't budge an inch.

The chilly vapor thickened and swirled, blocking out everything but the distinct aura of silent winter. My breath puffed out in white clouds. He was here, in this frosted dome.

"Come out, Damas."

Like a Greek god come to life, he appeared before me, tendrils of vapor curling away from him. His smile, the one I'd found genteel and kind and alluring, now only repulsed me.

"What's the point of all this?" I yanked on my web of confinements. "You know the prophecy. I must be at the gathering in three days, or you all die. Or don't you remember?"

"I don't plan to harm you, dear Vessel. I told you I never would." A glint of malice flared in his eyes and his too-wide smile.

My VS thumped in the distance, this vapor holding my power at bay somehow. I closed my eyes and willed it forward. Damas grabbed my jaw and shook me. I opened my eyes on a gasp, his grip a painful vise.

"It didn't have to be this way, Genevieve. I would've cared for you. I would've loved you."

"You don't know the meaning of the word."

"You could've taught me." His expression softened to such sincerity, an imploring plea glistening in his supernatural eyes. "You could've shown me how to love. You could've been my queen."

Someone pounded on the exterior of the dome, but I could see nothing through the white fog cocooning us from the mayhem. The screech of talons crossed the top of the dome. Mira was trying to get in. Whatever this was he'd created, there was no sifting in or out. I'd already tried.

"You're mad."

His intent gaze raked over my face, landing on my lips. If he thought to kiss me, he was sadly mistaken. "Let me go, Damas."

"I liked it better when you called me Thomas."

"But that was a lie. Just like everything else about you."

"Unlike your hunter? He's so honest. He never told you of his heavy sins, did he? I had to bring you that truth."

"He told me everything, how you seduced his will with the promise of revenge and led him to slaughter those people in that village. Yes, he did the killing, but you had as much blood on your hands as he did. And you only showed me that ghastly vision in order to lure me back to you. Well, it won't work. None of it. I will never be yours."

The pounding continued.

His smile slipped. "Yes. I know. You made your choice. Such a pity. All the pleasure that could've been yours will now only be pain. And remember, I gave you a choice."

"You said you'd never harm me."

"Physically…no."

Fear streaked through my veins like ice. "What do you mean? What have you done?"

"It could've been so different." His grip on my jaw slackened, and he dropped his hand. "You think the hunters could've kept them safe?"

He shook his head with a condescending arch of the brow. My knees buckled with the weight of his insinuation.

"Damas, what have you…?"

The web and the white dome vanished. I stumbled forward directly into Jude's arms. It had been him pounding. The vapor dissipated. Only silence weighed heavy where there had been clanging of swords and grappling bodies before Damas sealed me in his dome.

"Are you okay?" Jude asked, fear and rage marking his face.

A hazy cloud of ash and sulfur lingered in the air. Storm clouds still billowed, pressing down like a heavy cloak.

I couldn't answer as I scanned the misty scene. The bodies of demon hosts littered the ground. All was quiet, but not all was well.

Damas was still here. I could feel him.

Uriel tended to Xander. George knelt by my father, completely unaware of the demon prince inches away. Behind him stood Damas, a sword raised in a double-fisted grip. Lightning beat three flashes across the night sky, silhouetting the man, the demon, who'd once professed to love me, as he stared down at his target. My father.

"No!"

The blade fell hard and true, right into my father's chest. George flinched as the sword seemed to drop out of nowhere, not seeing or even sensing the perpetrator hovering over his shoulder.

A flash of lightning. The demon prince met my gaze once more, steel-hard with a promise of more pain to come, before disappearing into the night. George was already pulling the sword from my father's body by the time I ran to them and fell at my dad's side.

"No. God, please. No. *No!*"

My dad wasn't even conscious before, but now he coughed up blood, spattering his white gi.

"Dad…Daddy." I cradled his head in my lap. "Please! Uriel!"

He was already there at our side.

"Please help him. Tell me you can."

"This healing of the body is beyond me. I can only mend the soul."

Jude was already lifting my father in his arms. "I know someone who can. Hold on to me, Genevieve."

I wrapped both arms around the two men I loved most in the world, and we were gone.

A longer sift. The sun had already fallen, leaving a sliver of pink light on the horizon of a quaint town. This wasn't Arran. We stood in a familiar place on a wide green lawn. I turned and saw St. Mary's Church, where Jude and I had been married.

"Father Clementine?"

"Yes." Jude strode toward an unassuming stone building off to the right. "Come. Hurry."

He didn't need to tell me. I was pushing open the wrought-iron gate in front of him. We arrived on the back steps of the cottage.

"Go in. He'll know we're here."

I opened the door to find a short priest, nearly bald, with bushy eyebrows, walking toward us as if he'd expected us. Father Clementine.

"Come in, come in." He ushered us into his humble home,

through a cozy den and into a room where Dommiel was propped up in a twin bed playing cards by himself, staring at us in wide-eyed surprise.

Jude gave him a single glance, then set my father on the other bed. I hadn't realized this was the healer George had spoken of when he took the injured Dommiel away that night in London.

My dad hadn't come around once. Blood seeped from the gaping wound.

"The blade went through his heart," I whispered, choking on the words.

The man I knew as the merry-eyed priest who had led Jude and me through our wedding vows was now calm and grave as he held both palms over the wound in my father's chest.

"No, dear," he replied. "Whoever did this missed the heart."

"How can—"

"Let him work." Jude pulled me gently out of the way with an arm around my shoulder.

"Get my kit, Jude. You know where it is."

He let me go to fetch the kit in another room. I moved to the foot of the bed and knelt, placing a hand on my father's ankle, needing to touch him. Still warm. He wasn't gone yet.

Jude reentered the room and set a brown leather satchel on the nightstand. Father Clementine went to work, all the time whispering a Latin prayer. I'd seen wounds cleaned and stitched before. As a matter of fact, the first time I'd gone to

Jude's place in the French Quarter was when that asshole Fabio had stabbed me.

Jude had used his own home-nursing kit to take care of my injury. Fabio got what he deserved in the end. And I damn sure planned to make Damas pay.

"Damas paralyzed me in that dome," I whispered to Jude, who now stood at my back with his hand on my shoulder.

He didn't reply. I thought he hadn't heard me, but he finally replied, "We knew there would be a consequence of you accepting the power to sift from him. He's a demon prince, no guardian angel. He left some of himself behind. Perhaps it now prevents you from doing him mortal harm."

The thought that I'd relinquished my power to destroy the one man I wanted to blast into oblivion made my blood run cold. I would have my vengeance. One way or another.

Father Clementine had wiped and cleaned the excess blood, still praying. I'd noticed that the wound no longer bled as it should have. My father should be dead from blood loss alone, but his healer seemed to pray the wound closed.

His fingers moved with deft swiftness as he stitched with thick threading material. The wound was on the left side of his chest. Damas had meant to stab through the heart. But he'd missed. On purpose? Doubtful. Perhaps the heavens were on my side.

As he lay there, I felt a keen sense of déjà vu, remembering when I'd stood at Jude's bedside, studying every mark that had been made by demon fiends set on hurting him. Though not suffering the same ghastly whiplike wounds, my father was bruised badly.

His gi had opened, the black belt he usually wore stripped away. Massive contusions darkened his chest and abdomen. Both of his eyes were swollen. A cut opened his bottom lip. He'd fought and lost. He'd been used as a punching bag for the demons' entertainment.

"Did you kill Bellock?" I asked, rage rippling through me.

"No." Regret hung in that one-word reply. "But I will."

We remained quiet a moment while Father Clementine's prayer grew louder. I wondered if he'd prayed over Dommiel, a high demon, as he'd healed him. The image would've made me laugh any other day, but not when my own father lay on death's door. Dommiel said nothing from the bed beside us.

Jude didn't need to tell me that Father Clementine had a few gifts of his own. He wasn't simply a doctor or a man who was good at stitching wounds. His power as a sentinel, a Flamma of Light, surpassed the ordinary. He knew with all confidence that my father's would-be killer had missed his mark.

He spoke to the body, and the blood had stopped flowing from the wound. A supernatural gift of healing. Something I hadn't seen any other Flamma possess before now.

He snapped his satchel shut and turned to me. "That is all I can do now, dear," he said in his thick, clipped English accent. "Why don't we have a spot of tea to calm your nerves?"

I moved to the head of the bed and swept Dad's bangs away from his brow, then kissed him there, relishing the warmth under my lips. A tear rolled off my cheek into his hair. "Get well, Dad. Please," I whispered. "I love you."

No response. I followed Jude, who glanced back at Dommiel with a scowl. Dommiel held up one hand and one hook as if to say *I didn't do anything*. I hadn't the energy to chat with the high demon at the moment, especially knowing it was his own kind that had done this to my father.

Of course, it was Damas who'd put those nasty holes through Dommiel's wrists. The injuries were visible when he'd raised his arms in mock protest of whatever he thought Jude might do to him. The black stitching was the same that Father Clementine had used on my father.

I pushed Jude on when he stalled at the doorway, probably considering whether to interrogate Dommiel. But I knew the ousted demon had nothing to do with this.

"What about Xander?" I asked when we stepped into the den.

No television or computer anywhere. A wall of books and old furniture filled the room. A brown wingback chair faced the warm fire crackling in the grate.

"George must've had Xander watching over your father. They obviously ambushed him at the dojo."

"Yes. I'd asked him to put two guards on my dad and——"

Jude turned sharply. "And Mindy."

I nodded, a wave of fear swamping me again. Without a word, he grabbed my hand. We rushed from the house out the back door, through the gate, and beyond the wards that protected the house from any Flamma sifting directly inside.

"Jude," I practically cried, knowing what we'd find.

He pulled me hard into his embrace, and we were gone, sifting through the black once more, gray shapes blurring past. We landed outside my apartment in New Orleans. The street was quiet but for a dog yipping in the distance.

"No." Our apartment door was wide open, no lights on inside. I sprinted.

"Wait!" yelled Jude, following fast.

I ran inside and straight to her bedroom, seeing no one and nothing amiss in the living room. Her bedroom was empty. So was her bathroom and her closet. I looked every tiny place Mindy might've hidden from an intruder. Jude hadn't followed me.

I found him standing in the kitchen entrance, staring down at something. I rushed up beside him.

"No, Gen."

Too late.

"Is it Mindy?"

Blood smeared the kitchen floor, painting our white tile red. Crimson splattered our fridge and countertops. A young man's body lay on one side, having bled out from a stomach wound. Dave. Mindy's boyfriend.

Two large, male hands—chopped mid-forearm—lay on the floor a few feet away. Tarquin's head had been propped on one of our white dinner plates and set on the counter next to the toaster, facing the doorway, where sightless, glassy eyes would greet anyone who entered. Blood had pooled on the plate and dripped off the counter. Streaming rivulets dribbled down the cabinets, dripping steadily into a pool on the floor.

Our popcorn popper sat on the counter, untouched. A flash of Mindy came to mind, tossing a popcorn kernel into the air and catching it in her mouth. I could hear her tinkling laughter, then I could hear her screams as this horrific nightmare unfolded.

My stomach roiled. I clamped my hand over my mouth and ran to the bathroom and vomited in the toilet. Gripping the toilet seat, I emptied my stomach, sweat breaking out over my entire body. Jude was there. He pulled a dishcloth from the cabinet, wet it under the faucet, then pressed the cool rag to the back of my neck.

I stood upright and took the cloth to wipe my face, now fevered from the horror in my kitchen.

"He's killed Mindy, Jude."

"No," he said with confidence. "If he'd killed her, he'd have made sure to leave her body. He wanted us to see those he left behind."

"Poor Dave," I said, wiping my eyes. As much as he wasn't my favorite of Mindy's boyfriends, I'd never wish this on him. Or anyone, for that matter. "And Tarquin."

Jude's stony expression hid the anger simmering under the surface. But he could never hide his emotions from me. His fiery aura lit once more, the way it used to before he'd ever been to Lethe's lair. A dangerous flame burned around him.

"How could they have gotten in?" I asked. "The wards. They couldn't sift inside. After you were gone, I made George double your efforts so no one could. So how did this even happen?"

I'd known if the wards were strong enough, no Flamma of any kind could sift inside. Even then, I hadn't trusted that my so-called guardian angel, Thomas, wouldn't do something underhanded. Of course, he wasn't an angel at all.

Jude's expression was distant, pensive. "Mindy's boyfriend was killed first with no resistance. Tarquin must've been watching and saw something or someone come into the apartment, coming in after Dave was already dead."

"But who? Mindy would never have opened the door for a stranger. Never. She's not stupid. We've discussed this time and again."

"She let them inside, there's no doubt. You're right. With the wards, no Flamma of Dark could sift inside, but a sentinel working for a demon prince could walk in."

"But I know no sentinels."

"Apparently, you do. Someone Mindy would've trusted. What about that guy you dated, the study partner?"

"Malcolm? No way. Not him." Someone we both knew?

As if my world was sliding sideways, the truth knocked me off balance. I gripped the edge of the countertop.

"Oh God." There was only one person I knew who Mindy might let inside without hesitation. One person who fit the bill as a sentinel, a guard, but not for the Flamma of Light. For him. For Damas. "Erik."

"Who?"

"Erik. He works for my father. He's like family. He's like…my brother." I thought I was going to be sick again.

Damas had told me he'd watched over me my entire life. Erik had come into our lives right after my mother died. He'd been planted by Damas. The truth dug its claws so deep, the thought burning acid in my stomach.

"If Mindy knew him," said Jude, "then he could've let Damas inside."

"But, Jude, this isn't like vampire mythology. Damas couldn't walk in just because he was invited."

"No."

The timbre of that one word snapped my attention to him. I set the wet cloth on the counter. "What is it you're not saying?"

"Genevieve, when you accepted his gift of power, you opened yourself to him in ways I think we're only now beginning to comprehend. He paralyzed you back on that bayou and prevented you from using your power, isn't that right?"

"Yes."

"Then he left some of his essence behind. Who's to say he didn't take some of your own? Some part of you that was able to mask his identity, even to the wards created by the Flamma of Light. When I told you he was the master of deception, of lies, I wasn't exaggerating. He can hide himself in ways no one else can. He's had thousands of years to perfect his art."

I folded the dishrag over the edge of the sink, my hands trembling. "When Damas was standing over my father, George didn't even sense him, as if his signature wasn't even on his radar. Yet I could feel him the whole time. I knew he was there." I leaned forward on the sink, bracing my weight with both hands. "It's my fault my father is dying. It's my fault Dave is dead. And Tarquin. And possibly even Mindy."

Jude pulled me away from the sink and twisted me around to meet his gaze. He swept away a lock of hair sticking to my cheek from the wet cloth and curled his fingers around my nape, keeping my focus on him. His aura of flame and iron wrapped me in a cocoon of protection, the way it used to.

"Don't go there, love. Hear me now, and hear me well." He brushed his thumb along my jawline. "I've lived with the bitter fruit of regret. It will eat you alive till there is nothing but the black pit of hatred left behind. Every time you look back at a mistake you've made, wishing for a different end, wishing you'd been a better person, you give a piece of your soul away. If you want to live in the now, for me, for our child, then you must forgive yourself and let it go."

I wrapped my fingers around his wrist. "It's hard." I didn't want to cry. I was so sick of crying. I'd wept enough tears to fill a fucking river. Yet, even now, after all I'd seen of the Flamma of Dark and their evil, I longed to curl up and weep for what they'd done, for what they could still do. "My heart isn't hard enough, Jude."

His intense expression fell, softening with a half-smile and a look of complete adoration shining in his dark eyes. "Oh, my love. Thank God for that. Your good heart is what I cherish most." He cupped my face with both hands, angling so that I couldn't look away. "Your heart is warm sunshine in the cold winter. And I would want nothing else."

A tear slipped down one cheek. "Goddamn it." I couldn't help it.

Jude swiped my cheek with his thumb. "What is it?"

"I didn't want to cry."

His smile widened. "You're sensitive. It's natural."

"Are you calling me moody?"

"I'm saying you're human, and wonderfully feminine, and therefore fragile. In some ways."

"Great. I'm weak. That should help us out a ton to kill that fucker Damas."

"Genevieve Elizabeth Drake."

Well, that silenced me. How did he know my middle name? Wait. What was I thinking? This was Jude Delacroix, master of secrets and detection.

"Listen to me, woman. You marched into the deepest pit of hell, killed a demon prince, and dragged me back to life."

"I got you out, but Uriel brought you back to life."

He brought his face closer to mine. His fingertips combed farther into my hair. "When I was lost in the darkness of my mind, I dreamed of the stars and the moon. Over and over again. A sparkling canvas shone in the night wherever I wandered. The torture inflicted upon my body drove me far, far away. But I was never alone. It was the moon…the moon, Genevieve, that kept calling to me in these dreams. Her beauty and brightness shone like no other. I didn't even know my fucking name after I passed through the veil of Lethe. Under Danté's whip, I wished I'd never been born. So I let my mind wander. And always, *always* the night sky would appear. That luminescent beauty called to me, soothed me, kept me from losing my sanity. *Mea luna tenebris*. You have always been my moon in the darkness."

No point in fighting the tears now. How could a girl not cry when the man who owned her heart said such things? I wrapped my arms around his waist and let my head fall to his shoulder. He held me close while I let it all out.

"And you're my guiding star," I muffled into his shirt.

He tightened his hold and pressed a tender kiss to my temple. "Then we're a perfect pair, you and I. We belong together. And nothing, not even the demons of hell, will ever tear us apart."

And that was a truth I felt bone-deep. No matter what Damas and his demon brothers planned, my bond with Jude was strong enough to withstand anything. My heart might be human and fragile, but my will was iron and steel. And I had a fiery bad-ass Master of Demons who would always catch me when I fell.

Like now.

Dad still hadn't woken up, but his pulse was steady. I'd been at his bedside for hours. Jude had gone out to meet with George and Uriel. I'd dozed in the chair by my father's bed. When I opened my eyes, I found my katana leaning against the wall. I'd forgotten it. Of course, Jude had fetched it for me.

Father Clementine used oil lamps. I turned one up so I could check on Dad. After a few hours in this place, I realized he lived without electricity or modern technology of any kind. *"I like the simple life. It's easier to stay close to God this way,"* was his reply when I'd asked.

The local newspaper and visits with the townspeople were the only ways he knew what was going on in the world. But what was there to know other than the world was quickly going to hell? Literally.

Terrorist strikes increased across America, Europe, the Middle East, and even Russia. Riots had erupted in all corners of the US for no reason at all. Hatred and malice stirred humans into doing random acts of violence. Of course, I knew who was at the heart of every strike and every riot. Demons.

Dommiel stirred in the bed next to me. "I have something for you."

I stood with the quilt that had been draped over me while I slept by either Father or Jude and wrapped it around my shoulders. Angling my chair nearer to Dommiel, I sat again and finally observed him closely.

He had no piercings of any kind in his lips, nose, cheeks, brows or even his ears. It was odd. At the same time, the absence of all the metal revealed the face of the handsome angel he had been before the fall. Dark stubble was growing back on his shaved head.

"What is it?"

He opened a small drawer in the nightstand and pulled out my St. George medal, dangling it in the air for me to take. I took it and traced the figure of St. George and the dragon with my finger. I'd never realized I'd meet the man in the flesh.

"Why are you giving it back to me? Our blood bond remains."

"That belongs with you. I saw you wearing it the very first time I met you. Even while I had it in my possession, beneath the blood bond I sensed an emotion lingering within the small silver medallion. It belongs with you."

His hook lay in his lap on top of the quilt. He crooked the

other arm behind his head, propping himself against the wall. There was no headboard on these bare beds. He looked so vulnerable, different, somber, and yet…content.

"How much longer before Father Clementine says you're good to go?"

"The wounds are closed. That priest knows some healing tricks. Whoever made him gave him some good mojo. But the bones were fractured in my ankles."

I winced, remembering how we'd found him crucified to his own office wall. Damas was indeed a demon prince of hell, capable of all manner of tortures.

My pulse tripped faster, knowing Mindy was in his hands. But Jude and George had convinced me not to lose hope, that he would use her as some sort of bargaining chip with me. I'd already figured out what Damas planned to do, so I was keeping my shit together till the time came.

"So then you'll head back to New Orleans?"

He stared down at his hook. "No. I won't go back there."

"Wait. Why not? That was the whole deal. You helped me, and Jude would help you keep NOLA as your domain. A bargain is a bargain."

"You don't understand," he said, meeting my gaze. "Damas killed every minion who was loyal to me. Every one of them."

He paused, and if I wasn't talking to a high demon who'd worn a sinister grin every time I'd met him, I'd have thought I detected a note of remorse in his voice.

"Damas has branded me," he continued. "I am a traitor to my kind."

"Because of me."

"Because of my greed. I knew Bamal wanted the New Orleans territory. I knew he'd eventually come back and stake his claim. So I took your offer, in my own greed for power. None of this is your fault. You offered an opportunity, and I took it."

And there it was. True, heartfelt remorse lining every word that poured from his mouth. This demon was not the one I'd first met with his raven perched on the dragon's head above his throne in The Dungeon. This was a broken soul, humbled before fate and circumstances, accepting the consequences.

Uriel had spoken of a new age dawning when the Great War officially began. And Dommiel was a prime example. A creature of darkness with the foulest of sins on his soul, and yet, that prickly signature that had always accompanied him was gone, changed, morphed into something smoother, like a jagged stone washed smooth by time and the constant lapping of steady waves.

"You've changed, Dommiel."

He laughed. "Not so much."

Very much, from where I was sitting.

He glanced toward the small window set between the beds. Snow had fallen last night. A gray pall hovered, leaving the quiet landscape to keep us company.

"Maybe it's this place," he said. "It reminds me somehow of the time before the Fall."

My mother's adaptation of Gustav Dore's angels plummeting from heaven was rendered in vivid and vibrant colors, revealing the beauty of the angels as they fell from grace. I tried to imagine Dommiel as one of the many who'd taken the wrong path.

"What do you mean?"

He gestured with his hook toward the door. "The priest." He captured my gaze with a smirk. "He's actually a good man, you know."

"There are lots of good men."

"No, there aren't. People are too caught up in their own selfish desires. Trust me, I know."

"You spent the majority of your time in the club off Bourbon Street, Dommiel. I think you might have seen more of the bad than the good."

"No." He turned his somber gaze on me. "I've been alive too long and seen too much. My time in the city of New Orleans is only a blink of time in my life. Countless years, I've seen men take what they want—for politics, power, lust, for blood revenge. I've seen women abandon their children only to meet their own needs. I've seen children beat dogs because their father had done the same to them. It is a wicked world, Vessel. If you plan to attempt to defend and redeem those humans caught up in this war, you'd best prepare for the worst."

Dommiel's truth hit me so hard, I tried to keep my composure. Yes, he was a demon lord. He'd spent countless years luring humanity toward sin and his dark ways. But here he was, professing the world as he saw it, and it sickened him.

Did he realize he was more like me in this moment than one of his own demon horde?

"You may be right, Dommiel. But for every selfish human, I can offer a selfless one in their stead. The firefighters and policemen of 9/11. They walked into a burning inferno to save strangers, knowing they would probably not come out alive. Many of them didn't. The single mother who works three jobs just to keep a roof over her children's heads and food on the table. The homeless child who offers his scrap of bread to his younger sibling instead of keeping it for himself. These people exist. They do. I've seen them."

His expression was unreadable. "You are the one true Vessel, aren't you?"

There was no denying a truth I knew as I knew how to breathe air into my lungs. "Yes."

"Do you know what you look like to the Flamma of Darkness?"

Jude had told me I was a beacon to all Flamma. I assumed that meant I had some sort of white light around me to the eyes of Flamma.

"No," I finally answered, curious how he saw me.

"Your signature is so pure and clear, it radiates with a glistening aura. It feels like cool water to the dying man, like a balm to the blistered soul, like silence to the maddened mind which has no reprieve from discordant voices. But Flamma of Dark do not want to be saved. They want the sin, the frenzy, the chaos. They know they are welcome there. You beam with something they cannot touch, and it reminds them of what they could have had, could have been once."

I'd never thought of the world from their point of view. So strange. And so sad.

"That isn't how you feel anymore, is it? What will you do now?"

He looked out the window, where downy flakes had begun to fall again. "The priest offered to let me stay with him."

Dommiel and Father Clementine?

"And are you going to stay?" I asked, surprised.

"No. I like the priest. And I am grateful to the old man. I may be a creature of sin, but without him…I would not be whole again." He pulled up his sleeve to trace the mark on his wrist where the blade had pinned him to the wall. "Damas had injected his essence into the blades. He'd intended for me to rot from the wounds. A slow, painful death. He hadn't figured on you coming to the rescue."

"Why not? He knew you'd helped me. You were being punished for it. Why wouldn't I repay the favor?"

"Because demons don't think that way. They think only of their own gain."

The thought of Damas, as Thomas, smiling at me, kissing me, winning my favor by slow degrees, slapped me with regret. But Jude was right. I couldn't live that way. I had to let go and move forward.

"So if you're not going back to New Orleans and you're not staying here, then where will you go?"

"I'm not sure," he said with a funny smile. "It's kind of freeing, actually. What does that frown mean, Genevieve? Are you worried about me?"

"Maybe. A little."

"Don't be. I'll be fine. And the blood bond remains. If you need me, you can call. You still have my feather?"

"Yes. Of course. But how will you reach me if I keep the medal?" I didn't want to give it back, yet I thought it unfair he couldn't call me if he needed.

He held up his hand in protest when I started to hand the medal back, still cupped in my hand. "No. As I said, the necklace has some special meaning to you. I can sense it when I hold it. You've done enough already, more than any of my own kind would have. Now, if you don't mind, those wonderful meds the priest gave me thirty minutes ago are starting to kick in."

"Oh. Sure." I stood and glanced at my father, who hadn't moved, then left, clasping the medal back around my neck. As soon as I tucked it into my shirt where I'd worn it since my mother had given it to me, I sensed what Dommiel spoke of, zinging along the silver chain straight to my heart. My mother's love for me and mine for her still resonated here.

Her voice, soft and pure, whispered over the years gone by. *"It will keep the dragons away."* I went in search of Jude. The Blood Moon was fast approaching. I hoped my mother was right.

I stood in front of the window of our little room on the afternoon of the Blood Moon. Snow whispered down in soft flakes, falling to earth in peaceful quiet. The old adage, the calm before the storm, couldn't be truer at this moment. I was harnessed and strapped with a weapon wherever I could hold one.

Jude stepped up behind me and swept my hair to one side before placing a kiss to my neck. I shivered in response. His arms came around me. One hand cupped my belly. I still hadn't begun to show at all, but that was to be expected. I hadn't even crossed the five-week mark.

"Father Clementine wants you to eat before you go."

I chuckled. "It wouldn't be prudent to meet every demon and spawn of hell on an empty stomach, would it?"

"Not prudent at all." Another soft kiss to my neck.

I twisted in his arms and pressed a feverish kiss to his lips, demanding that he open for me. He did, his hands sliding to the small of my back. He groaned and pulled me closer. His tongue swept in and met mine, desire mounting in a millisecond.

He pulled back and touched his forehead to mine. "What was that?"

"I wanted to. Would it be prudent to shut that door and pull you onto that cot right there?"

"No. Not prudent at all. Let's save that for tomorrow. After our job is done. A celebration."

I scoffed. "You act like it'll be so easy, like we're just expelling a demon or two, and then we'll be back home in time for tea."

"It won't be easy. We have no idea what they have in store. Whatever it is, it will be very difficult, I imagine."

I had an idea what they planned to do. We'd see soon enough if I was right about Damas and if I could stop him.

"But we have something else, my heart."

"Yeah? What's that?"

"You. The only Vessel of Light to ever escape the clutches of evil. And we've arrived at our destination…the night of the Blood Moon."

"It all ends tonight."

Jude loosened his hold on my waist. "No, love. Tonight it all begins."

Yes. The Great War and battle for dominion over the earth.

The very idea was unfathomable, the thought too huge for me to comprehend. Better to take it one step at a time.

"All right, then. What has Father cooked for dinner?"

He took my hand and led me out of the room. "A hearty beef stew."

My stomach growled instantly. He glanced back with a crooked smile. "My girls are hungry."

"Oh, so now you agree with me it's a girl."

"I'm just appeasing you. Don't want to upset the mother unnecessarily." He winked.

I laughed as we entered the den, where a small round dining table was set up in the corner.

"Here you are," said Father Clementine, setting down a white bowl with a spoon and a basket of crusty bread.

I took the first bite and thought I was in heaven. "Mmm. It's delicious."

The twinkle was back in his blue eyes. "Well, now. That's music to my ears. You two eat up before you head out."

Jude and I practically inhaled the meal, ready to be off, ready to get things moving, a nervous energy filling the room. I sopped the last of mine up with a crust of bread, then wiped my mouth with a napkin, hoping this wasn't the last supper or something.

"Thank you, Father. Jude, I'm going to step in and see Dad one more time before we go."

He nodded. Father Clementine drew his attention back to a

front-page article in the paper. Another terrorist attack in London.

When I stepped into the bedroom, I felt something was different. Dad lay on his side, his eyes open, staring at the lantern on the bedside table.

"Dad!" I ran to him but didn't jostle the bed when I knelt before him.

His eyes were half-lidded but clear when they gazed at me, a spark of recognition shining there. "Genevieve," he croaked.

"Wait. Drink this." I poured him a glass of water from the pitcher Father Clementine kept on the bedside table. I held his head with one hand and the cup with the other. Some dribbled down the side of his cheek, but he gulped a good bit.

"Where am I? How did you find me?"

"Dad, what do you remember?"

"These…things…these creatures…attacked me at the dojo. They weren't human, sweetheart. They had red eyes. I don't know how to explain it."

"I know, Dad. I know." The cat was out of the bag now, and I couldn't be happier. He knew of the demon world. He'd seen it firsthand, felt it.

"They took me to this place and…there was another man, a good man, a fighter who tried to help me… Where are we now? This isn't a hospital?"

He was still fuzzy, his thought process irregular. Jude and Father Clementine were suddenly in the room. They must've heard my exclamation. Father rushed around me and placed his palm on Dad's forehead. Ordinarily, this looked like a man checking for fever, but I sensed the energy revving in the room, vibrating in the air.

Father Clementine smiled. "He seems to be doing much better, but he still needs his rest."

A sigh of relief whistled out of me. "You hear that, Dad? You're going to be okay."

Of course, he didn't even know he'd been stabbed through the chest with a broadsword. He still seemed out of sorts, unable to comprehend everything going on around him.

"Genevieve," said Jude with a hand on my shoulder. "We have to go."

Father Clementine turned up the oil lamp as the darkness crept in. I hated to leave my father, but he was in the best of hands.

I leaned over and kissed him, pressing my cheek to his, trying not to brush his wound and hurt him. "I love you, Dad. I've got to go, but I'll be back soon."

"Love you, sweetheart."

He didn't even ask where I was going. His eyes slid closed again when Father Clementine placed his palms over the wound and began his repetition of healing prayers.

"Good luck," said Dommiel from the darkened corner.

Jude and I both turned at the door.

"Thank you," replied Jude.

With all the animosity and history of nastiness between these two, it was the most humble and grateful *thank you* I'd ever heard. It was appreciation for more than Dommiel's well-wishes. It was for the demon risking his own life to help me.

Yes, Dommiel had admitted he'd done it for selfish reasons, but we all knew that wasn't all true. Mostly true, but not all. There was a seed of good in that cantankerous demon. I wondered what sort of life he would lead from here and hoped that he would change his ways, even just a little.

I slipped on my leather jacket at the back door. Jude had been wearing his for an hour, anxious to go. He was nervous. So was I. We marched out into the cold, crunching on the snow as we pushed open the gate and passed beyond the wards. Jude and I stood facing each other. He looked up. I followed suit.

The night was clear and bright, the moon a perfect silver globe hanging above us, so serene, casting moon shadows on the freshly fallen snow. Tonight was definitely the night. My VS tingled with anticipation of events to come.

"Before we're no longer alone and the world goes to hell, I wanted to tell you something," Jude said.

"Yes?" My teeth chattered, more from nerves than the cold.

"If anything should happen to me or if I should get into trouble and Damas tries to use me as bait to draw you into a vulnerable position, you must promise that you won't hand yourself over or pull some heroic bullshit of any kind."

I stifled a laugh. "Look who's calling the kettle black."

"What are you talking about? Why would I speak to a kettle?"

I blanked for a second. "Jude. Are you telling me you've never heard this expression, about the pot calling the kettle black?"

"No. That's a common expression?"

"Jude Delacroix. What the hell? I swear, for a man of your infinite years, you know very little about pop culture. Or even twentieth-century culture."

"Pop culture isn't relevant to expelling demons."

"Right. But still, it's kind of ridiculous the things you don't know compared to the things you do."

"So what does this mean? Calling the kettle black?"

"It means that you're one to talk. You're telling me not to do something that you've done a hundred times already."

"You're exaggerating. And I'm expendable. There are other Dominus Daemonum. There is only one Vessel of Light to lead the Great War."

I punched him in the shoulder, hurting my knuckles more than him. "*Ow.*" I shook my hand. "To me, you're not expendable. There is only one Jude, father of my child, and I will have you healthy and whole after this fucking night is over."

"Don't be angry. Your mood can certainly turn on a dime these days."

"Are you calling me moody again?" Didn't men know what not to say to a moody, pregnant woman? I was getting hotter by the minute. "And how the hell do you know the phrase 'turn on a dime' and yet you don't know the pot calling the kettle black? You just—"

He grabbed me by both arms, held me still, and slanted his lips over mine, silencing me with a toe-tingling kiss that had my head spinning into orbit. When my body grew pliant and melded against his, a soft moan humming deep in my throat, he nipped lightly.

Our breaths mingled. My senses reeled, my underlight primed and beaming like the moon above us.

"Better?" he asked in a husky whisper.

"Yes." I laced my fingers behind his nape. "But you won't be able to solve all our arguments by kissing me, you know."

"Oh, my heart. I have other weapons in my arsenal."

Before my head could fall into the gutter where that comment was leading me, we spun into the Void toward our destiny.

Jude and I waited on Southwark Bridge in London. He'd taken me for a long walk along the streets of London before we were to meet George. He didn't tell me why. I didn't ask. I'd thought we were meeting with George and Kat early to formulate a plan.

But what plan could we formulate when fate held the cards?

As we walked, hand in hand, the crisp night air awakening my senses, I spun a cast of illusion to cover my underlight growing brighter with every block.

Every now and then, Jude would say something like, "Never drop the connection with your Vessel power." He'd stop at a shop window. "Remember that I'm there. Though you must face Bamal's Vessel on your own, I'll still be there." I'd nod, and we'd walk on.

When we finally made it to our destination at the center of Southwark Bridge, the tiered lamps breaking through an unusual fog, he pulled me to a stop to face him.

"And know, Genevieve, that you are the Vessel of Light spoken of in the prophecy."

"But the prophecy only speaks of probable events, not definites. I may not win."

He paused, studying me the way he used to when we first met, a curious expression of keen observation crossing his features. "You will, *mon coeur*. I have no doubt."

I was glad one of us was so confident, but it did little to assuage my fears. One line from the prophecy kept repeating in my mind. *A sacrificial lamb must die; her blood must pool under darkened sky.* This didn't appear to be a possible outcome but something that *must* happen, ordered by the fates.

I looked up at the moon, shining like a silver beacon for the world to see. The hour of the eclipse drew near.

Footsteps approached. We both turned. I recognized Kat's slim silhouette and swinging ponytail as she emerged from the mist. George walked at her side, Xander and Dorian behind them.

Kat didn't even pause but pulled me into her arms at once. She said nothing, her green eyes swirling with black residue saying it all. This was it.

"Xander, are you well enough?" Jude asked.

"I'm well enough to kick the bloody hell out of a few demons."

George held up his hand. "There is no fighting until Genevieve has faced Bamal's Vessel."

"We know," said Dorian, his usual charming smile nowhere to be found.

"Where's Uriel?" asked Jude.

"He'll already be there," replied George. "As will others."

"It's time to go," I said, feeling my VS pulsing through my veins unbidden. She knew as well as I that it was time.

"The fog is fortunate," said Xander, glancing over his shoulder and finding no one within eyesight. "Come, sweet Katherine. Destiny awaits," he said, taking her by the hand.

His flirtation didn't seem to bother George at all as he took her other hand. No time for petty grievances.

"I'll lead the sift," said George.

The rest of us completed the circle, Jude gripping me tight. George took us through the Void at hyperspeed. Then we stood on solid ground, the air chilly and damp.

I gasped at the sight stretching across Dartmoor before us. Under the vibrant moon, I could see the moor rolling away in the distance, and upon every snowy hill stood hundreds, no thousands, of Flamma stretching into the distance. In front of me, the Flamma opened a path leading to a circle of standing stones approximately fifty yards away.

The Flamma of Dark stood to one side—red-eyed demons, black-scaled spawn, multi-clawed beasts. A dragon lifted its horned head above the horde and snuffed the air, blowing a great puff of steam into the cold.

On the other side stood row upon row of angels, beaming with a honey-hued underlight. Wings of white, gold, crimson, blue, and even black. All wore battle gear, but those with black wings were garbed in uniforms of red tunics and silver breast plates, appearing much like the archangels from mythology. All stood at attention.

"Who are they?" I whispered to Jude.

"Maximus's army." He pointed to a black-winged angel next to Uriel. "The archangel."

Uriel stood tall next to Maximus—a fierce looking archangel with piercing blue eyes and a face as hard as granite. With dark hair and a severe expression, he was ready for war. I swallowed but had no spit left in my mouth. The archangels had been building their armies for this moment. So had the demons.

Kat let go of my hand, but Jude kept me in his grip and led me down the open path. The others walked behind us, escorting me to the ring.

All eyes swiveled as we passed. I removed my cast of illusion, letting my presence shine bright. A female angel with royal blue wings and black hair gave me an approving nod.

The Flamma of Light had been told there was a Vessel on earth who may indeed fulfill the prophecy, but now I was here to prove the rumors true. I held my chin high. Whether I won or lost, this was the moment to begin the Great War.

As we drew closer to the circle, I saw Damas standing in a line with four other high demons who resonated with his level of power—the kind that threatened to buckle my knees and toss me like a rag to the ground. Only my constant control using my VS kept me upright.

My heart stuttered at the demon standing to the right of him. Standing nearly seven feet tall with long black hair, he looked mostly human. If you could ignore the ram's horns curling out of his head, the black claws on his hands, and the fangs peeking from his mouth.

"That's Vladek."

A demon prince in his true form, no glamour to hide the beast within.

"The one next to him is Calliban," added June, squeezing my hand, understanding that seeing all of these beings in their true forms was freaking me out.

Calliban had a swarthy complexion, no horns or fangs. That I could see anyway. He might be using glamour. He smiled with a seductive lure as a sheik would to one of his harem. The two standing to their right made my pulse quicken with dread, like a rabbit in a snare when the wolf is drawing closer.

"The other two are Rook and Simian. Twins."

Jude and George had said these two held no domains on earth, and I knew why. There was no stitch of humanity in their pallid, black-veined faces or their crimson eyes.

With long black hair and wearing full-body metallic material over black leather, like double-layered chainmail, they had the look of ancient barbarians, monster vampires, and modern-day bikers all at once. They were not of this world.

So these were the demon princes—all but Danté, who no longer walked any realm, and Bamal.

Damas stood on the edge of the ring of stones, his dark hair perfectly set, sea-green eyes glinting in the moonlight. Ominously beautiful.

At his back stood Bellock, malevolence rolling off him in waves. Jude's grip tightened on me. This was the first time he'd encountered Damas since learning he'd masqueraded as my guardian angel, Thomas. I knew Damas wouldn't let the moment pass without saying some asshole-worthy comment.

"Judas, how wonderful to see you so healthy," he said in greeting, proving my premonition immediately.

He called him the Roman equivalent of his name, but it was obviously an innuendo linking him to the great betrayer.

"You must've had an attentive nurse."

You'd have to be stupid to miss the dripping sarcasm and suggestive tone. I waited for Jude to respond with an equally biting greeting or a punch to the face. He did not. He held the gaze of the demon prince, rage lining Jude's features with tension, before finally peering down at me.

With a tender smile, he let go of my hand, then mouthed *I'm here*.

Jude rose above Damas and his baiting by refusing to acknowledge him at all. I was so proud, I wanted to throw my arms around his neck, but now was certainly not the time or the place.

I walked into the circle of stones, which had been wreathed with tall torches set just beyond the monoliths. Nothing and no one was here. Only a slab of slate rock elevated knee-high sat at the center of the ring.

Jude took his place opposite Damas but kept his sights on me.

I unsheathed my katana, readying myself for whatever came next.

A crackling snap announced someone sifting down the path. I watched from the center of the stones as Prince Bamal walked with a steady gait, holding the hand of a red-cloaked woman, her head down and hood up—his Vessel.

His henchmen Gorham and Razor, the assholes who'd tried and failed to kidnap me for their master, walked at his back, all arrogance and swagger.

When they reached the edge of the circle, Bamal faced his petite Vessel and whispered low to her then pressed a kiss to her forehead.

I couldn't hear what he said and stepped forward out of curiosity. He pulled the mantle of her cloak from her head, revealing waves of blond hair and the beautiful silhouette of—

I sucked in a breath. My world stopped. My vision hazed. Mouth agape, I couldn't move, couldn't breathe, couldn't think beyond the beating of my pulse pounding in my ears.

He cupped her face and planted a lover's kiss to her lips. She reciprocated.

"No," I whispered to myself, pain lacerating my insides. "It can't be."

Jude stood behind her and couldn't see her face. Damas grinned from his view of both me and the woman kissing Bamal. He'd known all along. She stepped into the circle, and I clutched my chest, praying my heart didn't stop right here, right now.

"Mom?"

She made no sign of recognizing me. But I knew her. It had been ten years, but I still knew her. She hadn't changed a day. Clear blue eyes mirroring my own held me in a state of shock and devastation and disbelief.

"How?" I asked her. She still made no response.

From the outer ring, Bamal had crossed his arms in smug triumph, relishing every heartbreaking second of this reunion.

I turned my question on him, since she refused to acknowledge me. "How is this possible? I saw the video of the day she died, the day she jumped from the Mississippi Bridge. No one could survive that fall."

"Who said she reached the bottom?" he asked in response. "My spawn can fly, pretty Vessel." He gestured to the left toward another dragon, red-scaled and orange-eyed, stamping along the perimeter of the standing stones.

Jude wanted to come to me, I could see it in his tight stance, his imploring eyes. An invisible barrier kept them outside the circle. The prophecy demanded that the two Vessels duel unimpeded.

I was to duel my own mother to the death? No. I couldn't. I couldn't do it, which was exactly what Bamal had counted on.

I caught Jude's gaze and shook my head. "I can't."

He nodded once, encouraging me, clenching his jaw. Fists balled at his sides.

She approached the flat stone at the center, red cloak billowing. She stopped on one side and stared upward toward the moon, waiting for something. Transparent clouds slipped across the sky, a sheer blanket sweeping between earth and the stars. The very edge of the moon began to darken. The eclipse had begun.

A shaft of lightning cracked a resounding boom down from the heavens, vibrating the ground. It struck between two of the stones. A slit of black opened, slowly gaping wide from another dimension, a dark abyss I knew too well.

The first to step forward was Acheron, the ghastly black-boned skeletal creature who held a bargain over my head. I inhaled a deep breath, remembering who Acheron would seize to fulfill said bargain if I failed to deliver a demon prince. I'd be damned before I let Jude fall prey to the underworld again.

The air shifted as the banshee cry of Cocytus wailed across the moor. She too slipped from the void. The Flamma of Light and Dark backed away from the circle, making way for Cocytus, who floated around the ring with ratty raiment billowing in the wind.

Third came Styx, her transparent silken white gown slicked tight to her voluptuous frame. She floated to the ground with grace and beauty that belied the black-eyed hatred in her gaze.

Lethe whispered out of the black maw, a ghostly hag who floated to the other side. I refused to look at her a second more than I had to, making sure she didn't approach anywhere near Jude.

And finally, a fiery beast I'd not yet laid eyes upon shook the earth when he stepped hooved feet from the other dimension. The opening sealed closed with a crackle.

"Phlegethon." I knew his name, though I hadn't imagined one of the soul eaters looking more like a demon lord himself.

With two black extended horns and a body like a minotaur, rippling with massive, bulging muscles and fire licking over his red skin, he was the fiercest creature I'd ever beheld. His slitted yellow eyes glowed with the lust for violence. In his gargantuan fist, he held a Thor-sized hammer, molten red and ready to crush the skulls of any beast that drew near.

The pulse of sorrow, woe, and hatred rippled from the other-world beings in one great symphony of despair. They each took a stance, spaced equally apart, around the ring of stones, facing the mass of Flamma.

Every time I'd come in contact with a soul collector, I'd lost the ability to hear. Their presence sucked sound from the air as if into a vacuum. This time, it was the same, but also different. I couldn't hear the murmurings of angels or demons or the stamping of claw-footed dragons dotting the moor. I couldn't hear anything outside the circle of stones.

It was as if they'd shut a soundproof door where I could only hear whatever passed on the inside. *A ring of wordless, mighty breath; amidst the clutch of endless death.* They completed another part of the prophecy, acting as referees to be sure no one interfered within the stones.

Once more, I set my attention on my mother—heart in my throat and still in disbelief—then dared to step closer. Trembling from the second I saw her, I touched my fingers to the medal around my neck, the one she had given me, and prayed for the strength to endure this trial. One of us must die. This was impossible. The world asked too much of me.

"Mom?"

She stopped watching the sky and looked at me. "Why do you call me that?"

Bamal had wiped me from her memory. Another stab to the heart.

"Because…you are my mother."

A frown puckered her brow, and I nearly collapsed. This same look of concentration on her face when she painted in her studio was seared in my memory.

"I am no one's mother." Though her expression was passive, my VS detected a vibration of dark power radiating outward. "I am my lord's queen."

I glanced toward Bamal. He could hear nothing, but the scowl on his face told me he didn't like whatever he saw.

"You may not remember. But once, you were my mother."

Curious eyes followed me as I stepped closer. I still held my katana, though it was useless. The will I'd had to kill Bamal's Vessel vanished the second I saw who she was.

"I would watch you in your studio. You painted the most beautiful things. Always bright colors."

Her gaze left mine to watch the sky once more, apparently deeming me no threat. A rising wind whipped through the ring, lifting her golden hair. The wispy clouds rolled above us, revealing the silvery orb between patches of darkness. The shadow of the earth eclipsing the moon grew greater, dividing the moon in half.

Sun and Moon, eye to eye; immortals await one battle cry. For within each heart of Moon and Sun, lies key to rule over all and one.

I was the Moon. My mother was the Sun. I'd never understood this cryptic aspect of the prophecy, believing it to be something to do with the eclipse. It was us—my mother and me.

"You painted this one painting of the day I was born. You stood in the window, cradling me close in a white blanket with the midnight sky beyond. Dad hung it in the house. Your husband…he loved you. He never loved another."

Her gaze dropped from the sky again. "Love?"

"Yes." I opened my VS, letting it slide outside my body, holding the memory that had always made me strongest when casting any spell. The one where my mother—the woman standing before me as a stranger—held me in her arms with such affection and read nighttime stories with such love in her heart that I knew she'd loved me, no matter that I'd lived with the weight of her suicide all my life.

But it hadn't been suicide. It was a sacrifice.

"I know who you are," she said, voice steady, gaze hard. "You are the enemy. The one to take me from my lord. I will not allow this to happen."

"Please remember." This was much harder than pulling Jude from the abyss of Lethe. She had been under Bamal's hand for a decade. "My favorite was Dr. Seuss."

I called my VS, commanding it to obey my will in a way I'd

never asked it before. At first, it would not come. The pain of seeing my mother smothered my thoughts. I closed my eyes and found the memory that had been the one to give me the control over my power.

When the familiar heat pulsed through my body, I opened my eyes. The glow of my skin brightened until the light filled the circle and my memory came to life.

There, a sort of hologram in transparent form in shades of gray and white, stood my childhood bedroom, and my mother sitting on the bed, one arm around my ten-year-old self.

Propped on my belly was a book. My memory mother smiled sweetly and crooned the singsong words. *"Today you are you. That is truer than true. There is no one alive that is you-er than you."* She touched my nose, and I giggled. The visible memory washed away in an ethereal cloud, but the sound of my childish laughter remained within the circle.

"This is a trick of the mind," she said, though her voice shook. "My lord warned me you would do something like this."

"He is not your lord. At least, he wasn't always so. You had a family, a husband who loved you more than anything in this world."

With a wave of my hand, I called the power of Light forward again and revealed a second vision, the one I cherished most. My dad twirled my mother in his arms in the kitchen, singing an Elvis Presley song.

He crooned, *"But I…can't…help…falling in love with you."* My mother in the memory tossed her head back, golden locks swinging. This time when the memory faded into ether, my mother's lip trembled.

"That isn't real," she said with less confidence than before.

A guttural roar raised our attention to the sky. A great black dragon beat its wings, soaring closer. Its silhouette against the half-eclipsed moon raised chills on my skin. It swooped closer till I could see it carried something, someone in its claws. A rush of wind filled the ring when the beast hovered over us and dropped its quarry toward the stone slab.

"No!" I screamed, not wanting her to fall to her death.

My mother thrust out an arm, and a black mist caught Mindy before her body hit the rock. She floated gently onto her feet right inside the ring of stones.

Barefoot, wearing jeans and a pink sweatshirt—apparently what she was wearing when Damas had taken her—Mindy walked, zombie-like, to the stone slab, never even glancing my way, and lay down on her back.

"She mustn't die until the appointed time," said my mother. "We will wait until the Blood Moon is full."

I was right. Damas had taken her to use as the prophecy's sacrifice. I was ready for this, though anger seethed through me just the same. But Mindy didn't even try to get up and escape. Her head lolled to the side like she was drugged. Swirling black clouded her irises.

I'd seen this before—the girls in Gorham's club House of Hades, the ones who'd been infected with demon essence to control their will. Damas apparently had given Mindy to Bamal to prepare as a willing sacrifice.

"Your tricks and visions will not fool me," my mother said. "My lord warned me of you."

"Your lord is a liar." Fury swelled inside me. "He erased Dad and me from your memory. But I know…I know in your heart, you must remember."

The shadow of the earth had nearly enveloped the moon above us. Only a sliver of white remained, the red-tinged eclipse swallowing the globe whole.

My mother slipped from under her cloak a black-boned dagger and raised it above Mindy, who passively awaited her fate.

"No!" I dropped my katana and leapt across the stone slab. I grabbed hold of my mother's wrist, and we tumbled to the ground.

Her blue eyes transformed, darkening to bloody red. She opened her mouth and released a black mist, which snaked into a web of tendrils, wrapped my wrists, and pulled me off her. She rolled to her feet, losing her red cloak, dressed in full black tights and shirt beneath.

"*Flamma intus!*" I commanded.

A pulse of white splintered the black web, releasing me from the bonds. I jerked to my feet.

Catlike, my mother circled the slab, the black-boned dagger still in hand. "She must die. You know the prophecy."

"I won't let you hurt her."

"Then you offer yourself as the sacrifice? Blood must pool under darkened sky or all will perish. You will. So will she.

And anyone else you love on this earth. All of us will perish and be lost unless the sacrifice is made."

I glanced over her shoulder, seeing but not hearing the jeers of Flamma from the other side. Demons screamed their taunts, but I could hear nothing. Jude remained solid and still, watching with his broadsword in his fist.

I couldn't sacrifice myself, because it was no longer just me at risk. There was my unborn child, even now a warm reminder deep within my womb as my VS flooded my veins. I couldn't kill myself without killing the life within me. Plus, I was positive I could use my Vessel power to help us win the war.

"No," I said. "I won't sacrifice myself."

"Then she must—"

"Do you know why I won't sacrifice myself?" I cut her off.

"Because you are not brave enough."

"No, Mom."

She narrowed her eyes. "Don't call me that."

I circled the stone. Mindy still lay there, helpless and oblivious to her fate.

"You are my mother. Your blood courses through my veins. Bamal doesn't understand that a mother's love is stronger than any spell of darkness he cast upon you."

She stopped circling. "Enough. I will do as my lord commands." My real mother was buried deep in the dark, having been under Bamal's control so long. She'd been conditioned by fear of her lord and master and forgotten the truth of who she was.

She raised her dagger high and sliced toward Mindy's chest. I launched myself toward her again. The dagger embedded in my shoulder as we rolled to the ground once more. A vibration resounded outside our protected shell. I rolled my head sideways to see a myriad of fanged demons roaring outside the circle. I couldn't hear anything.

My mother tried to raise herself, but I clutched her by the wrist and forced her back to my side. With the other hand, I pulled the dagger from my shoulder and tossed it to the ground.

My VS pooled around the wound, blocking Bamal's poison from seeping into my body. I touched my fingers to the gash and jerked my mother's arm forward, wiping a streak of blood on her pale wrist.

"This is my blood…and yours. Can't you feel it?"

My VS rose from within me, singing with a vibrancy I'd not felt before.

"No," she cried, her crimson eyes bleaching pale blue. Her gaze shot upward once more, panic filling her small frame. "The Blood Moon is full. It must be now…or we all perish. My lord will be angry."

"Mother!" I screamed. "Come to me. I am blood of your blood."

Her trembling hand came out to touch the blood streaking her skin.

I spoke not to her but to the power swelling in my core. "Flame within, if you have ever been mine, show her what is true and divine."

Closing my eyes, I shot like an arrow a stream of images laced with the power of Light straight to my mother's heart.

Making s'mores by the fire with Mom and Dad…riding a bike for the first time…watching her paint from the stool in her studio…dressing up for Halloween, both of us smiling for Dad when he took the picture… blowing out candles on my seventh birthday while she laughed and kissed my cheek: "May all your wishes come true, princess." A swirl of dark, then Mom standing on the rail of the Mississippi Bridge. A bystander yelled, "Lady, don't do this. It's not worth it." My mother's haunted face turned to the camera, the gusting wind lifting her hair in golden streams around her delicate face. She replied, "Yes. They are. They are worth it," and disappeared over the edge.

I yanked us from the memory. Her woeful gaze held me, though she said nothing at all. I took her hand and placed it on my belly. "Your grandchild grows here. Your blood…and mine. I cannot sacrifice myself. And I can't let you kill my best friend."

My vision blurred from the amping of power building to a boiling point and from the tears pooling in my eyes.

"But there must be a sacrifice," she said, her eyes glistening with unshed tears. Then sudden, painful recognition. "Genevieve."

I sobbed at the sound of my name on her lips. "Mom. There must be another way. There *must* be."

I hated the whole world at this moment when there was no way out, no way around a fucking prophecy that demanded death to unleash heaven and hell on humanity.

She lifted her hand to my cheek and smiled. "Shhhh…don't

cry, princess." With a lightning-swift move, she grabbed the dagger from the grassy ground and plunged it into her heart.

"No!" I shrieked, my power pulsing outward with my cry, bouncing off the dome and the standing stones.

She fell onto her back. I pulled her into my lap and grabbed the handle of the dagger, but she stopped me, her hand over mine, our blood mingling.

"No, daughter… I remember." Her smile was both sad and serene. "I tried to sacrifice myself once…and failed." She coughed. A line of red poured from the corner of her mouth.

"You didn't fail, Mom. You saved us. I'm safe. I'm alive." Tears slipped down my face.

"Your father," she said, desperate eyes searching mine.

"Yes. He's okay. He loves you still. So much, Mom. He never stopped loving you. Not ever."

"And I him." Her mouth quivered into a smile, scarlet staining her teeth. "My lord kept him from me, from my thoughts. He took me away from you both…but now… you've brought me back again." She coughed. A thicker stream pooled from her mouth and the heart wound. "You freed me, princess." Another cough, her voice cracking when she whispered, "I'll free you."

"Mom, don't talk."

She smiled, and I saw there in my arms the mother who'd cradled me a hundred times, wishing the bad dreams away, singing me to sleep with the greatest love in her eyes—uncon- ditional and eternal and pure.

She reached up and touched her fingers to my cheek. "Today you are you. That is truer than true," she whispered.

Her eyes rolled heavenward. The moon slipped out of the earth's shadow, the sun's light casting the lunar orb in a radiant glow, as if the sun were letting her go. I grabbed my medal and jerked, breaking the chain.

"Look, Mom. Remember?"

Glazed and content, no longer filled with fear or malice, her gaze landed on the medal I held above her. A slow blink. "Yes." She smiled, and my heart crumbled. "It keeps…" She stilled. Her head turned and eyes closed. She was gone.

"It keeps the dragons away," I whispered through a shaky sob.

I curled the medal into her hand and pressed my lips to her forehead, my heart aching for her sacrifice. Greater than her death, she had sacrificed a decade under the tyrannical, sadistic hand of Prince Bamal.

I let my head fall back and screamed, the sound cracking the dome, my voice echoed to the heavens.

The shadow of the earth slipped off the tip of the moon and faded into the night. A violent storm of clouds rushed over the moor. Outside the ring, I could see the grappling bodies of Flamma. Lightning streaked with a crackle, splintering the sky. A shaft bolted from the sky and struck me with Flamma fire. My arms flew back, spine arched as the heavenly power pounded into my bones. Within a few seconds, the lightning vanished.

A new burn flooded my body, like a waterfall of light pouring into every cell till I thought I would burst. When the flood subsided, I found myself still alone in the ring with the exception of my mother's lifeless body.

The protective veil was gone. The soul eaters waited for their repast, watching the battlefield. While lightning flashed and thunder rolled, a powerful gale swept over the snow-covered moor, whipping it up in stinging blasts.

Before I could even lift myself off my knees, Prince Bamal was there, swinging a sword over my head. I ducked out of his strike zone and scooped the hilt of my katana in hand. As he twisted, I clutched him by the throat and froze him with the new power tingling to my fingertips.

"No more, Bamal. Your time is done."

Fear skittered behind red eyes. He hissed and bared razor-sharp teeth as his beast rose through the mask of beauty. I stuck him straight through with my blade, my face close to his, fearless of his devil's grimace. I could whisper the command of destruction, obliterate him into smoky ash and charred bones.

But I had other plans. He shook and writhed, trying to wiggle off my blade, desperate to pull away.

"Be still," I commanded, and he was. By my will alone, he obeyed. "*Acherontis pabulum.*"

"No!" shouted the once-fearsome demon lord who'd preyed on my mother and made her a slave.

"Yes," I said with quiet finality.

The ghastly reaper with a black death's head and crimson eyes whispered into the ring.

"A demon prince to pay my debt, Acheron."

The unnatural creature nodded and opened his arms. I retracted my blade from the Bamal's guts and ordered, "Go to him."

Without hesitation yet screaming defiance the whole way, the great demon prince walked into the arms of Acheron, who opened his yawning mouth and fed on him head-first. I'd not seen Acheron feed like this on the last demon, but perhaps a prince was one to be savored.

Some creature snorted and grunted behind me. I spun to see that one-horned, ugly spawn that had attacked Jude and me in his courtyard once. Three more the same as him charged into the ring for me.

I held out one hand and pulsed once, my VS severing them in half as if with a laser. Their top halves, chest up, spun like tops away from their torsos and running legs, all crumpling into flailing piles.

Another darted in, going for Mindy, who still lay there, unmoving.

"No!"

I barreled toward her only to stop when Xander leaped forward, slicing off the creature's head with a swift and graceful swing. Xander sheathed his sword and leaned over the slab of stone where Mindy lay still and quiet.

"I've got her," he said, giving me a nod before sifting Mindy to safety somewhere.

I walked out of the standing stones, fully awakened. Electric fire poured through flesh, blood, and bones. Kat was right. I felt the change in my very soul…like falling in love.

My love.

From the elevation where the standing stones stood, I scanned the horde of angels and demons among clanging swords and grappling bodies, seeking out Jude.

Mira swooped over the mass, diving and scratching with her powerful talons where she could. Dragon fire lit up a distant skirmish. A flash of a graceful fighter with platinum ponytail swinging alongside the figure of George I knew so well. They fought a dragon together. Perhaps there was hope for those two after all.

The soul eaters gorged on the wounded, those too helpless to flee. Phlegethon raised his fiery hammer above his horned head and let it fall, crushing the skulls of two fallen demons at once. I turned away, my stomach queasy at the sight of him scooping up the crushed remains in his clawed hand.

Dorian battled Bamal's man, Gorham, to my left. And just beyond was Jude, engaged with Bellock. I took one step beyond the stones to find Razor standing his ground with a line of twenty demons behind him—some humanesque, some monsters—standing tall with swords drawn.

"You're going to pay for Bamal, bitch."

Razor was actually crying. But I had no pity. And I would have no mercy.

I remembered the hundreds of innocent tourists and Parisians running from the scene of the Eiffel Tower bombing while Razor had smiled at his handiwork from the sidelines. I remembered the father who fled with his screaming toddler in his arms, the child's blond curls bouncing, his face a mass of tears and fear a second before they were blown apart.

"No, Razor. You're going to pay…for every soul you struck from this world. For every innocent you defiled to please your master."

Razor stepped forward, his demon horde closing in. I laughed. They all froze, puzzled by my maniacal response to a face-off with twenty-one demons, weaponless.

But I had a weapon. It was me.

"Get her, Razor," called one of the larger fools standing in the crowd. Razor launched into a run.

"Goodbye," I said, sucking in a lungful of air and blowing my power straight at him.

White crystals blew with a gale-force wind. Razor screamed as his skin melted away upon impact. The others followed, howling in pain as they clawed at the skin falling from their flesh. I waved my hand. Razor's monstrous form fell backward as did the rest like dominos.

"Be gone," I whispered.

Their bodies liquefied into the ground. Nothing left but twenty-one piles of steam.

Beyond them stood Rook and Simian, the scary-as-hell demon princes. They tilted their heads in the same direction, like curious dogs at a strange sound. They turned to each other, mirror-like, and sifted away. Creepy but smart demons.

The roar of a dragon Titan filled the battlefield. I gazed across the moor, angels and demons entangled in combat as far as I could see. The black-winged army of the archangel Maximus fought with violent ferocity and skillful precision.

Sparks of blue and white Flamma fire shot into the air as a multi-headed beast in the distance fell to the ground, shaking the earth. A streak of white zipped across the night sky as Mira dove and swept triumphantly over the mammoth creature.

My lovely hawk had taken down a Fury. And twenty yards away, Jude was getting the best of Bellock.

I smiled and took two steps before I was slammed onto my back, my head cracking against a protruding rock. Dazed, I touched my fingers to the back of my head. Warm stickiness.

"Sorry, love. Did that hurt?"

Damas knelt beside me, one hand clutched in my hair, the other pressing hard on my abdomen.

"You are one brave son of a bitch," I said. I paid my debt to Acheron, so there was nothing to keep me from blowing this fucker into oblivion and ridding the world of him once and for all.

He yanked my hair, stinging the injury on the back of my head.

"Ah!" I cried out.

With my mouth open in pain, he swept down and pressed a wet kiss to my mouth, so fast there was no need to react, for he was off the ground and standing above me in a blink, gray clouds sweeping above him.

"I wanted one last kiss."

"Before I kill you? Hope you enjoyed it."

He pressed his foot to my chest, shoving me down.

"I saw what you did, what you said to your mother," he said, angling his pretty face with a grin. "I might not have had much luck with you. Perhaps it will be different with your daughter." He winked.

Suddenly, a thick blade of steel ripped through his chest, sword protruding a full foot. His mouth opened in gaping shock as he looked down to see a blade sticking out of his chest. He coughed. Black blood splattered.

George loomed close over his shoulder. "You'll never know, bloody fucker. You'll never twist anyone to your will again." George glanced down at me, where I lay still trapped under Damas's foot. "Finish him, Genevieve."

I grabbed Damas's ankle and thought the word *death*. His mouth opened in a soundless scream right before I obliterated him into ash and charred bones, the wake of Vessel light blasting across the moor.

Demon shrieks of terror squealed at the flare of power blowing over the battlefield. I didn't consign him to some deep well of hell from which he could one day crawl to torment more victims. To try and seduce others—my own daughter—to his will.

No. Fucking. Way. He was gone for good. Finally.

I jolted to my feet, coughing on the ashy remains of the third demon prince I'd wiped out of existence. What looked like a shriveled femur bone rolled down my torso as I stood. I gave it a swift kick.

A slick stream of blood oozed from my head wound down the back of my neck, and my eyesight hazed. Spots dotted my peripheral vision.

George grabbed one arm, but I focused ahead at the man running toward me through the mayhem.

Jude. Sprinting full speed, jaw clenched, gaze locked…on me. As my knees buckled, he caught me in his arms before I hit the ground.

"I've got you, *mon coeur*," he said, his deep voice filling me with the promise of protection. "I've got you."

"I'm okay," I said, my words sluggish. "We have to keep going."

"You've done enough for today, my heart." He swept an arm behind my knees and lifted me. "It'll wait till tomorrow."

I wanted to go on, but using my new power had drained me dry. Spots hazed my vision. I wound my arms around Jude's neck and rested my head on his shoulder as he strode away from the battle and sifted to safety.

I didn't fear the dark this time when it swept me under. I never would again. Why, you ask? Two reasons.

One, old Murdoch was right. Nothing could ever drown my spirit in sadness again unless I let it. No matter what tragedy struck me next, I was content within myself. I would face life the way Jude had taught me—strong, confident, and battle-ready.

And two, I'd found my compass under the stars, always pointing me true north. His strong arms wrapped around me tight, promising never to let me fall and to always keep me safe.

Always.

EPILOGUE

NINE MONTHS LATER

I stood at the window of our cottage, holding our pink-cheeked cherub in my arms. Mira coasted in the updrafts over the cliff under the relentlessly gray sky. Uriel was right. We were now in a new age, some called the Age of Gray. But my sweet bundle knew no difference. She smiled nonetheless.

"Do you see Mira?" I asked my newborn. "She's doing tricks for you."

My daughter cooed, her hazel-gold eyes lighting with a supernatural spark. Jude walked up behind us, wrapping my waist with a protective arm. I leaned back, reveling in the solid strength of him.

He cupped our daughter's head with his broad hand, completely covering her skull with his wide palm and long fingers. She lit up with a smile for her daddy.

"Sweet Seraphina," he crooned.

When he chose her name, I balked at first, thinking it a tad long and lofty for such a wee thing. But then Jude had said, *"It means fiery-winged and comes from the word 'seraphim,' the strongest of angels."*

I looked at her coppery cap and eyes of flame and whispered, *"Seraphina."* It was a perfect moment.

A far-off rumble dragged our attention out the window. In the distance on the mainland, a stream of gold light a mile wide flooded from the heavens to the earth below.

"Another chasm," I said.

"Yes. Another."

The chasms had opened from above and below, flooding earth with new armies of Flamma every few hours the first days after the Blood Moon. They'd dissipated after several weeks. But every month or so, another would open up somewhere and dump another army onto earth.

"Shouldn't we go and help Uriel and the others? I feel much stronger now."

"No need to hurry." He bent and placed a kiss to the top of Seraphina's sweet head. "The war will wait. Even for you. Besides, we're winning."

For several months following the Blood Moon, we battled the Flamma of Dark armies cropping up all over the globe. Wherever the fighting was heaviest, we went.

Word spread that the Vessel of Light was on the warpath and that with my newfound power, I could kill at will any Flamma of Dark within reach.

The demons were driven back, but many fled to the underworld. Toward the end of my second trimester, as I stood on a Mongolian plain, staring at a field of decimated demons, I fainted on the spot.

That was when Jude had told George and Uriel they could fight without me for a while. I didn't bother arguing. When Jude made up his mind, that was it.

I was disappointed to learn that Bellock had escaped the night of the Blood Moon. So had the other demon princes. Four of them were left, but they'd kept themselves well hidden since that fateful night.

And there never was any sign of Erik. He'd vanished and escaped punishment altogether. But the world was getting smaller. He couldn't hide forever.

Jude had secluded us here with our burgeoning child, keeping us far from the war. The others brought us news from time to time. The constant battling of heavenly and demonic hosts had changed the ways of the world. Humans had taken up with either side and fought beside the Light or the Dark.

There were thousands of human casualties, sending survivors into hiding. The modern world crumbled under the weight of worldwide war.

When my time came, going to a hospital was out of the question. What hospitals were still functioning acted more like triage emergency facilities—a chaos of wounded constantly flowing in and out. I couldn't have my child in such a place.

Father Clementine had helped with the delivery at his protected cottage in Sussex. I had to channel my VS without the aid of an epidural. Even though I dulled the pain with my VS, the agony was horrific. But it was worth it.

It was difficult to explain my clandestine marriage to Dad. He was hurt that I'd kept my marriage from him, at first.

I'd never tell him who'd sacrificed herself at the altar of the Blood Moon so that I and my child might live. So that we all might live. The pain of knowing she'd suffered for a decade at the hands of Bamal would likely kill him altogether. I just couldn't do it.

Then Seraphina came, and all seemed right with the world.

Mindy remained in Father's care for a few weeks after the Blood Moon too. Kat would frequently check on her. Her spirits were low. She was more subdued than before, spending most of her time learning to cook from Father Clementine. And to stitch up the wounded that were brought to his care.

War and death had a way of making people reset their priorities pretty damn fast. Trivial things of our lives before didn't matter anymore.

We'd set up Mindy and her mother in a nearby cottage outside Brodick. My father elected to keep a cottage in a more secluded spot near the Glenashdale Falls. I wanted them all close as the war raged and the world changed. Outside the Isle of Arran, humanity was falling beneath the iron fist of constant bloodshed, terror, and battles.

And on the edge of the forest where Jude and I walked and the deer roamed, there was a small stone marker under a rowan tree, reading: Beloved wife and mother, who returned to the Light and to Love. Surrounding this nondescript epitaph was a Celtic heart with interlacing knots that circled and wove into the script in a neverending line. Just as my love for her would never end.

I kept her name from the marker, so no wandering Flamma of Dark—in search of the Vessel who failed them—would try to desecrate her remains. Her bones were now hidden and protected in a shaded place on an island far away from the rest of the world.

When fall swept through, the rowan tree's leaves flamed to life in vibrant orange, red, and gold, reminding me of the woman whose zeal for art and beauty and love now rested in peace beneath its boughs.

That was when Seraphina came. I glanced out the window at the chasm pouring Flamma of Light onto the mainland, glad it was not one of the others opening up nearby. I could just make out the warrior angels beating their wings, entering this dimension from wherever they'd existed before the war.

George and Kat were busy, organizing and acting as liaisons with the constant flood of angels spreading across the globe. Jude had also hinted that Kat had taken up residence with him in London. When I demanded to know more, he simply smiled and said, "Seems Kat finally realized that even a demon hunter's life is too short to waste any more time without the man she loves."

Seraphina cooed and gripped my finger with her pudgy little hand. I carried her away from the window and sat on the bed, my knees bent, cushioning her between my thighs.

"That's right, my love. Today you are you. That is truer than true. There is no one alive that is you-er than you."

Seraphina's mouth opened in a toothless smile, and she gurgled in response to the poem I'd recited so often. Her golden eyes sparked with mirth, marking her as something other. And so she was.

She was the daughter of a Vessel and a Dominus Daemonum who loved her more than life itself. No matter what the future held, she would have us both to guide her into this strange new world that was changing, falling, building into a mysterious unknown.

I glanced up at Jude, who leaned against the windowsill, watching me with arms crossed and a heart-stopping smile in place. Seraphina yawned.

"I think she's ready for a nap."

"Mmm. Good. I'd like to take her mother to bed as well."

"I think that can be arranged. I'm a bit tired myself."

"No, you're not. I was the one to feed her three times in the middle of the night."

He walked over and scooped Seraphina out of my lap and tucked her in the bedside crib, but not before pressing a soft kiss to her dainty head. His gaze lingered on her a few seconds before he spread out alongside me on the bed. The mattress dipped. I turned sideways to face him and slid my hand under his shirt to his back. "I appreciate you taking full baby duty last night."

"Do you?"

"Yes." I kissed him. Instant heat sizzled between us, as always. My body still wasn't ready for sex, but we'd found other ways to pleasure each other for the time being.

He swept his lips lightly over mine. "How about I show you how much I appreciate you?" He melded his mouth to mine and stroked his tongue once before pulling apart. "Would you like that?"

"Yes," I said, breathless and wanting.

Then Jude made me forget about the worries of the world the best way he knew how—with his hands, his body, his mouth…and his love.

"Fuck, yes," growled Jude, thrusting inside me from behind.

One of his hands gripped me tight, fingertips digging into my fleshy hip, the other stroking my clit in maddening circles while he fucked me hard.

I whimpered, falling forward, chest and head hitting the quilt. We were both still standing on the side of the bed, right where Jude had pinned me when he caught me getting dressed and decided to interrupt.

I wasn't complaining.

He rumbled a growl and removed his hand on my clit then lowered his body to press me into the mattress, still fucking me good and hard.

He gripped my ponytail and pulled it aside, my face turning to face the wall while he bit my nape then sucked my earlobe.

"Goddamn, Jude," I muffled, clenching my hands into the quilt.

"I needed you, baby," he groaned. "Needed this sweet, tight pussy." He sucked the side of my neck hard.

"Ah!" I cried, knowing that would leave a mark.

His roughness and dirty words sent me flying toward my orgasm with remarkable speed. And he knew it.

"That's it. Squeeze my cock just like that." He slammed inside me harder, his heavy sac smacking my pussy with every thrust. "Fuck, woman, you feel so good."

"I'm coming!" I cried out right before I did, my sex pulsing around his thickness.

"Yes. That's my sweet girl," he breathed into my ear, before lifting his torso off of me and wrapping my ponytail around his fist, tightening his grip.

He pounded in once, holding his cock deep, tugging on the ponytail to arch my neck so my heavy moans through the orgasm weren't muffled in the mattress.

I knew that's why he did it. He liked to hear me coming, and I was a bit of a screamer I'd realized. With my back arched, my hands planted on the mattress, I rode out the orgasm I'd been needing so badly.

Seraphina's new antics had kept me awake most nights these days. I was constantly going to her new bedroom that Jude had built onto the cottage to see if she was still safe in her crib. I'd been too tired for sex for over a week.

But, fuck, I needed this magnificent orgasm rippling through my body, tightening all of my muscles as pleasure pulsed deep and hard. I'd needed this release just as much as Jude did.

When my moans subsided, he pulled out. "Knees on the mattress and spread wide."

Obeying as quickly as my jellified limbs could move, I did as he told me.

He smacked my ass. "Wider," he growled.

I half-laughed, half-moaned at his dominant command. I loved it when he got bossy in bed. My clit tingled when he spanked me again.

Craning my neck to look over my shoulder, I asked, "What was that one for?"

Because, hell, I was as wide as I could go with my ass perched and ready for him.

He grinned. "That was because I like the way your ass looks with my handprint on it."

Then he thrust inside me, and I clenched my eyes closed on a hiss. He'd never let go of my ponytail and hauled me up by the hair, not too hard to hurt but rough enough to get my juices going again.

My torso upright, back to his chest, while he thrusted at a leisurely tempo, he mounded my breast, pinching my nipple till it was hard.

Mouth at my ear, he whispered, "Play with your clit, baby. Want you to come again when I fill you up."

On a breathy moan, I circled my clit and flicked it the way I liked. I felt his gaze over my shoulder as he gripped my breast and my hair tight, groaning while watching me. His tempo picked up, his thick cock swelling even more as it always did right before he climaxed.

"Feels so good," I murmured, working my fingers faster.

"Delicious," he grated against my nape and licked my skin.

Then he thrust deep, his grip on me hard as he speared me deep. I was a few seconds behind him, my body convulsing, wanting to fall forward. But Jude let go of my hair and breast, wrapping both arms around my chest, burying his face into my neck as he bit that spot again and pumped me till he was empty.

When my brain came back around to reality, I was panting, still basically sitting on Jude's cock on the edge of the bed with his arms caging me against his chest.

"I love you," he whispered into the hair at my temple, nuzzling sweetly.

I laughed, always jarred by Jude's naughty/sweet Jekyll and Hyde routine. Something about an orgasm made him suddenly want to snuggle and whisper sweet things to me. Again, I wasn't complaining. I had the best of both worlds.

"Something funny?" he asked, still inside me.

"Not at all." I twisted my head around and kissed him, tasting the mint tea he'd had before he found me dressing for the day. "Just happy."

He smiled and kissed me deeper, his cock twitching inside me.

"Now I actually need to get dressed and check on Seraphina before you think we have time for another round."

On a grunt, he pulled out of me and gave my ass a smack.

"Hey!" I shouted, standing and rubbing the stinging spot. "Don't get any ideas of that becoming a regular thing."

He flashed me a devilish grin as he pulled on his boxer briefs. "Oh, I've got lots of ideas."

Trying to ignore the delightful shiver his tone and that expression gave me, I bypassed him to the bathroom to clean up and dress quickly as I'd left my bra on the door handle after my shower last night.

Before Jude had even snapped his jeans, I was walking back through our small living area and the kitchen where Jude had knocked through the wall and added a bedroom for Seraphina.

"Good morning, Princess," I sing-songed as I made my way to her crib.

Then I gasped. A streak of panic seized my chest when I found it empty.

"Jude!" I screamed. "It's empty! She's gone!"

"Fuck!" he called from our bedroom, stomping fast through the cottage in his boots.

We both looked everywhere. I opened cabinets. He shoved the corner chair aside to look behind it. Then we both froze, hearing the rumble of a deep voice outside the cottage. Glancing at each other, we ran to the kitchen window. I blinked at the strange and somehow sweet sight in the yard.

The Archangel Maximus stood in the thin blanket of snow, his hands on his hips, his black wings spread wide, frowning down at Seraphina. She was bundled in her favorite blue blanket, still wearing the full-body onesie I'd put her to bed in, her arms held up to the severe-looking archangel.

Jude and I rushed into the yard. Maximus turned his frown at us. Mira perched on the woodpile against the house, watching Maximus with narrowed eyes.

Good thing Mira had taken her nanny duties pretty seriously. Ever since Sera had started to develop powers that were scaring the bejeezus out of both me and Jude, I'd put Mira on permanent babysitting detail.

"Why is your infant outside in the cold all alone?" asked Maximus, his accusing glare fixed on us.

"She wasn't supposed to be," said Jude, scooping her up, her copper curls bouncing in the wind.

She patted Jude's cheeks with both palms, "Da Da."

"You're not supposed to go outside by yourself," he scolded gently.

She giggled and turned her upper body toward Maximus again, reaching out both arms toward him.

Jude and I exchanged glances. Sera didn't typically like strange men. When we'd brought her into Brodick, she shied away from even our friendly bartender at our favorite pub. Up till today, the only two men she reached out for hugs from were my dad and George.

"Why is she doing that?" asked Maximus, his hands still on his leather-clad hips, his scowl still in place, looking at her like she was a strange bug or something.

He was dressed in leather pants and a military-style thermal shirt, his unusual plate of armor over his chest as always. It had been restyled since our battle of the Blood Moon. He'd apparently found a modern tailor who happened to dabble in warrior-wear. Interesting.

His sleeveless plate of armor sealed tightly to his chest and back, form-fitting. It was made of thin material, bearing an intricate design of a circle of warrior angels, wingtips touching.

"She's doing that," I told him, arms crossed in the chilly morning air, "because she wants you to hold her."

"I don't hold babies." He sneered at Sera. "And how did she escape outside?"

He looked at me, zoning in on the bite mark on my neck, his glare turning accusing. Like Jude and I decided to have sex while our one-year-old wandered in the snow by herself. That wasn't the case.

Suddenly, Sera disappeared and reappeared with her hands clinging to Maximus's chest armor. Jude and I both lunged forward, but Maximus quickly drew his arms up beneath her to keep her from falling.

"That's how," said Jude.

Maximus had both arms beneath her. Sera settled with a giggle and babbled some nonsense up at him, patting her fingers on his armor. One word I recognized was "say-say." That was how she said "safe place." Jude and I had been pointing and showing her all the safe places she was allowed to sift. It wasn't really working.

The archangel stared down at her with a mix of wonder and horror.

I grinned, moving to lean against Jude who wrapped a hand around my hip. "I thought you didn't hold babies."

Maximus's glower popped up, his blue eyes glittering with annoyance. But he also didn't hand over his charge.

"She's sifting? A human infant?"

"Neither of us is human anymore," said Jude. "And we understand as little as you. She just started popping in and out of sight this past month."

That's why I couldn't sleep. I kept fearing she'd sift somewhere dangerous. Somewhere we couldn't find her. But so far, she had only sifted close by.

Usually, it was to sift onto the kitchen counter to get a treat she wanted or to sift into a tree to pet Mira. That one had nearly given me a heart attack. Jude had caught her when she toddled off the limb, but from then on, I couldn't sleep more than a few hours at a time.

"Interesting," murmured Maximus, now staring down at Sera who was cooing something to him none of us could understand.

"She also starts fires," added Jude.

Maximus glanced up. "Truly?"

Jude nodded. "It's a gift I have as well. Apparently, she's inherited certain powers of ours."

Maximus's annoyed expression transformed to interest as he

tugged on one of her copper curls. "She will be a mighty warrior when she's older."

"Don't even try to recruit her," I said, moving forward to take her from the archangel.

Sera babbled something to me as she always did, none of her words making sense. But she was happy about whatever it was. Then she turned her adoring gaze back to the angel, blinking her amber-gold eyes at him sweetly.

For a moment, Maximus stared and blinked back at her.

"What have you come for?" asked Jude.

Originally, Jude had kept his cottage a secret from everyone but us. But matters changed when this became our permanent residence. Still, there were very few who knew the location. Those within out tight circle we could trust. Maximus had become one of them, having helped Uriel in many battles.

Over the past year, we'd wiped out all of the stronger, organized forces under the demon princes with the help of Dommiel, Xander, Uriel, and others now aligned on our side.

When my presence was necessary, Jude and I would sift to the thicker battles and I'd wipe out all that I could. Now, we were winning. Archangels were taking up seats of diplomatic power to protect the humans still alive after the apocalypse had descended on earth.

Those demons who decided to play nice were under the watch of the Flamma of Light taking seats of power. If the demons stayed in line, they could go about their lives of sin and debauchery, similar to how it was before the night of the

Blood Moon. Only, there was a much smaller human population.

"I've come to let you know I'll be leaving this territory. George and Xander have the UK well in hand. Uriel and some others are watching over Europe."

"Where are you headed?" asked Jude.

"America." He looked at me. "Actually, I will be based where you once lived. In New Orleans. I'll be in charge of the southern region of the US."

"Really?" I smiled, remembering the city I loved so much, but also knowing it wasn't the same since the apocalypse had started.

Maximus gave a tight nod, gaze skating to Sera in my arms. His frown returned. "George asked that I inform the two of you before I set off. Once I have my base set up and the legion settled in, I'll send word so you know where to find me should you need."

"Thank you, Maximus." Jude stepped forward and offered his hand. "We know you've never hesitated to answer the call with your legion. No matter our odds."

His marble expression cracked, a slight smile tugging his lips. "We've had quite a few bloody battles, haven't we?"

"Understatement," agreed Jude as they shook hands.

He walked over to me and shook my hand as I shifted Sera to my left hip. Then he chucked her under the chin lightly.

"Goodbye, little one."

She reached up and wrapped her fist around his forefinger.

His smile widened, marveling at her. Sera had that way of mesmerizing people.

Then he whispered, "I'll recruit you for my army yet."

"Like hell," grumbled Jude.

Maximus stepped back, still smiling. "When she's older, of course."

I shook my head, not even bothering to engage in that argument. Jude was already insanely protective. I couldn't imagine him ever allowing Seraphina to join an archangel's legion.

Of course, stranger things had happened since all of this began.

With a tight nod to Jude, Maximus turned, walked to the edge, and dove off the cliff.

Sera gasped, blinking her bright eyes when he disappeared.

Then Maximus flew straight up into the sky, black wings flapping. He was magnificent to behold.

"Say, bye-bye." I took her little wrist and helped her make a goodbye wave with her hand.

She babbled something again. This time, I caught the word "Mus" in there, knowing she was trying to say the serious archangel's name. Then she added, "say-say."

Then he disappeared and sifted away.

"Let's get you both inside." Jude wrapped his arm around us and headed for the door. "And no more sifting outside without our permission," he told Sera.

She laughed and said, "DaDa."

"You heard me, little girl," he grumbled.

No telling what the future held for any of us. And what raising a child with untold powers stirring inside her would be like. An adventure, to be sure.

But for now, I smiled at our here and now. Most of the world was at peace and trying to rebuild what we'd lost. I looked forward to the days ahead, raising our extraordinary daughter with the man I loved in our little world on the Isle of Arran. For now, life was good and beautiful and perfect.

THANK YOU FOR READING THE VESSEL TRILOGY. If you enjoyed this series, you might enjoy Juliette's dragon romance series set in a dangerous fantasy world. It begins with the NIGHTWING novella trilogy about three best friends falling in love with men of the dragon hybrid race called Morgons.

It continues with the full-length VALE OF STARS series, where human women are being mysteriously kidnapped and killed by Morgons. When Moira delves into the underworld of Morgonkind with her guardian Kol Morning, they will discover a darker plot against humans than either ever imagined.